WRITTEN IN THE STARS

A CHARITY ANTHOLOGY OF FESTIVE SHORT STORIES

BLOODHOUND
— BOOKS —

www.bloodhoundbooks.com

Print ISBN: 978-1-5040-8012-5

Contents

PART TWO
HOLLY JOLLY CHRISTMAS

PART THREE
IT'S A CHRISTMAS MIRACLE

CHRISTMAS BONUS

FOREWORD

Dear Reader,

By choosing to read this very special anthology, you have made a donation in aid of two amazing charities: Great Ormond Street Hospital Charity and The Butterfly AVM Charity.

I was inspired to create this anthology in 2021, on what would have been my daughter's third birthday. Sofia passed away, very unexpectedly, in 2020 aged just one and a half, due to a brain AVM (arteriovenous malformation) – something my family and I knew nothing about until then. It is a rare condition that she was very likely born with, but had shown no signs or symptoms.

I have done a lot of research since learning of AVMs, and this is how I found The Butterfly AVM Charity. They were the first UK charity to focus on raising money to fund research into AVMs and supporting families, and I've followed their journey ever since. Sofia spent five days at Great Ormond Street Hospital before we had to say goodbye. She was shown so much love and care by all the staff, and her nurses helped us make hand and foot cast imprints with her; something we will treasure forever.

With the support of my partner Daniel and my son Leo, I wanted to do something for other families who find themselves in the devastating place we were two years ago. And so, as a lover of the written word, I reached out to my publishers, Bloodhound Books, and my fellow authors, asking them to join me in making this anthology a reality. I was overwhelmed by the kindness of so many authors and must give a mention to *everyone* who submitted a short story.

I wanted there to be something for everyone in this anthology; be it stories that make you wonder whodunit, make you laugh out loud, or shed an emotional tear. While they are all based around a Christmassy theme, the stories themselves are so varied, I'm confident you'll find something you love.

As well as the fabulous contributing authors, the team at Bloodhound Books have been unwavering. This anthology really wouldn't have been possible without some selfless people donating their expertise and time: editors Clare Law, Ian Skewis and Morgen Bailey; proofreaders Abbie Rutherford, Heather Fitt, Shirley Khan and Maria Lee; as well as marketing and publicity queen Hannah Deuce. A special thank you to Betsy Reavley who has been by my side throughout this entire project. She's offered advice, been a sounding board and given unending support.

The two chosen charities are very close to my heart. Everyday they support thousands of children and families face uncertainty and life-threatening illnesses. And now you have helped them to continue their important fight.

Tara Lyons,
Sofia's (and Leo's) mum, Bloodhound Books' editorial and
production manager and author

To find out more about either of these charities, visit the following websites:

The Butterfly AVM Charity: www.butterflyavmcharity.org.uk

Great Ormond Street Hospital Charity: www.gosh.org

Great Ormond Street Hospital Children's Charity. Registered charity no. 1160024.

For Sofia Lyons-O'Sullivan

PART ONE
A CHRISTMAS CRIME

Follow That Star

by A.A. Abbott

Although they were both wearing wigs, only she knew her hair was fake.

Marc didn't. For sure, he appreciated his Santa outfit was a disguise. He clearly had no idea Milly wasn't who she appeared to be.

No one looked further than blonde hair, in her opinion. At this luxury hotel, the best in town, the gentlemen certainly preferred blondes. Especially after a few drinks, they leered, pinched her bottom and made offers. She laughed it off. Drake, the manager, would never support her if she complained. He'd claim the CCTV was broken. Anyway, these men weren't her prey.

'Why do you do this?' Marc asked, as they vaped together outside the delivery bay.

'I'd prefer a cigarette, but Drake will smell the smoke.' Milly shivered in the cold night air. Her uniform was overly traditional: a white blouse and black skirt, below which she was expected to wear sheer tights. She suspected the dress code was aimed at the clientele, or at least, the ageing male bosses who influenced their companies' choice of party venue.

'Here, let me.' He put down the vape pen and removed his fur-trimmed coat, placing it around her shoulders. 'I meant, why waitressing? You're a bright girl.'

'It's a job. Thanks for the coat.' It felt cosy and she approved of Marc's anarchy T-shirt. Somehow, it suited his stick-on beard.

'No worries.' He peered at his watch. 'Twenty past nine. Ciderhead Sid had better be quick. I cadged a turkey sandwich for him.'

'You too?' She fished a foil-wrapped packet from her bag.

As if on cue, Sid shuffled into view. Dishevelled and dirty, he slept out most nights with a bottle for company, staying just far enough from the main entrance to stop the security guards getting shirty.

'Them for me?' he slurred, grabbing their offerings as though he hadn't eaten all week. A brewery smell clung to him. It remained long after Sid mumbled his thanks and shambled off to pester passers-by for change.

Marc spun around to face Milly. 'Has anyone told you that you have the most beautiful blue eyes?'

'Often.' They hadn't, but she wasn't admitting it. Inside the hotel, with its flashing coloured party lights, no one could see your eyes properly. Milly made a mental note to try green contact lenses at the next place.

She edged away from him, finished vaping and returned his coat. 'Must get back. They'll want their coffees and mince pies.'

She could feel his gaze upon her as she pushed the door open, returning to the warren of rooms and corridors the guests would never see. Here, the odd mouse blinked in the fluorescent light; tattooed kitchen porters swore and Drake wielded his metaphorical whip. An otherwise unremarkable middle-aged man, Drake appeared to have the superpower of being in several places at once.

He sidled up to her as she collected a groaning tray of mince pies. 'Hurry up, slowcoach. You're thirty seconds over on your break.'

'Sorry. It won't happen again.' Milly flashed an appeasing smile rather than telling him to stick his job. She didn't wish either to burn bridges or be memorable in any way, let alone for the wrong reasons.

In the function room, its faded paint hidden by swags of tinsel, the Capital Chemicals party was in full swing. Few guests had stayed seated. Those who were had played musical chairs and moved to different tables. The rest gathered in small groups to drink and chat. Their beverages were stronger than the pots of stewed coffee she left with the pastries.

Drake had followed Milly in, no doubt to check up on her. Luckily, he was soon distracted by the Capital Chemicals CEO. The sleazy fellow, who had told Milly 'Call me Jim' while ogling her cleavage, asked when Santa would arrive.

Drake mounted a small stage. A DJ would use it later to play cheesy favourites. Meanwhile, an armchair and microphone had been reserved for Father Christmas. Drake grabbed the mic. 'Who wants to see Santa?' he bellowed.

'We do,' yelled the revellers, so lashed that Milly thought they would have cheered for Satan instead.

It was the signal for Marc to set off a sparkly party popper at the rear of the stage. He bounded through the glitter to applause from the crowd.

'Happy Christmas,' Marc announced, seizing the mic and seating himself in one fluid motion. 'The first little boy I've come to see goes by the name of Jim. Does anyone know where he is?'

Call Me Jim marched forward.

'Oh dear,' Marc said. 'You're a rather big little boy. You needn't sit on my knee, Jim.'

'Thank God for that,' Call Me Jim muttered.

'Has Jim been naughty or nice?' Marc asked the crowd.

'Naughty,' they roared.

Milly could believe it. Call Me Jim had left his jacket on the chair where he'd previously held court. She bumped into it, shaking the garment onto the floor and noticing a twist of paper fall out. It looked like a wrap of cocaine to her not inexpert eye. Evidently, Call Me Jim planned a white Christmas.

She picked up and straightened the jacket while the guests cackled at Call Me Jim's discomfort. Marc informed the CEO there might be a little something in the sack if he helped to give presents to the other boys and girls. A secretary produced a box of Secret Santa gifts. Call Me Jim and Marc distributed these with much innuendo.

By now, the meal was over. Watched over by Drake, Call Me Jim and his team continued with the serious business of getting out of their heads and into each other's knickers. Milly cleared tables and escaped to the kitchen. Thankfully, the staff dish of the day wasn't turkey, as Chef had no intention of serving 'the same thing every blinking night'. They tucked into curry, plus half-full bottles of wine snaffled by the servers.

Marc arrived, pulling off his whiskers with a wince. He was a good-looking lad under the white curls, with sandy hair and twinkling brown eyes. That twinkle had won him the job, he explained. 'I'm twenty-five, so it's not as if age matters.'

'Size?' Chef interrupted. A fat, balding man, he had a traditional Santa's girth, if not the hair.

'Nope.' Marc grinned. 'You've got to look cheerful. That's easier with office jollies than kids. Never work with children or animals. These parties are a piece of cake by comparison.'

'Seasonal, though, isn't it?' Chef said. 'What do you do

after December 25th?'

'As an actor, I take whatever I can get. I'm only Santa when I'm resting.'

'Been in anything I'd have seen?' Chef asked.

Marc laughed. 'Maybe, if you like Shakespeare. But my dream is breaking into Netflix. I've applied for a leading role in a new series. Fingers crossed.'

'Indeed,' Chef agreed. 'I do enjoy the Bard's work from time to time. I thought you seemed familiar.' He turned to Milly. 'How about you? What do you do for the rest of the year?'

She could have lied and claimed to be a student. Unusually, she elected to tell the truth. 'The outdoor life. Ski resorts and beach bars.' Milly was always moving, following her star. Christmas was the sole exception. It was when she returned to give something back. She hadn't forgotten where she came from.

She noticed Marc's bright eyes assessing her, and that decided it. She giggled, as people expected that from blondes. Then she added, 'I'm giving my notice as soon as I see Drake. There are jobs in Austria, and I can take my pick.' It was almost true. She'd already arranged to fly out for the New Year.

Later, when she broke the news to Drake, his face revealed that waitresses came and went all the time. He didn't try persuading her to stay.

'Coming on the staff bus?' Marc asked.

'No thanks, I've booked an Uber.' The staff bus was free, but it wiggled all around the city as it dropped everyone off.

The road outside was quiet apart from the purr of the Uber's engine and requests from Ciderhead Sid for spare change. Milly thought about giving him a fiver. She was flush, having filched forty pounds from Call Me Jim when she tidied his jacket. Do-gooders always told you not to give cash to the homeless, supposedly to avoid facilitating their addiction. Milly regarded addiction as a sensible response to a dismal life. She'd been there. In the end, she handed Sid half a pack of cigarettes, which pleased him greatly.

When Milly returned to the hotel two days later, Sid didn't recognise her. Nor did Drake, or anyone else. She was no longer blonde. Her natural brunette colour failed to turn heads and her LBD was similar to eighty per cent of the dresses worn at tonight's corporate Christmas party.

She arrived after the mince pies had been served, which, she knew, would have been at 9.30pm precisely. Drake was a stickler for detail and Chef, although loved by the staff for his fine cooking, ruled them with a rod of iron.

Marc was dishing out the company's Secret Santas, using the same old jokes she'd heard each night. They'd been funny once.

She found a semi-abandoned table. No partygoers were sitting there, but they had left jackets and handbags on their seats. The bags were dinky and black, just like hers. How easy it would be to pick up the wrong one by mistake, leaving hers behind. She did so three times, visiting different ladies toilets in the vast, maze-like building. Then she moved on to another table.

She had an escape route in mind, just in case. Even the hotel's long-dead architect would have been hard-pressed to navigate the service corridors as well as Milly. Ditching her bag would be no hardship, as her valuables were stashed in a hidden money belt. However, she was in luck. At a large corporate bash, half the merrymakers didn't know each other. Nobody challenged one more honey in a black dress. Only once did

Milly sense eyes upon her, but when she cautiously looked around, all the party animals were gawping at Father Christmas.

Before putting each bag back, effusive apologies at the ready, she took ten pounds here and twenty pounds there. It was a sum that well-off people wouldn't miss. They'd assume they hadn't counted properly, or they'd bought a round and forgotten about it. She was recycling their wealth, she told herself: taking from the rich to give to the poor. Milly had a very good evening, fruitful enough to return the next night, and the next.

It was when she left that party, as she was about to step into her Uber, that Santa appeared with a sobbing girl.

He waved, and Milly's heart skipped a beat. The message in his gaze was inescapable. Marc had spotted her.

'Hey, you're going south of the river, aren't you? Be an angel and take Joanne home. Some scumbag's nicked her taxi money.' Marc's glare said he'd worked out who had taken it.

'Of course.' Milly pointed Joanne into the cab, and got in beside her. She made sympathetic noises.

'This is so kind of you.' Joanne dabbed at her tears with a tissue.

'Don't mention it.' Reflecting, Milly recalled a couple of bags with very little money in them. She had raided them anyway. Next time and in the next hotel, this particular hunting ground being off limits now, she would be more careful.

Joanne lived in the poorest part of town, near the fleapit where Milly stayed. Milly considered booking an earlier flight, but decided Joanne posed no threat. She'd had her taxi home, after all. No, there were more hotels in town, all desperate for casual staff at this busy time of year. She would spend her ill-gotten gains and then find another job.

❄

It gave Milly a surge of pleasure to shop for a Christmas feast. She bought books and little treats too, then boxed up her purchases with pretty paper. Having asked around, she knew which families were in dire need, and she staggered to their homes with hampers. It brought a tear to her eye when the pinched faces of young mothers and their children lit up at the sight of food.

'I'm delivering for a friend,' she told them.

'Snap.' It was a familiar male voice.

Milly, about to say goodbye to a grateful single father, jumped with shock. She looked over her shoulder. Next door, Marc was handing over a basket of groceries to a woman with four toddlers clinging to her ankles.

'So we meet again. I knew it was you the moment I saw you strut down the street.'

Milly blushed. 'Really? Just from my walk?'

'That, and those blue eyes.' Marc gazed into them. 'You fooled Drake, but I'm an actor. I study body language. Anyhow, this is my last drop. How about a cuppa?'

Milly thought about legging it. However, Marc looked fitter and his expression was friendly. She found herself agreeing.

'Good choice.' He motioned to a greasy spoon café on the corner.

Over tea with three sugars, Marc suggested they pool resources. He didn't mention how she financed her largesse, but he did explain that he spent all year saving up. In his view, they should both change their approach and seek crowdfunding for their food parcels. 'So, what do you say?' he asked.

Milly managed a tight smile. 'That won't be possible. I'm leaving soon for the mountains and the sun.' She might have been raised in the inner city, but the best lesson she'd learned was that she didn't need to stay.

'I'm leaving too,' Marc said. 'I got the Netflix gig.'

'Congratulations.' Her smile broadened with genuine delight for him.

'Come with me. We're filming in Wales. I'll pull strings and get you a supporting role. We can work on your movements together.' He laughed. 'I've seen how you blend in anywhere. You've got raw talent.'

Milly stared at him. He understood her better than she'd realised.

Marc's eyes twinkled. 'By the way, I'll tape my wallet to my body. And tell everyone else on set to do the same. Seriously, if you're earning good money, do you really need to steal it?'

'You're on. Just one condition.' After all, she couldn't sense if he'd meant acting talent or something else. 'No casting couch. I'm not that way inclined.' The last statement wasn't quite true though. He really was cute.

Marc frowned at first, then grinned. 'Agreed. But there's also one condition from me. No wallets. Or handbags. Deal?'

'Deal.' Milly high-fived him, enjoying the brief touch. There would be sunshine as well as mountains in Wales, she was sure.

When you got the chance, you followed your star.

***

A.A. Abbott – known as Helen to her friends – is a British crime thriller writer. She has lived and worked in London, Bristol and Birmingham, and uses her knowledge of these cities as locations for her fast-paced suspense novels. Her latest psychological thriller, *Lies at Her Door,* is set in the shadow of the iconic Clifton Suspension Bridge. She is a member of the Alliance of Independent Authors, Bristol Fiction Writers' Group and Birmingham's New Street Authors.

THE COLLECTIVE NOUN
FOR SANTAS

BY ALEX AND HELEN WALTERS

SPARKLE, sparkle, sparkle. Death to all the damned sparkles.

Crystal couldn't have felt less festive as she walked along the road back to her house. Fairy lights, inflatable Santas, a plastic Rudolph that played carols in rotation. The neighbours had gone overboard this year.

It grated on Crystal's nerves. What had she got to celebrate? Her boyfriend had dumped her, her vile boss had come within inches of sacking her, and her cat had chucked up all over the carpet that morning before she'd had her first coffee.

That hadn't even been the most revolting mess she'd had to deal with that day. Working at a cheap and cheerful gastropub in the run-up to Christmas was an endless round of mopping up spilt lager and scraping Christmas pudding off the floor. Not to mention the horror of inspecting the bathrooms.

Not for the first time, she contemplated chucking it all in and quitting work after Christmas. That was a decision for another day though. For now, all she wanted to do was kick off her high heels, have a bath, put on her pyjamas and slippers, and crash out on the sofa with a bottle of wine and a takeaway. She couldn't think of a better way to spend a rare evening off.

The difficulty with that plan became clear as soon as she stepped into her living room. There, on the sofa, with her cat snuggled up to him, was a man she'd never seen before in her life. She had no idea who he was, although the way he was dressed suggested certain possibilities.

He was wearing black boots with a fur trim, his legs were stuck out in front of him and his chest, under his bright-red tunic, went up and down as he snored. On his head was a red hat with a big white pom-pom.

'Santa!' she said.

The man groaned, snuffled and started snoring again.

Crystal looked at him aghast. Why on earth was there a strange man on her sofa? And why was he dressed as Santa? And, more importantly, what was she going to do about it?

She shook his shoulder. 'Um, excuse me.'

'Shnur – nuffle,' he said.

Less gently she poked him in the arm. 'Wake up! What are you doing in my house?'

The man continued to snore, but stirred by his mistress's voice the cat sprang up, arched his back and jumped onto Santa's chest.

Santa screamed. Crystal screamed. The cat yowled.

'Who are you?'

Crystal took a deep breath. 'I live here. This is my house. Now, who the hell are you?'

The man rubbed a hand across rheumy eyes that, along with his white beard, made him look older than Crystal suspected he actually was.

'I'm... well, I'm...' The man looked bewildered. 'I'm...' He looked down at his red costume then lifted a hand to touch his fluffy white beard.

'You're not actually Santa, are you?' Crystal offered. 'I mean, apart from anything else, Santa isn't real.'

'I know that. But people *have* been calling me Santa.'

'I think you'll find that's because you're dressed as Santa.' Crystal couldn't work out whether this man sitting on her sofa dressed as someone who doesn't exist was insane, or if maybe she was. All she knew was that the prospect of a quiet evening with a chicken chow mein and a glass of Merlot was slipping swiftly away.

The man looked down at himself again, then put his hand up to where the pom-pom swung from his hat. 'Right.'

'But you must have a real name?' she pressed.

'Yes.' The man fell forward and put his head in his hands. 'But I don't know what it is.'

'You don't know what it is,' Crystal echoed, feeling like an idiot.

'The last thing I remember anyone calling me is Santa.'

Crystal sighed. 'Let's try something else. What are you doing in my house?'

'Your house?'

'Yes,' she said patiently. 'My house, my sofa, my cat.'

'I don't know. I don't remember.'

'What *do* you remember? You must remember something? What was the last thing you remember doing?'

The man stared into the distance. Well, as far as it was possible to stare from his position on Crystal's sofa.

'I remember putting this on.' He indicated the costume. 'I remember people calling me Santa.'

'Where were you?' Crystal suddenly had an idea. Maybe the man had been a Santa in one of the local department stores. 'Were you giving out presents to small children?'

'No children. Lots of other Santas though.'

'What?' Crystal dropped down onto the sofa next to him,

the weariness of the day and the inexplicability of the situation catching up with her. She was pretty sure this confused man wasn't an actual danger to her. But the problem remained. She needed to get him out of her house.

'Lots of other Santas,' he repeated. 'Yes, we were all dressed as Santa.' He looked ridiculously pleased with himself to have remembered that.

'All of you?' Crystal said. 'Who were the others?'

He was shaking his head now. 'I don't remember. I just remember being in this outfit, and being surrounded by other people all wearing the same. Lots of people in red with white beards milling around.'

'But you don't know where you were? Or who the other people were? Or how you came to be sitting in my house on my sofa?'

'No,' he said, sounding defeated. 'I really don't.'

Crystal didn't want to do it, but she realised she had no choice. It was starting to get dark outside and she wasn't sure what else to do.

'I'm sorry,' she said. 'I'm going to have to call the police.'

I don't believe in Father Christmas. I mean, obviously I don't. I'm thirty-two. I play rugby and drink pints. I'm a burly police constable. Obviously, I don't believe in Father Christmas.

Yet here he was, sitting in front of me.

I suppose I'd envisaged Father Christmas as more jovial than this downbeat figure. I'd have expected rosy cheeks, a large fluffy white beard and a general air of cheeriness. What I was looking at was a gaunt face, grey stubble and an overwhelming sense of misery.

Maybe not the real Santa then.

'Okay,' I said. 'Let's try this again. I'm PC Gibbs. What's your name?'

'I've told you. I don't know. All I remember is Santa.'

'If you're Santa, where's your sleigh? Reindeer? All that malarkey?'

'I don't mean I really am Santa. It's just that I can't remember any other name.'

'I hope you're not yanking my chain.' It had been a long day already, and it was nearly the end of my shift. The last thing I needed was Father Christmas taking the proverbial.

'I'm really not. I don't remember anything except–'

'Being surrounded by other Santas.' The householder here, a Ms Hadley, had already told me all this when I arrived. She was now sitting on the far side of the room, watching the two of us. She'd made it quite clear that what she really wanted was just to get Santa out of her house. I didn't blame her. The only problem was where to take him. I could take him back to the station, which would at least make it someone else's problem. But he hadn't really committed any crime. Not even breaking and entering, since he'd apparently just used a key he'd found under the doormat.

Another consideration was that if he really was suffering from amnesia, he might need medical attention. But for the moment all I could think of was to keep him talking, in the hope either his memory might return or – if he was trying to pull a fast one – he might let something slip. 'Tell me about these other Santas.' I felt a fool even saying the words. 'Where was this? What sort of place?'

He thought for a moment. 'Something's coming back, I think. We were in a room. Not a particularly large room. Not for so many Santas anyway. It was a bit cramped.'

'And everyone there was dressed as Santa?'

'I think so.' He closed his eyes. 'Though some of them were still getting changed.'

'Getting changed?'

'Into their Santa outfits.'

'Of course. And what were they wearing before?' This was beginning to feel as if it might get us somewhere.

'Before? I don't know. Just clothes, I guess.'

'But what sort of clothes? Smart? Casual?'

'I don't know. Smart-casual?'

I sighed. 'And these Santas were all men?'

'Well, yes, obviously. They were Santas.'

'Obviously. Silly of me.' There didn't seem much to be gained from debating the point. 'Can you remember anything about the room? Was it a house? An office? A changing room?'

Another long pause. 'I'm not sure. Not a house. I mean, not somewhere like this. More like a changing room.' He closed his eyes again, as if to envisage the scene. 'There were benches.' He offered this information with a note of triumph, as if he'd finally given me what I needed.

'Like in a gym?'

'Something like that.'

Another thought struck me. 'What are you wearing under that outfit?' If he was still wearing some of his normal clothes under the costume, there might be something to help identify him.

He looked surprised by the question. 'I don't really know.' He unbuttoned his top and peered inside. 'Looks like a vest.' He slid his hand tentatively inside his red trousers. 'And a pair of boxers, I think.'

That made sense, I suppose. I don't imagine Santa went commando. 'You don't have a wallet? Keys? Anything like that?'

He patted the places where he might expect to find pockets. 'Sorry.'

I was trying to think this through. It was a freezing cold day, and the Santa costume looked pretty flimsy. He was wearing a pair of sturdy boots – as Santa does – but if he hadn't been wearing a coat and was wearing only a vest and boxers under the uniform, it seemed unlikely he'd have walked very far. Either someone had driven him here or he'd come from somewhere close by.

Perhaps I should call back to the control room and check if there'd been any sightings of multiple Santas in the vicinity. The only problem with that plan is that the call handlers would think I was either drunk or having a laugh. Quite possibly both. Maybe save that as the last resort then.

But I was quickly running out of other ideas. I looked at my watch. My shift should have finished fifteen minutes ago. Why was it that this kind of problem always came up at the end of the shift? I couldn't really see any other option than to drive him back to the station and see if anyone else had better luck with him. I was already envisaging the reaction I'd get when I walked in with Santa in tow. I wouldn't be allowed to forget it this side of Christmas.

'Okay,' I said wearily. 'I think we'd better–'

He looked up suddenly, a new light in his bloodshot eyes. 'Football.'

'What?' It seemed increasingly possible he'd lost his marbles as well as his memory.

'A pitch. A football pitch. Outside the place we were getting changed. I remember seeing it through the window.'

I'd not been on this beat for very long and I didn't know the area particularly well. I couldn't immediately think of anywhere that met his description. I looked over at Ms Hadley. 'Any football pitches round here?'

'There's the park,' she said. 'There are a couple of pitches there. And some kind of hut they use as a changing room.'

I looked back at Santa. 'Okay, St Nick. I think we'd better go and take a look, don't you?'

Since it was obvious Santa couldn't remember where the football pitch was, and PC Gibbs didn't know the local area very well, Crystal led the way across the main road, through the park and over to the flat-roofed hut that served as a changing room for the local groups who used the football pitch.

As she walked, Crystal asked herself how on earth she'd got mixed up in this mess. The PC, who looked like he should still be at sixth form, had confirmed what she'd suspected. That Santa hadn't actually committed a crime. In fact, he'd ticked her off about her security arrangements.

'Doesn't everyone leave a spare key under the doormat?' she'd asked.

'It's not something we really recommend, madam,' he'd said.

In the end she thought she'd got off lightly when he'd handed her a card for the local nick's crime prevention officer and suggested she get in touch.

Now, as they all stood outside the hut in the park, she wondered what was going to happen next.

Gibbs turned to Santa. 'Is this the place where you and the other men got changed?'

Crystal was starting to feel sorry for Santa. Yes, he'd invaded her home, but he clearly didn't mean her any harm. She couldn't see him as a hardened criminal.

'I'd need to see inside really,' he said.

Gibbs tried the door handle. 'Locked,' he said, in a disappointed tone.

'You could always check for a key under the doormat.' Crystal held back a giggle.

Gibbs gave her a look, but stooped down and lifted the edge of a piece of sacking that obviously was the closest thing to a doormat that the hut could manage.

He coughed, then stood up with a key in his hand. This time the look he gave Crystal very firmly told her to keep quiet.

The key turned in the lock and they all trooped in. As Crystal looked around her, she saw a scruffy but unremarkable room with benches down the middle as Santa had described. 'Yes, this is the place,' he said.

'Right,' Gibbs said. 'So, you were in here with a bunch of other blokes and you all got changed into Santa costumes. Then what?'

'That's what I can't remember.' Santa sank down onto one of the benches and took his hat off. That's when Crystal noticed it.

'What have you done to your head?' she asked.

'That looks like a nasty cut.' Gibbs approached Santa for a closer look.

'Does it hurt?' Crystal asked.

'Not really.'

'It would account for the memory loss,' Gibbs said. 'The next thing we need to do is get you to hospital. We'll get your injury looked at and decide what to do next.'

'Okay,' he said. 'Guess I don't really have a choice. It's not like I have anywhere else to go.'

He sounded so forlorn that Crystal felt even more sorry for him.

'But before I do that, I'm just going to have a quick look

around in here to see if there's anything that could give us some idea of what's been going on,' Gibbs said.

Crystal looked around her. There was a row of lockers on the far wall. She watched as Gibbs tried various handles but the lockers were clearly, well, locked.

'Can't do much more,' he said. 'I've no grounds to break into them.'

Santa was still sitting on the bench with his head in his hands, but at that moment he looked up. 'There's something under the bench.'

Gibbs reached down to pick up a piece of paper, crumpled as though it had fallen from someone's pocket. As Gibbs picked it up with a begloved hand, Crystal gasped. 'I know what that is.'

'It looks like a restaurant flyer to me,' Gibbs said.

'Yes, but it's a flyer for the gastropub where I work. You see that photo of the genial host smiling behind the bar? That's my boss.'

She decided this wasn't the moment to explain how far from genial her boss actually was.

Gibbs frowned. 'That seems like a bit of a coincidence.'

Then Santa chipped in. 'That man.'

'Yes, what about him?' Crystal asked.

'I remember him now. He was one of the other Santas.'

It was a dilemma, to be honest. All my instincts were telling me I ought to get St Nick here seen by a medic. I didn't want to be the one who had Father Christmas die on his watch. The head injury didn't look serious in itself, but he might be suffering from concussion or some internal injury.

On the other hand, it was clear Santa himself was as keen to solve the mystery as anyone. I suppose that was understandable. It must be disconcerting to think you might be stuck as Father Christmas for the rest of your life.

'Look,' he said, 'let's at least go and check this pub out. If that doesn't give us the answer, then I can go and – well, get my head examined.'

You might not be the only one who needs his head examined, I thought. 'You're sure you feel up to it?'

'I feel fine. Well, fine-ish. Head's a bit sore, but I haven't got an actual headache or anything like that.'

I turned to Ms Hadley. 'Where is this place?'

'Just a few minutes away. I can take you.'

We left the hut and made our way back along the high street, Ms Hadley leading the way. We were beginning to attract some attention from other pedestrians. It's not often you see a woman leading a police officer and Father Christmas along the street. It occurred to me that when we arrived at the pub, people might think we were a strippergram service.

In the event, the pub was in too much of an uproar for us to be noticed at all. That was the first surprise. The second was that the pub was full of Santa Clauses. I mean, it wasn't that every customer was Father Christmas. But there seemed to be a surprising number of them.

And they were all arguing, some with each other, some with customers who were more conventionally dressed. They didn't sound like friendly arguments. There was a lot of shouting, finger jabbing, even the odd half-hearted push and shove. Some of the language was the kind you wouldn't expect Father Christmas to know. Rather stronger than 'Donner and Blitzen', if you get my drift. In short, it wasn't quite a riot, but it was heading in that direction.

And I was the sole representative of law and order in the room.

I decided there was no point in trying to quieten the mêlée from the doorway. I pushed my way towards the bar, closely followed by Ms Hadley and my own personal Santa. At least he wouldn't be feeling self-conscious in this place.

I finally reached the bar, where the noise seemed even more intense. The man whose image had been on the leaflet was standing behind the bar. By now, it seemed inevitable that he was also dressed as Father Christmas. He was stabbing his finger angrily towards a group of other Santas who were haranguing him with equal fury. I heard him say, 'Well, it must have been one of you lot!' Except that he didn't say 'lot'. The word he used was one I never expected to hear emerging from Father Christmas's mouth. I felt as if part of my childhood had been sullied.

I edged my way along the bar towards the angry group. As I approached, he caught sight of me and shouted, 'Look, it's the law.'

The group of Santas duly took the hint and, at least for the moment, fell silent. I moved along the bar until I was standing immediately before the man. 'What's going on here?'

'We've been robbed, that's what's going on. Eight hundred quid at least. Robbed by Father Christmas.' That's a redacted version of what he said anyway. His actual words were liberally interspersed with expletives.

'Please calm down, sir. Just tell me what's happened.'

'I've told you. We've been robbed. Eight hundred quid out of the till.'

'You had eight hundred pounds in cash in the till?'

For the first time, he looked unsure of himself. 'Something like that. It's Christmas, isn't it? Place has been heaving all day. I hadn't had a chance to take the cash back to the safe.'

I nodded, wondering how much cash had really been in the till. 'And what happened to it?'

'I had to go down to change a barrel. There were a couple of other staff behind the bar, so it hadn't occurred to me there was any risk. But while I was in the cellar, the two idiots both decided to go out to collect glasses.'

A young man at the far end of the bar held up his hand. 'It wasn't our fault. We had a bit of a quiet spell and we were running out of glasses. I thought you were–'

'I told you not to leave the bar,' the Santa manager said.

'You didn't. You said–'

'It doesn't really matter for the moment,' I said. 'Just tell me what happened next.'

'The cellar door's at the far end of the bar. Behind you. As I came up, I saw Father Christmas at this end of the bar with his hands in the till.'

'You saw Father Christmas with his hands in the till?'

'Well, not *the* Father Christmas, obviously. *A* Father Christmas. One of these people.' He gestured towards the group around me. Again, he didn't actually say 'people'.

I could see the argument was about to resume, so I intervened quickly. 'Did you try to stop him? This Father Christmas, I mean.'

'Of course I did. I came rushing over. But he vaulted over the bar and disappeared into the crowd.'

Normally, the idea of someone disappearing into a crowd while dressed as Father Christmas would have sounded absurd. In this place, he'd have been more conspicuous if he'd been dressed in jeans and a T-shirt. 'Ah. I see the problem.'

'Well done, PC Sherlock. So what do you suggest we do now?'

It was a good question. 'Could you describe this man at all?'

On reflection, that was a less good question. The manager said sarcastically, 'He had a big white beard, was dressed in a red outfit, and had a big red hat on his head. What do you think?'

'No, I meant–' I shook my head. 'It doesn't matter.' The truth was I had no real idea what to do. I suppose I could try to search several dozen Santas, but it was quite possible that the guilty Father Christmas had already left the building.

It was at that point that my own personal Santa spoke up from behind me. 'It was him. He was the one who told us all to dress as Father Christmas today. This was all his idea. I've remembered it all now.'

It was clear from the manager's expression that he'd have much preferred personal Santa to shut up. 'Okay,' I said wearily, 'you'd better tell me what you remember. But first, I'm calling for backup.'

Crystal watched Santa's face as he looked confusedly at her boss. There were signs of comprehension dawning, but he was still clearly as bemused at the situation as she was.

'Right,' said Gibbs, 'backup have arrived. I'll just brief them on the situation, then I want a chat with you, Santa.'

He gestured to a table in the corner of the pub, just beyond the continuing chaos of Santas now being nabbed by police officers.

Santa led the way and Crystal winced on his behalf as he hit his head on a low and very fake wooden beam as they approached the table.

'Ouch,' said Santa as he collapsed into a chair.

'Oh God, are you okay?' Crystal asked. 'The last thing you needed was another bump on the head.'

Santa sat with his head in his hands, rubbing his eyes, then he looked up at Crystal.

'Oh, it's you.'

'Yes,' said Crystal. 'It's definitely me.'

'Aren't you normally behind the bar?' Santa asked.

Crystal was confused. 'Well, yes. But you also turned up at my house earlier. Don't you remember?'

He rubbed his eyes again. 'I do. But I also remember seeing you in here. Behind the bar, serving tables.'

'That's weird,' she said. 'I recognise you as well now you've lost the beard and the funny hat and you're looking less peaky than you were earlier.' She saw so many people in this place, especially in the run-up to Christmas, but now she thought about it, this man had been in a few times recently. He wasn't exactly a regular, but he seemed to know some of the regulars so he was probably local at least.

Santa took a deep breath. 'I think my memory must be coming back.'

'That's good news, sir,' said PC Gibbs. 'Because I've got a few questions for you.'

'I can't remember everything yet, but I'll try my best.'

'Let's start at the beginning, shall we? The gentleman behind the bar?'

'My boss,' Crystal chipped in. 'Miles Carter.'

'Yes,' said Santa. 'I don't really know him personally, but, well, this place has a bit of a reputation. No offence to the lady.'

'None taken,' said Crystal. It wasn't exactly news to her that this place didn't have the cleanest slate.

'What sort of a reputation?' said PC Gibbs.

'It's the sort of place where people come to make dodgy deals. Everyone knows the manager turns a blind eye. But every now and then he calls a few favours in.

'There's this mate of mine, comes here a lot. Anyway, a couple of weeks ago he let me know there was something going down. A few of the locals, who owed him a favour, were going to help the manager pull off a stunt to steal the takings from his own pub. Someone had a job lot of Santa outfits – rejects from a costume manufacturer. So, they got the bright idea of everyone dressing up as Santa to cause confusion.'

'They certainly managed that,' said PC Gibbs. 'But how did you get involved, and how did you end up in Ms Hadley's living room?'

'That's where it gets embarrassing.' Santa looked at Crystal with a blush spreading across his cheeks.

'We're all grown-ups here,' said PC Gibbs.

Crystal wasn't sure about that, given that she still thought he looked about twelve, but she was willing to let it pass. And she couldn't wait to hear Santa's explanation.

Santa put his head in his hands once more, and then seemed to make a superhuman effort to sit up straight and look Crystal in the eye. 'I've been coming in here for a while. I can see how badly that man treats you. He's a pig.'

Crystal couldn't argue with that.

'So, when I heard about the plan, I thought I'd get involved and do a bit of sabotage. Make sure it went wrong. Make sure he got arrested. Something like that. I turned up at the meeting place earlier. You know, that football place. And I got into my Santa costume.'

'Then what?' Crystal asked.

'I think you'll find it's my job to ask the questions,' said PC Gibbs. 'Go on, sir.'

'That's where it gets a bit hazy again. I remember leaving the changing-room hut with the others. Then, I don't know.' He paused, screwing up his eyes in an attempt to remember. 'Something hit me, maybe a bike, I fell and banged my head. That's why I didn't make it here.'

'Right, sir. It's starting to look like you may be innocent of any crime. The people we need to arrest are Mr Carter and whoever actually took the money. If we can ever work out who that is.' He threw a despairing glance at all the Santas who were still milling around. 'I'll see how my colleagues are getting on.'

Crystal turned to Santa. 'I'm not sure whether I should thank you for doing this on my account or not.'

'Nor am I.'

'There's one thing I still don't understand,' Crystal said. 'How did you end up in my living room of all places?'

'Ah, that bit's even more embarrassing. I don't know if you remember, but a few nights ago he got really angry with you. You clocked off to go home and a few seconds later I saw him leave as well with a face like thunder. I followed you to make sure you got home safely.'

'Again, thank you... I think.'

'I suppose when I lost my memory, I must have just automatically retraced my steps from that night.'

'But how did you know there was a spare key under the mat.'

He smiled at her. 'Everyone does that, don't they?'

'No harm done, I guess,' Crystal said.

'Except to your boss,' said Santa.

'I doubt they'll have any evidence to prove he did anything wrong amongst all this confusion,' Crystal said.

'Ah, now that's where you're wrong.' Santa pointed at one of the other Santas. 'See the red-haired Santa with glasses?'

'Yes.'

'That's my mate. He volunteered to take the money out of the till. He was supposed to quietly slip away during the confusion and pass the money back to Carter later. But instead he planted it in Carter's office. He just tipped me the wink. Your boss is going to be in pretty big trouble once the police, and the owners of this place, work it out.'

Crystal still wasn't sure what to make of her new best mate, or the situation, but she couldn't help liking him.

'One more thing,' she said. 'I don't suppose you remember what your name is?'

'Funnily enough I do,' he said. 'It's Nick.'

***

Alex Walters has written many crime thrillers, including the DI Alec McKay series. He lives in the Black Isle in the Scottish Highlands where he runs the Solus Or Writing Retreat with his wife, occasional sons and frequent cats. This short story is his first collaboration with wife Helen, who's a widely published short story writer and regular columnist for Writing Magazine.

Maude

by Caron McKinlay

MAUDE SHUFFLED down the bus steps and into the snow. Fingers fumbled with the buttons of her old tweed coat. Everything was so difficult these days. Strands of grey hair were stuck slick to her face. With a sharp tut from the corner of her mouth, she brushed them away and bent down to pick up her carrier bags. There were a few bits and bobs for Christmas inside and she hoped they hadn't been ruined by the icy sludge that squelched under her feet.

'Excuse me? Are you all right or do you need a hand? It's absolutely freezing, eh?'

Maude smiled at the pretty brunette dressed in the Saturday night uniform of minidress, thigh boots and black puffer jacket. About twenty years old, plastered with make-up and thick black eyebrows. Kind eyes, hidden in shadows. 'Ach, I'm okay, love. It's just age, you know, and this awful weather. Used to be a time I could run up and down these roads with my shopping, but those days are long gone. I'm Maude, by the way.'

'I'm Sharon. Well, my mates call me Shazza. Have you got far to go? I'm waiting for my boyfriend to get off the next bus, but that's not for another fifteen minutes. I could help carry your bags a wee bit to your house?'

Maude's eyes crinkled in delight. 'Oh, that would be great, love. My hands are aching carrying these. The plastic digs into your fingers and that hill seems to get steeper every day. I'm only at number ninety-six, the house that stands by itself just after the bridge.'

As they walked, Maude spoke of her two grown daughters. 'Laura's a successful solicitor in an Edinburgh firm and Eliza's a social worker in Bethnal Green. Both are busy with their new careers and fresher husbands.' She paused to catch her breath. 'Neither has time for visiting, not even at Christmas, but I'm proud of them both.'

Sharon's breath etched the frosty air and she smiled wistfully. 'It must be hard for you not to see them at this time of year.'

Maude's eyes glistened. 'It's my husband I miss the most. We were married thirty-five years, always in each other's pockets. We did everything together. He even went with me to Sunday night bingo. He's been dead two years now and oh, how I miss him.' She fumbled for a tissue in her pocket and dabbed her puffy eyes. 'Ach! I'm a silly old fool, dear. I still leave his tartan slippers beside his favourite chair, and I've not washed his last whisky glass. It's less lonely that way. He loved a wee whisky while he watched the horses on the telly. Those damn slippers though. I must trip over them twice a day. Then I scream, 'John, you've left your slippers lying about again!' Of course, there's no one to respond.' She glanced at Sharon. 'Oh, I didn't mean to upset you, dear.'

Sharon wiped the tears from her face with the plastic cuff of her jacket. 'It's just so lovely, Maude. Not everyone finds someone that loves them like that. Some men...'

Maud frowned at Sharon. 'Some men give you black eyes, eh, love?'

Sharon lowered her face towards the ground, avoiding Maud's dark gaze.

'Love, there's no need to hide yourself. I saw them earlier when you picked up my bags. The ones on your wrists look fresher.'

Sharon pulled the sleeves of her jacket down further. Was it the bite of the cold or the sensation of shame that was reddening the girl's face? Maude looked closer. They passed under the old bridge in silence until Sharon finally spoke. 'Robert doesn't mean to hurt me. It's my fault. Sometimes I make the wrong thing for dinner or say something stupid. I always screw up and he's under so much pressure at work. His new boss is a bitch and nitpicks his work. I love him, Maude. I just need to listen more to his needs. It's really great when he's happy with me. Honest.'

Was this new boss a bitch or was it just something he'd told Sharon? She stopped at her garden gate. The roses were as overgrown as the weeds, and old crisp packets decorated the thorns like baubles on a Christmas tree. 'Look, this is me. Why don't you come in for a cup of hot tea and a chat? Leave the beggar waiting around for a bit.'

Sharon's head shook. 'Oh, I can't! I need to be there. Maybe some other time.'

'Come on, love. Look at the state of you, teary and freezing from the snow. You need someone to chat to and a hot cup of something to warm you up. In fact, I have that fizzy wine that you young ones drink. We could have a wee tipple together. Wouldn't that be fun?'

Sharon bit her lip. 'I really shouldn't. Robert is expecting me... but...' Her voice trailed off.

A black car slowed down beside them, music blasting. From

the open car window, two men with their faces hidden in grey hoodies shouted, 'Want a shag, hen?' Sharon stuck her middle finger up and they cackled and laughed. As the car revved off, a flash of dirty cold slush drenched the pavement. Sharon stepped back to avoid it, but Maude slipped on a patch of ice.

Sharon's eyes widened and she grabbed Maude's arms. 'Maude. Maude, are you okay?' she whispered. 'Ignore those arseholes. It happens sometimes.'

'I'm fine, I'm fine. Just a wee dizzy spell. I must have forgotten to eat lunch again, and that car gave me such a fright. Could you see me to my door please, love? Maybe help me sit down in my chair before you run off to see your fella?'

Sharon nodded, placing her palm at the old woman's elbow, but flinched back when her phone rang in her pocket. She grabbed it and answered. 'Oh, hi Rob! Yes, sorry, sorry... I've been watching the time, yes... Yes, but this old woman needed some help and well, she just fell. I'm just going to help her into her house... What? No, Rob! I'd never do that! Her name is Maude. We're just at that big house at the end of the bridge... uhm, number ninety-six... Okay, okay. I'll wait for you here. Rob, I'm so, so sorry. I was just...'

Maude rubbed the back of her neck and her face paled. 'You deserve better, you know, Sharon. But off you go. I'm fine, really. No point in him walking all the way up here. I might be tempted to give him a piece of my mind and that would make matters much worse.' Picking up her bags, she closed the garden gate and shooed Sharon off. 'Take care and thanks for the help. Look after yourself.'

Sharon dragged her hands through her hair. 'I'm sorry. I can't seem to do anything right.' She turned and fled back towards the bus stop.

The front door slammed. Maude trudged along the drab hall to the kitchen. The stench of old grease was thicker there, but it always clung to her straggly hair no matter which room she was in. A fly buzzed around a teacup. She batted it away, switched the kettle on and opened a new packet of Rich Tea.

From the hallway, the cupboard door creaked open, and Maude clenched her fists.

'You can come out now, John, but put the rope back in the toolbox. You won't be needing it tonight. The stupid bitch gave our address to her boyfriend.' She rinsed her mug under the hot tap. Grey lumps of jellied food floated around dirty dishes. 'And next time, get off your lazy arse and catch your own little playthings. I'm too old for this.'

Dipping a biscuit into milky tea, Maude sagged into the once pink sofa. Lights twinkled on the Christmas tree. Bought to brighten up the room, they only accentuated what was missing. She sighed and turned up the volume of *Coronation Street* to muffle the ache inside her.

They always said red was the colour of rage, but they're wrong. It's drab grey.

***

Caron McKinlay grew up in a mining town on the east coast of Scotland. When not blogging, reading, and writing, Caron spends her time with her daughters. She doesn't enjoy exercise – but loves running around after her grandsons, Lyle and Noah. Caron had three childhood dreams in life: to become a published author, to become a teacher, and for David Essex to fall in love with her. Two out of three ain't bad, and she's delighted with that.

DEATH AT CHRISTMAS

BY D. S. BUTLER

I'LL NEVER FORGET the Christmas I spent at Thornberry Farm.

Christmas had always been my favourite time of the year – the decorations, fairy lights, the smell of a real Christmas tree, and the taste of mince pies still warm from the oven.

I wasn't looking forward to working over the Christmas period. I'd miss the celebrations at home. No sharing a box of cherry liqueurs with Nan, laughing at Dad snoring in his armchair after the Queen's speech, and no teasing Mum about the rapidly emptying sherry bottle. I'd even miss the old tinsel and foil decorations that I'm sure my nan had kept since the eighties.

All families had their own traditions, and the Thornberrys were no different.

Most of the Christmas preparations fell to me. I'd bought the children's advent calendars, ordered the tree, a large spruce from another local farm, and decorated it with the Thornberry children, Tom and Philippa. We'd draped garlands over the mantelpiece. Christmas chocolates, wrapped in brightly coloured foil, nestled in crystal bowls on the kitchen dresser and coffee tables. The children weren't supposed to eat them until Christmas Eve, so when I noticed the level getting a little low, I secretly topped them up.

Technically, most of what I did for the Thornberrys wasn't in my job description, and it certainly wasn't in my employment contract, but over the year I'd worked for the family, my role had expanded, until I was no longer an accounts and administrative assistant for the farm, but a general helper and part-time nanny for the children as well.

I didn't really mind. If I had done, I suppose I would have put up more of a fuss. I was very fond of the children, and I happily took them to their choir practice and sewed their outfits for the nativity play at their primary school.

My first impression of their mother, Gretchen, was a sweet but harried woman, always rushing about but never seeming to get anything done. She wasn't suited to being a farmer's wife. A creative type, she preferred to be immersed in her studio. Sadly, though she spent a great deal of time working on her art, the paintings weren't a commercial success. More than once I'd heard Ed, her husband, grumbling about the studio being in debt. He was right, of course, I'd seen the accounts.

But, under Ed's control, the farm had also been making a steady loss. That, together with the fact the Thornberrys still insisted on a luxurious lifestyle, including shopping at expensive delicatessens, and ordering clothes from boutiques with eye-watering prices, meant money was in short supply.

Ed Thornberry didn't own the farm. Everything was still in his father's name, and the fact father and son didn't get on well only added to the tense atmosphere around the farm. Ed's father, Charles, was known in the village as Old Man Thornberry. On my first trip to the village shop I'd been given the family history by Mrs Applewhite, a friendly woman, partial to gossip.

She first told me about Marcus Thornberry, the tearaway younger son, who drank heavily, lived in London, and had a reputation in the village as a woman chaser.

She also told me Charles had run the farm as a thriving enterprise. He'd employed many of the locals and had been much respected and admired. In recent times though, after Ed took over the day-to-day running of the farm, the old man had turned into a recluse.

Mrs Applewhite, stacking tins of beans, had asked casually, 'I don't suppose you've seen him?'

At that point, I'd only been working at the farm for a week. I knew he lived in an annexe on the opposite side of the farmhouse to my smaller annexe, but I hadn't met him.

I shook my head. 'Not yet.'

She sighed. 'He doesn't come to the shop anymore. He gets his groceries delivered. Such a terribly sad situation.'

That piqued my curiosity. 'Why, what happened?'

Mrs Applewhite surveyed me carefully, perhaps weighing up whether I could be trusted. 'Charles has always been a bit eccentric, but...' She put down the can she'd been holding and looked at me directly. 'I'm worried about him. He used to come to the pub a few times a week, but I can't remember the last time I saw him there.' She shrugged. 'I'm sure there's nothing in it. But there are rumours.' She gave a nervous laugh. 'It's ridiculous, I know. But you do hear about this sort of thing.'

'What sort of thing?' My grip tightened on the metal handle of my shopping basket. I had picked up on some tension between Ed and Gretchen, but this sounded like something far worse than a marital tiff.

'People say his sons have locked him away. That he's lost his marbles, gone quite mad.' Her eyes were wide as she watched me closely.

Was she really worried about the old man or was she trying to get information to feed the local gossip circle?

'I don't know anything about that,' I said briskly, determined not to show that her words had rattled me. I had to admit, I found it odd that I hadn't met the old man yet. When I'd offered to take his post to him the day before, Gretchen had insisted that was not part of my job and practically snatched the letters from my hand.

I left the village shop feeling uneasy, but after the children got home from school, I was too busy to dwell on Mrs Applewhite's gossip.

Unfortunately, it wasn't long before I had my first run-in with Marcus Thornberry and realised there was more than a grain of truth to Mrs Applewhite's description. I soon learned to go to bed early when Marcus was visiting.

I first met Charles Thornberry in March. It was a sunny morning. The sky was an intense blue and the lawn shimmered with frost. I had taken my coffee into the garden to look at the cheerful explosion of daffodils.

I wasn't sure it was him at first. I'd expected him to be a doddering old man, but he didn't appear as elderly as I'd expected. His face was weather-beaten and wrinkled, but his hair was still dark, though greying at the temples. His blue eyes and bushy eyebrows were so like Ed's, I couldn't miss the family resemblance.

Feeling unnerved at Charles's sudden appearance, I forced myself to smile. 'Good morning.'

'Who are you?' he snapped back.

His penetrating gaze made my mouth grow dry. 'I'm Lily Gold. I work here at the farm. Admin and accounts, but I help out with the children too, and well...' I trailed off. I had held my hand out for him to shake, but he looked at it as though it was a rotten fish.

I let my hand return to my side, irritated at his rudeness and my lack of backbone. Why did I let him get away with snapping at me like that? Did he think just because I was an employee he could...

'How long have you been here?'

'Not long. I just popped into the garden to look at the flowers while I had my coffee.' I'd been on the go all morning, getting the children ready and taking them to school. This was my first coffee of the day. Surely, he wasn't going to complain about me taking a few minutes for myself.

He batted my words away in irritation. 'No. I mean how long have you been working at the farm?'

'Oh, I see.' I flushed. 'About two months now.'

He frowned. 'Why haven't I seen you before?'

I didn't know how to answer that question. Should I say because he'd locked himself away? Or because Gretchen had warned me to steer clear of 'the old curmudgeon'. I didn't think he'd appreciate me telling him that, and Gretchen certainly wouldn't.

So, I simply shrugged.

He grunted. 'Are you sure you're qualified to do the accounts?' He looked me up and down.

'Yes!' It was my turn to snap. 'I have a degree in accounting actually.'

He lifted his eyebrows. 'Glad to hear it.' I couldn't be certain, but I think he smiled. 'I didn't mean any offence. I'm just surprised I haven't seen you before.'

'No, well, perhaps I should have introduced myself, but Gretchen said–'

He barked out a laugh, and I stopped talking.

'She told you not to bother me, eh?'

'Something like that.'

'Hardly surprising. Did Ed tell you the farm is mine?'

'Yes, he did.'

He grunted again. 'It was successful when I ran it, but now it's losing money hand over fist. If I were a few years younger, I'd take it back.'

I wasn't Ed's biggest fan, but I couldn't help feeling sorry for him. The industry had changed in the last few years. His father running him down in front of me, an outsider, seemed unfair.

'I think he's trying his best,' I said, feeling the need to be loyal.

Charles snorted. 'I thought, having a degree, you'd be smarter than that.'

I ignored the jibe. 'Times change. It's hard to run a successful farm these days.'

He shook his head. 'They have you fooled, don't they?'

Then, without another word, he walked away.

After that, I saw him from time to time, standing by the window at the front of his annexe. I'd wave, and if I was lucky, would get a nod of acknowledgement, but we didn't talk again for another week. Gradually as the months passed we built up a friendship.

It was my first Christmas with the Thornberrys, and over the school holidays, the children made more demands on my time.

To their delight it had snowed for the past two days, and a white Christmas was looking very likely.

I'd persuaded them to gather around the crackling fire in the sitting room, intending to read them a story. But the children had other ideas. They complained stories were boring. They wanted to have fun. To do something exciting, go outdoors to play in the snow.

They'd been outside earlier, but now the sky was darkening and the temperature had dropped. I looked out of the window, doubtfully.

'Please, Lily. Can't we play outside again. Just for a little while?'

I felt some gloves I'd left to dry on the radiator. They were still a little damp, but not as sopping as they'd been earlier.

Tom added his wheedling to Philippa's.

'All right,' I said. 'But only for a little while. It will be dark soon.'

'Yes!' The children rushed to put on their coats, scarves and gloves and I did the same. I didn't have to go with them. They were perfectly safe in the garden, but I preferred being outside where there was less chance of me seeing Ed or Gretchen. Late the previous night, they'd had a humdinger of a row. Today, no one had mentioned the argument, but the atmosphere was tense.

Outside, the children returned to their snowman. They'd made him almost as tall as Philippa, with a carrot nose, and dark pebbles for his eyes and the line of his mouth.

'Grandpa!' Philippa shouted with glee and ran past me.

Tom followed suit and they both rushed over to Charles Thornberry who was walking towards us holding a tray with four mugs, wobbling a little under the weight.

He chuckled as the children each took a mug of hot chocolate, topped with whipped cream. Then he said to me,

'Thought you might like one too. It's a bitter day.' He winked. 'Extra marshmallows. Hot chocolate is not the same without them.'

I took it gratefully and listened as the children chattered away happily, telling him about their snowman. He spent some time helping the children pack more snow around the base and find sticks they could use for the snowman's arm.

He straightened with a groan, and winced, pressing his hand into the small of his back.

'Are you all right?' I asked.

'Arthritis. Gets me sometimes. Feels like burning hot knives.' He shook his head. 'Take my advice, don't get old.'

'Getting old is better than the alternative, I suppose.'

He grunted.

'The hot chocolate is delicious. Thank you.'

'No problem.' He shrugged and looked down at his boots, dark against the snow. 'How have you been getting on?' He looked back at the farmhouse.

'Fine,' I said cheerfully. 'Things are going well. And I've grown attached to these two.' I nodded at the children who were making snowballs.

He smiled at them with affection.

'I should get them inside. It will be dark soon.'

'Ah, let them play. It's nice to see them having fun, a bit of normality. That's what they need. Especially after last night.'

So, he'd heard the row all the way over in his annexe.

'Yes, I suppose they do,' I agreed.

The children's breath left their mouths as steam as they laughed and threw snowballs at each other.

'Are you spending Christmas here?' Charles asked.

'Yes.'

He frowned. 'A young woman, like you... Do you not have your own family to spend it with?'

42

'Yes, but Gretchen needs me to stay on the farm.'

'If she spent less time in the studio and more time with her children–' He broke off. 'Sorry, not your problem.' He put his hands in the pockets of his coat. 'Must be hard to meet friends stuck on a farm out here. Ed gives you time off, doesn't he?'

I hesitated a bit too long before replying.

'I'll have a word if he doesn't,' Charles added ominously.

'Oh, no, you don't need to. I do have time off now and then. I went into Oxford a few weeks ago.'

He looked sceptical. 'Well, you need to see people. It's not natural to be cut off from the world.'

He was being dramatic, Thornberry Farm was isolated, but Oxford was only ten miles away.

'Like you, you mean?' I softened the words with a smile to show I was teasing.

He stared at me, then laughed. 'Fair point. But I'm an old bloke, hobbling around with arthritis. I've lived my life. You're young. You haven't.'

I smiled. 'You're not *that* old.'

'Tell that to my hip,' he grumbled.

After a few minutes standing in silence watching the children, he suddenly said, 'I wish Carole could see them like this.'

'Carole was your wife?'

He nodded. 'Yes, she died before Tom was born. She'd have been proud as punch of those two.' He grinned as Philippa threw a snowball that grazed her brother's ear causing him to shriek in surprise.

Charles turned to look at the farmhouse again. 'She'd have sorted out Ed and Marcus, make no mistake.'

I wasn't sure what to say to that, so I said nothing.

'Ed's drinking a lot, isn't he?'

How was I supposed to answer that? Ed certainly enjoyed a drink but saying that to his father felt like telling tales.

When I didn't reply, he said quietly, 'Sometimes I think they'd like to get rid of me.'

'I don't–'

'If they could get away with it, I think they would. Ed and Marcus would love to get their hands on my money.'

I shivered. Did he really believe his children felt that way?

'Perhaps it's because you don't understand each other. Maybe a chance to clear the air and mend a few bridges could solve a lot of problems.' My words were hopelessly naive.

'I don't think they want to mend bridges, Lily. They want the money.'

'I don't know what to say, Mr Thornberry,' I said honestly.

'Call me Charlie. And I don't expect you to say anything.'

Was he really worried his sons would hurt him? I couldn't see Ed committing murder, but Marcus? I didn't like him. He was cold and calculating as well as being a lecherous pig.

'If you're really worried, maybe you should tell someone. The police?'

'Don't you worry about me, Lily. I have a backup plan.'

'Children! Come in immediately!'

We all turned to see Gretchen calling from the kitchen window.

Charlie rolled his eyes, the children trotted off to the house obediently, and I gathered up the empty mugs.

'I can wash them,' I offered.

'That's all right. It gives me something to do.' He took the mugs from me, and I followed the children into the house.

'What on earth were you thinking, Lily?' Gretchen scolded as soon as I walked in the door. 'It's almost dark and the children are freezing.'

Tom and Philippa, pink-cheeked and stripping off their

coats, turned to watch us curiously. I forced down a sharp retort.

'The children wanted to play. We don't get snow often and so–'

'And what were you talking to him about?' Her eyes narrowed.

'Grandpa was just helping us with the snowman, Mum,' Tom said.

'Get out of those wet clothes and warm yourselves by the fire in the sitting room,' Gretchen ordered before turning her attention back to me.

'I can't believe you'd behave in this way, Lily. After we welcomed you into our home... after everything I've done for you.'

I stopped unbuttoning my coat. Welcoming me into her home? I wasn't a guest. I was an employee, and not a very well-paid one, especially considering the hours required.

My anger bubbled to the surface. 'Gretchen, I look after your children without complaint, though it isn't in my contract. I cook for them, pick them up from school. I do the accounts, the filing.' I spread my arms to indicate the kitchen, that I'd cleaned only a few hours earlier. 'I keep your house tidy, which certainly isn't in my contract. I start work at seven and I'm rarely finished before seven in the evening, so I think it's *me* who does rather a lot for *you*.'

I held my breath. Though most of the time I was happy with my job, there was no doubt it wasn't the job I'd expected when I'd signed up.

I'd mentally packed my case, my chest tight at the thought of having to leave the children, when Gretchen's eyes filled with tears. She slumped into a seat at the kitchen table.

'Oh, Lily, I know you work hard. You've been wonderful,

an absolute angel. I couldn't cope without you. But you know how he is... If he'd seen you just now–'

'Who? Ed?'

She nodded, brushing a tear from her cheek. 'Yes, you know how he gets. You must have heard him last night.' She looked up at me.

'Well, I didn't like to mention it...'

'It's hard, dealing with his temper. And seeing you cosying up to his father could make things so much worse for me.'

'But why?'

'It'll make Ed angry.'

I hesitated before asking, 'I know he's been drinking a lot and you've been arguing, but has he ever hurt you?'

Gretchen shook her head. 'No! He would never hurt me physically, but his moods are unbearable at times. And seeing you out there talking to his father would have set him off again.'

'I wasn't doing anything wrong. He brought hot chocolate. The children seemed happy to spend time with their grandfather.'

Gretchen's lips tightened. 'You don't understand the situation. You really shouldn't interfere.'

I pulled off my coat, hung it on the back of a chair and sat down. 'That's not my intention.'

She ran her hands through her hair. 'I know. None of this is your fault. Charles likes to punish his sons. He withholds money. The farm is in desperate trouble, but Ed has a way out. He's going to turn a quarter of the land over to farm high-value crops – things like berries. There's a lot of money in it, but we need investment to make a start, and Ed's father refuses to help. Marcus's business is in trouble, and he's frustrated by Charles's lack of support too.'

'Does Charles have the money?'

'Oh yes,' she said bitterly. 'He's swimming in the stuff. He just holds back out of spite.'

'Are you sure? He didn't seem–'

'You know him better than us, do you? A few chats in the garden and now you're firm friends?'

'No, of course, not.'

She took a deep breath. 'I shouldn't be taking this out on you. Forget I said anything.' She stood up. 'I'm going to work in the studio. Can you get the children's dinner tonight? Oh, and by the way, there'll be one more for Christmas. Marcus is coming to stay.'

I suppressed a shudder. Last time Marcus was at the farm, he got very drunk and kept putting his arm around my shoulders and whispering dirty jokes.

An hour later, I was adding pasta to a saucepan of boiling water when Philippa walked into the kitchen.

'Lily?'

'Yes.'

'Why do you want Grandpa's money?'

I put down the pasta packet and turned to face her. 'What do you mean?'

'I heard Mummy and Daddy talking. They said you were after Grandpa's money.'

I wanted to know what else she'd overheard, but it wasn't fair to involve the children. I put on a bright smile and said, 'I don't want your grandpa's money. Now, do you want tomato sauce or pesto with your pasta tonight?'

Christmas was shaping up to be a subdued affair. I tried to make it fun for the children, but I missed the relaxed festive atmosphere of my parents' house.

At half past eight on Christmas Eve, the children were in bed, Ed and Marcus were huddled in the study drinking whisky, and Gretchen was in her studio. I'd tidied the kitchen as usual and was preparing to go to my annexe, a cold lonely one-bedroom apartment with a tiny en suite bathroom.

Feeling sorry for myself, I stuffed the children's stockings and hung them over the fireplace. As I turned, I noticed a small stack of mail on the dresser. It was all addressed to Charlie.

I hadn't seen him for almost a week, and I was worried about him after our last conversation. I grabbed the letters and headed back to my annexe. To remind me of my nan, I'd bought a box of cherry liqueurs for Christmas, intending to eat them after the children went to bed the next day, but on a whim, I decided to take them to Charlie. It was getting late, but the lights were on, so I decided to knock.

When he didn't answer, I thought perhaps he'd gone to bed early and mistakenly left the light on. Instead of turning away, I stepped into the small flower bed and peered in through the window.

Charlie was on the floor. The beige carpet was soaked with blood and a knife was embedded in his chest.

I dropped the letters and the box of chocolates, staggered backwards, and screamed.

The investigation that followed was a very dark time. Ed accused me of his father's murder. He told detectives I had been manipulating Charlie, intending to steal the family's inheritance.

I was questioned in a small stale room with no windows at the main police station in Oxford for over an hour. When

Charlie Thornberry's will revealed he'd left me fifty thousand pounds, it only added to the detectives' suspicions.

He left the rest of his wealth in trust for his grandchildren, though Ed was to manage the farm until the children came of age.

A week after Charlie's death, I learned Mrs Applewhite had come forward and given a letter to the police. In it, Charlie had detailed his fears that his sons might kill him to inherit his wealth early.

I guessed Mrs Applewhite's letter and the trust for his grandchildren was all part of Charlie's plan to make sure his sons didn't benefit from his murder.

I didn't sleep well after I'd found Charlie's body, which was hardly surprising. But my insomnia wasn't only because I was a suspect, or because I thought I should have done more to help Charlie.

There was something else bothering me, but I wasn't sure what.

I missed Tom and Philippa a great deal and couldn't help worrying about them. My family encouraged me to move on, and though I knew they were right, I couldn't resist driving back to the village to speak with Mrs Applewhite.

The bell above the shop door rang out as I stepped inside. Mrs Applewhite was behind the counter and her eyes widened in surprise.

'Lily, I didn't expect to see you again.'

'I didn't hurt Charlie,' I said in a rush. 'I know there must have been a lot of talk in the village, but I had no idea he'd left me any money.'

She walked out from behind the counter, put her hand on my arm and squeezed gently. 'I know. His family are a cruel lot. Selfish and greedy. I was very close to him at one time. Before he and his wife met.' Her cheeks flushed. 'Not many people remember that, but I always had a soft spot for him. I worried about him after Carole died. He came to see me last year, gave me that letter and said I'd know what to do with it when the time came.'

'Did he tell you he thought his life was in danger?'

'Not in so many words.'

'He told me,' I said softly. 'And I didn't do anything to help him.'

The door opened and one of the detectives, DS Clarkson, who had interviewed me in Oxford, walked in. Her eyes narrowed when she saw me.

'What are you doing back here, Miss Gold?'

'I came to see Mrs Applewhite.'

The detective took a can of lemonade from the chilled cabinet. The three of us stood in awkward silence as the detective paid Mrs Applewhite for the drink.

Finally, Mrs Applewhite asked nervously, 'Are you here to arrest Ed Thornberry?'

'I can't discuss the case with members of the public,' DS Clarkson said coolly.

'I don't think Ed killed his father,' I blurted out.

Both Mrs Applewhite and the detective turned to me in surprise.

'No?' Lifting an eyebrow, the detective said, 'Is there something you have to tell me, Miss Gold?'

'Actually, yes. I think you need to question Gretchen.'

Mrs Applewhite gasped, but the detective looked annoyed and bored. 'Thank you for your input, but we have already done that.' She walked to the door.

'Wait!' I said. 'Don't you want to know why I suggested that?'

The detective sighed. 'All right. I'll bite. Why?'

'It's the letters.'

She frowned. 'The letters you dropped?'

'Yes. How long was Charlie dead before I found him?'

She hesitated. 'Four days, we think.'

I nodded, going through the dates in my mind. 'The postmarks on the letters. Gretchen always insisted on taking Charlie his mail. It was the one thing she didn't allow me to help with. I think because they worried I was after the family fortune. They didn't like me spending time with him, but that doesn't matter now. What's important is the dates on the letters.'

'You're not making any sense,' the detective said.

'I think Gretchen knew there was no point in taking Charlie his mail because she knew he was dead. And if she knew that, perhaps she was the one who–'

'–who killed him,' the detective finished my sentence.

I couldn't be entirely sure Gretchen was responsible. There may have been an innocent reason for her not taking Charlie his mail, perhaps she'd simply forgotten. Although forgetting the mail for four days in a row when she'd never done so before was unlikely. She could also have known he was dead, but not necessarily have killed him. Ed or Marcus could have killed Charlie and confided in Gretchen.

But it turned out the letters were the key clue to the murderer's identity. Gretchen crumbled during questioning and confessed to killing Charlie because he refused to help them with their money troubles.

I didn't attend Charlie's funeral. But a few months later, I visited his memorial in the crematorium. It was March and bright yellow daffodils lined the entrance path, reminding me of the first day I'd met him. Feeling a little self-conscious, I stood beside the memorial stone and told him that I used the money he left me for a deposit on a small flat, and that I'd applied to train as a primary school teacher.

My time at Thornberry Farm had made me realise how much I enjoyed working with children. I liked to think Charlie would have approved of my new career choice.

On my walk home, I popped into a small cafe to warm up.

I smiled at the woman behind the counter as I scanned the drinks menu.

'I'll have a hot chocolate, please. Extra marshmallows.'

***

D. S. Butler, who also publishes under the names Dani Oakley and Danica Britton, writes mysteries in many different flavours — some grittier than others. So far, she's written two standalone psychological thrillers: Lost Child and Her Missing Daughter, and two detective series.

Around the Gas Stove

by Jen Faulkner

'Is she coming?'

Lights glitter from the inside out. I smell the concoctions of everything put in place to make this Christmas party go with a bang. To outdo the last one, the one I had hosted. Water scented with cinnamon and star anise boils on the stove in a tiny copper saucepan, next to the homemade mulled wine simmering alongside. A tad extravagant to have both, I think, but am not surprised. Everyone always goes over the top in this village.

The house stinks, which is why Laura, the host, has opened the sash window a crack. Laura stirs and sniffs the wine before ladling the deep red liquid into gigantic bowled glasses and handing them out.

'She hasn't replied.'

Standing around the gas stove, five women sip the hot spicy wine while ignoring the awkwardness that shrouds them all whenever *she* is mentioned. Sudden flashing from a Christmas tree reaching all the way to the ceiling breaks the tension and they lose themselves in the familiar for a while – talking about

Christmas plays and their child's starring role. For each of their children has a starring role, of course.

And I need them to stay there, around the gas stove. Huddled together like witches around a cauldron, the urges to cackle dulled for now. But as they drink, as the wine loosens their wicked tongues, they'll move onto other subjects, the ones I came to listen to, the ones where I can grab onto the information I came to glean. The closure.

'Have you seen her at all, since, you know?'

A chill whips around me, the warmth of the log burner not able to reach this far, the heat being lost through the gap in the window. One of them glances over, as though I should be the one to answer this question, but I remain mute. There are no words left I want to speak on the matter, only ones I need to hear over the crackle of the flames and the roar of the wind.

They turn to look at each other and shake their heads one at a time, their lips downturned as though even the thought of seeing her, or admitting to it, disgusts them. But I know no one has seen her. I know a lot of things. A shiver runs through me as I stand here, pushing thoughts of *her* away. I lean in and listen.

Outside, the dark night air gusts around the house, nestled on the end of a cul-de-sac seen as *the* place to live in this village. The houses are large enough to hold three or four families and yet scaffolding is erected around most of them, covered in twinkling fairy lights, like a status symbol. 'I have more money than I need,' the cold hard metal screams at those who walk by, 'More money than you, but I still don't know how to be happy.'

With high hopes, I'd moved my family here five years ago, and since then had paid my dues, had got involved, had bitten my tongue. These women, all five of them around the gas stove, are my friends. Our children are friends. And yet, still they aren't telling me what I need to hear.

'If she's not careful we'll stop inviting her.'

They all laugh then, smiles wide and artificial white teeth with a filling or two on show. I wonder which one of them will be the first to start the exclusion. Will it be Melanie? Or Caroline? Or maybe they won't need to reject her, I think. Maybe *she's* already ejected herself. Again, I need to hear more, to stay here a while longer, alongside the witches as they toil and trouble. I need to remove all blame. To have proof that *she* is not at the party tonight because of them. Not me.

You learn to watch your mouth in a place like this. You are not allowed to speak your mind, you are not allowed to challenge others, you are not allowed to be offended if the person doing the offending didn't mean to offend. There are rules here. Rules designed to keep everyone sane, even though they are anything but.

'She was rude.'

'She really was.'

'I know, right? I mean there was no need.'

'You were only trying to help.'

'I *was* only trying to help.'

'You've done so much for her.'

'We all have.'

'And yet still she bangs on that we don't understand.'

There are huffs and eye rolls and vigorous nods, and I find myself nodding along with them even though I don't agree. They haven't tried to understand. They've broken the rules themselves. They are offended.

'Well, I'm not going to apologise.'

'You shouldn't have to.'

'You've done nothing wrong.'

'She's a bitch.'

There, I think. This is what I came for. The truth. To learn what they really think of her. What they say behind her back when the rules don't count. When they can't be caught out.

A spark lights a piece of kindling inside me. My tongue burns with everything I want to say. But I swallow and wash the words away and dampen the fire in my stomach.

There is a gift in my hand, for the party. And they've all brought one, the women around the gas stove. Mine is a carefully chosen item designed to maim the person who chooses to unwrap the parcel. As the recipient cries out in pain, my hand will go to my mouth in mock horror, and I'll cry crocodile tears and say that I hadn't known the knives inside weren't safe in their protective sheaths. Claim I hadn't looked. I have my alibi all sewn up. A nasty accident, they'll say when they talk about what happened at next year's party.

Poor, poor so and so. Heads will tilt in sympathy. Eyes will narrow in pity and I don't care which one of them opens my Secret Santa package and slices their flesh. I don't care whose blood will be spilled.

Fuelled with rage, I turn the present in my hand and toy with putting it under the tree with the others. The wrapping paper is smooth with sections of rough green glitter. A bright red bow holds everything together. I puff out the edges of the ribbon, making the present look as attractive as I can, and pull at a loose thread. *Not yet,* I think, *I'll keep hold of it for now.*

The first time I hurt someone on purpose was at primary school. I was six. My friend, Jess, was sitting on the table in front of me and we were sewing decorations to make mobiles. I was crafting a rainbow, my needle threaded with bright yellow ribbon. The metal glinted in my hand and without pausing to think I drove it hard into her leg, felt a pop as the sharp end passed through her tights and skin.

She screamed and I laughed. Then when the teacher shouted at me and the guilt kicked in I wasn't sure why I had done it. There was a part of me, one I couldn't admit to at the time, which had wanted to hurt her. She'd left me out during the playtime before the lesson and had instead skipped around the playground with Becky, who she knew I hated. Maybe that's why my hand had thrust the needle into Jess's leg. Maybe not. The important thing to remember is that first time I'd felt guilty. The time I hurt someone after that, not so much.

'Should we text her?'

'Or call?'

My phone is on silent. My video doorbell uncharged. The fear of being forced to be sociable when I'm not expecting to be is very real. They know this, my friends around the gas stove, and yet they still call by unannounced or send irritated texts when I don't answer my phone after the first ring. *She* won't answer them tonight if they call. I know that. I know her.

'Maybe. She might have forgotten.'

'She might be busy.'

'She's never busy.'

'We're her only friends.'

'What about her parents?'

'I'm not sure.'

'She didn't say.'

Her parents are coming for Christmas, not beforehand. Not tonight. She told them that. They never listen. She's right, they don't understand. The present burns in my hands. I can't decide what to do.

The last time I hurt someone I swore it would be the last time. The police had been called. The dent on the bonnet of my car too big to cover up without suspicions being raised; a right leg broken in three places. The bruises would fade. My mother would survive.

The police believed me when I'd explained how the car on the other side of the road had its lights on full beam. No, I told them, I couldn't remember the number plate. No, I couldn't recall the make or model. Black, maybe?

No guilt that time. A little now maybe, when Mum limps if she's tired. But then, she shouldn't have left Dad.

And tonight, when whoever opens my present is injured, there'll be no guilt as there'll be no reminder. I won't be at next year's Christmas party to see the scars. Where I will be I don't know, but not there. Not here. Not with the witches around the gas stove.

The saucepan of mulled wine is empty now. The women all have a tinge of red around their lips and I rub my mouth hard as though wiping every stain away. The skin on my hands where it touched my mouth is rough and dry. My nails are bitten so far down that my nail bed bulges over the top of the jagged edges, angry.

'She won't change. She does it on purpose.'

'She's got a lot going on.'

'That's no excuse.'

'I know, but maybe we don't listen enough.'

'Right, so you're saying this is all my fault then?'

'No, of course not.'

'She's rude.'

Round and round and round they go until they come full circle again. I think maybe I've heard all I need to hear. They won't change. And nor will I.

In small movements, so as not to reveal my intrusion, I move away from outside the open window at the back of the kitchen from where I've been watching and listening to them bitch about me. Backwards I walk, further into the dark garden, the wet grass flattening beneath my feet. The flashing lights of the Christmas tree inside dim as I move away, the window now framing the women around the gas stove. The ones I had argued with last week.

I *do* listen. I'm *not* rude. And I don't care anymore. I'm stood alone outside the house because of them, not me. My Secret Santa present will come home with me. The women around the gas stove are already damaged; the knives in my gift won't deepen their wounds.

And hurting them will not heal mine.

But then I hear a cackle and the fire inside me ignites again. I can't help myself.

Seething, I take the alcohol-soaked Christmas pudding out of my handbag, the one I'd already stuffed with a rock. I light a raisin poking out of the side. Then, as the bright flames take hold and the scent of cloves and cinnamon burns my nostrils, I run forwards and hurl the blue and orange flamed ball through the sash window, at the women stood around the gas stove.

And walk away.

***

Jen Faulkner completed an MA in Creative Writing at Bath Spa University in 2015, where she was shortlisted for the Janklow and Nesbitt Prize. When she is not writing she can usually be found in the kitchen baking, or out walking her dog. She is currently plotting and writing her next novel, about how a shared traumatic event can affect two people in very different ways.

THE FAMILY TREE

BY JOY ELLIS

'THANKS FOR HAVING the girls for the afternoon, Mum. It's the only time I have to get out and buy their Christmas presents. I should be back by four. I really appreciate it.'

Liz's daughter Harriet was very good about not overburdening her with the grandchildren, and Liz — rather guiltily — felt grateful for it.

Liz Brownlow had served her full term as a police officer with the Fenland Constabulary and had been determined to enjoy her retirement, and that did *not* mean taking on the role of open-all-hours childminder. She loved her granddaughters, Alice and Pippa, to distraction, and when she did look after them she enjoyed it immensely, but she had already been through the agonies of juggling a home and child with a workaholic husband and a demanding career of her own. Now she was alone, she had decided to do all the things she'd wanted to do but never had the chance. She had spent her life serving others, now it was her time. Luckily, Harriet understood and they had found a balance that worked for them both.

'I should warn you,' her daughter went on, 'Alice has a school project, and she's going to be asking for your help.'

'That sounds interesting. Of course I'll help if I can,' said Liz.

'There's one drawback,' added Harriet cagily. 'It concerns our family tree.'

Liz took a deep breath and exhaled, slowly. 'Ah, I see.'

'She landed that little gem on me at breakfast this morning, Mum. I'm not sure how we should play it. Any ideas?'

'Well, I guess it had to happen one day, Harry. Leave it with me and we'll discuss it later.'

After her daughter had hung up, Liz made a cup of tea and took it through to her study. She had a good hour and a half before Harriet would be dropping the girls off, and she needed to think.

From the bottom shelf of a big oak bookcase Liz lifted out a heavy old photograph album. She returned to her desk and opened it up.

One look at the first picture sent her back decades, to a time long ago, when little Lizzie Lawson, as she was then, had arrived home from school, excited about the new class project for the summer holidays . . .

'Millie! For the tenth time! It's got nothing to do with the cherry tree!' Lizzie threw her school satchel on the floor and flopped unceremoniously onto the sofa. 'Mum! Will you please tell micro-brain here what a family tree is.'

'I'm not a micro-brain! You said you had to study our family tree, and we only have one, the little cherry tree in the front garden.' Millie looked furious.

'Girls, girls!' Their mother laughed as she handed them each a glass of milk. 'Okay, well, for starters, Millie, a family tree isn't a real tree.' She went on to try to explain genealogy to her red-headed six-year-old.

Later that evening, when supper was over and Millie was tucked up in bed in her Rupert the Bear PJs, Lizzie made her 'big pitch' to her parents.

'It's really important, honestly! Miss Hallam says that if I do well, I'll get a merit prize for the class, and we need it to beat the others in the end-of-term competition. Will you help me?' She looked imploringly from one to the other, endeavouring to use a technique that seemed to work for Jake, her cocker spaniel.

Her father was the first to crack.

'Of course, sweetheart. Your mother and I have often said we'd love to see if there are any skeletons in the family closet, but we've never got around to it. This could be fun!'

With great relief, Lizzie recognised a light in her father's eyes that meant he was off on one of his missions. When her dad, a fiery Scotsman, got the bit between his teeth, there was no stopping him. With his help, her project could be very good indeed.

His enthusiasm must have been infectious, because soon Jenny, her mother, was getting out notepads and pencils for each of them.

'There are rules,' said Lizzie, trying to emulate her teacher's voice, 'and we have to follow them with no cheating. We have to go the oral history route. I can ask anyone in the family to help me, but we can't contact any of those companies that trace your ancestors for you. It has to be word of mouth through the family.'

'Then we need to make lists of the surviving relatives on both sides,' said her mum, practically. 'William, you are in charge of the Lawsons, and I'll make a list of any of the Lindens on my side who might be able to help. And we need a chart, a big one. We'll start at the bottom with Lizzie and Millie, and your brother's kids, our nephews and nieces, and work upwards.'

Her dad thought for a moment, then grinned. 'I know! I've got half a roll of wallpaper left over from when I decorated the lounge. We'll use the back of that.'

So it had begun. A family enterprise, all enthusiasm and dogged determination to both trace their ancestors and make Lizzie's tree worthy of a merit prize.

Liz sipped her cooling tea, recalling that the Lawson side had been easy. Her father had a lot of relatives who were happy to talk and share their memories. She smiled to herself when she pictured in her mind's eye her father's horrified face when he got the telephone bill for that quarter. But even so, it had been a masterclass in discovery, especially as one of her uncles had done a lot of research himself and had traced the family to Fifeshire as far back as the seventeen hundreds. By the time it was taken as far as they could go, she even had a print of the Lawson coat of arms and a swatch of their tartan.

Young Lizzie would have been over the moon, except for the fact that her mum's family, the Lindens, had proved very difficult indeed. Lizzie's grandmother was in poor health and her grandfather had passed away some years before, as had his brothers and two of his sisters. All Lizzie's mother could discover were rumours, old tittle-tattle and unsubstantiated stories from some of her cousins. Jenny recalled a rumour or two herself, but they were next to useless — after all, it was never proven that Auntie Gladys had run away with Travellers, or that something terrible happened to crazy cousin Barbara.

Then, just as Lizzie was beginning to believe her merit prize was never going to happen, her mother had made the statement that would change everything. She declared that, although she had hoped it wouldn't come to it, they were going to have to visit Great Aunt Elizabeth the very next day.

Liz looked down at the album of photos, then turned her eyes away again. She decided that her tea was too cold to drink, and went to the kitchen to make another. She was putting off going back into the past again, but it had to be done. The children would be with her in under an hour and she needed to know what to say.

Back in the office, armed with a strong cup of tea, Liz forced herself to remember her great aunt Elizabeth, the woman she had been named after . . .

As young Lizzie and her mother fought their way up the overgrown path to the front door of Linden House, Lizzie wondered how long it had been since she had seen her great aunt. No one visited regularly because the old lady was as mad as a box of frogs and more often than not refused them entry. Generally, her mother came alone, believing that her aunt's outbursts were unsuitable for her young daughters, so it was years since Lizzie had been there.

Now Jenny saw that there was precious little paint left on the woodwork, and what there was had been bleached colourless by the weather. The letterbox was rusty and the defunct bellpush dangled from the door frame by two wires.

'Oh my!' exclaimed Jenny. 'I had no idea she'd let things get this bad. I really should come more often.'

'Don't feel too bad about her, Mum,' said Lizzie. 'Last time you came you said she was throwing things from the upstairs window at those welfare workers and yelling that she needed new blackout curtains, not charity. Whatever that meant?'

Her mother gave her a sad smile. 'She's firmly stuck in the

past, my love. She should be in a home, being cared for, but getting her to agree would be a battle I'd not want to engage in. And heaven help her nurses!' She gave a little laugh. 'But, if we do make it through the door today, you'll be surprised at her parlour.' She puffed out her cheeks. 'Here goes nothing. Let's just hope we aren't back in the car in less than a minute.'

Jenny hammered on the door.

Lizzie heard a bolt being drawn back and felt a shiver run down her spine. Then the door was flung open and they were confronted by a wild-haired and distraught Elizabeth.

'Whatever is the matter?' asked Jenny.

The old lady was absentmindedly wringing the hem of her apron in obvious distress. 'It's terrible, dear! Really terrible!'

Jenny and Lizzie followed Elizabeth through a maze of musty-smelling, dusty corridors until they reached what she called her 'parlour.'

The door swung open and mother and daughter stepped into a time warp.

Life for Elizabeth had stood still in the forties — the war years. Great Uncle Frederick had gone away to fight for King and Country in 1939, and his remains now lay in a corner of some foreign field. But Elizabeth still waited for him. Every day she took a duster to the heavy oak furniture with lavender-fragranced wax polish. She washed the lino and made sure that clean antimacassars were placed over the backs of the armchairs and the settee. She gently dusted the old Bakelite radio, being careful not to move the delicate knobs, and checked whether the gramophone needed a new needle. She wanted the place nice for his return.

Lizzie was dumbfounded. The rest of this wreck of a house was falling to bits, yet this room remained pristine.

Gently, Jenny asked Elizabeth what had upset her, and the

old lady dabbed at her eyes and wailed, 'Glenn Miller's dead! I heard it on the wireless.'

'Oh lord,' muttered Jenny to Lizzie. 'She's back in 1944!'

It took two cups of carefully brewed strong leaf tea to pacify Elizabeth. Then she had a period of comparative lucidity. She completely understood Jenny's request for information about their family history. Suddenly she was in full flow, darting from one branch of the family to another and showering them with names, places, dates and all sorts of remarkable facts.

Jenny and Lizzie tried to get down as much as possible in their notebooks, until Jenny tentatively asked if she had any photographs.

To Lizzie's surprise, Elizabeth came back with a resounding, 'Oh yes!' Then she stared at Lizzie, and in a schoolmistressy voice stated that in her view the young *should* take an interest in the generations that had gone before. She knelt down with surprising flexibility, opened the door of an aged sideboard, and pulled out a faded cardboard box.

The box read, 'Oxydol laundry detergent.'

'You can take them, but remember to return them before Frederick gets home. After his demob, I expect he'll want to relive the good old days before the war, and I'll need them back so that we can reminisce together,' said Elizabeth.

Lizzie watched her mother remove old sepia and black-and-white photographs, postcards, letters, shopping lists, handwritten recipes and heaven knew what else. This was perfect! Lizzie was so excited she gave the old lady a big hug, which was not her usual way, but it seemed appropriate.

'How sweet!' Elizabeth hugged her back. 'Now, I've tried to write on the back of the snaps — names, dates and places — in case my memory fails, so that should help. If you want to ask me anything else, just pop back, as long as there's not an air raid on, of course.'

And once again Elizabeth was back in the war years. She suddenly shooed them out, making Lizzie promise to Dig for Victory, as all patriotic youngsters should.

They sat in the car, slightly dazed. Lizzie held the treasured box on her lap and was amazed to find that it still gave off a faint smell of soap powder. 'She can't go into a home, Mum,' said Lizzie suddenly. 'She's clean and she eats well. When I hugged her she smelt nice and she wasn't skinny. She just lives in a different time to us.'

Jenny agreed. 'Her living room is immaculate, and her bedroom is too. She is simply still in the past, waiting for her beloved husband to come home from the war. If we moved her out, I think it would kill her.'

Lizzie thought about it. 'We should come more often, Mum. We need to look out for her. She was right, we younger ones should care about the older generation, shouldn't we?'

They drove back home, each deep in thought.

After supper that night, they all sat around the table and sorted through the contents of Elizabeth's box. Both girls giggled at the Victorian love notes, but were fascinated by the intricate little greetings cards with envelope flaps that lifted up to reveal delicate posies of forget-me-nots and violets beneath. Lizzie's dad found a recipe for 'a cool and tempting brawn' that required half a pig's head with the brains removed. This he insisted on reading aloud, while Millie made retching noises, and Lizzie, pulling a face, told her father to please shut up before she was sick!

It was the photographs that caused the most excitement. Jenny managed to get them into some sort of order, then, with the aid of the names on the back and Elizabeth's notes, as well as a long and laborious letter Jenny had received from a cousin who had done a bit of ferreting for them, they now had five generations to add to William's wallpaper family tree.

Millie, who was very late for bed, begged to have one last look at her great-great-grandparents' family portrait. She stood with her thumb in her mouth and stared thoughtfully at the cloudy, brownish picture. 'So why does everyone have a name on the back except Lizzie?'

Frowning, Jenny went over to the tired child. 'What do you mean by Lizzie, darling?'

Millie pointed to a dark-haired child with a rather sour expression. 'That's Lizzie. But she really shouldn't be in that old picture, should she?'

Lizzie took the photo from her and, yes, like it or not, the dark-haired girl did look very much like her! She turned the photo over and saw that Millie was right, it was the only figure in the picture that hadn't been named. For some reason she didn't like that sombre-looking girl at all.

While Jenny got Millie to bed, Lizzie and her father looked through all other photos again, and sure enough the sad-looking young woman was in two more. In one she was much older and had become quite a beauty, although again she was unnamed.

'What do you make of this one, Lizzie?' her father asked. He held up a larger photo, which had a ragged tear down one side.

She looked carefully and saw it was a large family gathering, with all the participants listed on the back, but just before the tear, you could make out a shoulder, and some dark hair.

When Jenny returned, she and William went through the whole list of names on the family tree, and finally had to admit that Lizzie's doppelgänger was the only one whose name they couldn't find. Lizzie felt really disgruntled to discover that the only person she could identify with — who looked like her — must have been the black sheep of the family. She was clearly disliked and, what's more, looked like a right mardy cow.

Then she saw her father smiling at her. 'Cheer up, kiddo! You've found a mystery woman! Everyone wants a nameless, dark, enigmatic character to turn up in their family tree, but they rarely find one! This is brilliant!'

She had gone to bed accepting that the woman had added an element of intrigue and excitement to her tree, and it might even give it the edge for the coveted prize.

There was still half an hour until the children arrived, and Liz knew that she had an even darker memory to revisit before she could put the album back in the bookcase. She skimmed through it and stopped at the clearest picture of the dark-haired young woman.

Liz felt a kind of sadness, tinged with something that she hated to admit to. Guilt.

Her mother had gone back to the 1940s house the next day with the intention of discovering who the mystery woman was. Sadly, she couldn't get past a cantankerous Elizabeth, who was ranting about the air-raid warden having stolen her ration book. Undeterred, Jenny returned the following day, and this time succeeded in getting inside, although it had taken a ten-minute conversation to convince Elizabeth that Jenny wasn't the lady from the munitions factory come to enrol her into her jolly band of women workers. Elizabeth did tell her a few pieces of new information, but stiffened and looked angry when questioned about the unnamed girl. Lizzie's mum said that Elizabeth had immediately pitched into a complaint — the grocer's delivery boy hadn't brought her the Mazawattee tea she had ordered. She then berated her for coming out without her gas mask. Jenny had left with the distinct feeling that the old woman knew exactly who the mystery girl was but had absolutely no intention of sharing that knowledge.

In the end, young Lizzie had won her merit prize, and received a great deal of praise from her teacher. The blank box on her family tree had caught the imagination of the whole class, and Miss Hallam had set them a competition for the best story based on the strange anonymous creature in the photograph. She also made Lizzie promise to tell them if ever the mystery was solved. She assured her teacher that she would, but this had turned into a promise that, as an adult, she would break.

Conscious that she didn't have long to get her story straight, Liz ploughed back into the past.

Her father, never one to give up on a mystery, had used every tool available to him, including a local history buff who knew the best ways to study ancestry. It had taken three weeks until one evening, on opening the post, he had sighed with satisfaction and declared that he had finally got the answer. The dark-haired young woman was called Eleanor Lawson, and was the step-daughter of Elizabeth's uncle. Lizzie's mother had been shocked at the news, and had exclaimed that if the girl was Elizabeth's cousin, why on earth had she denied knowing her? At that point mother and daughter knew they would be taking another trip back to World War Two . . .

As they walked up the path, pushing aside the encroaching shrubbery, Lizzie could hear the crackly sound of Elizabeth's ancient gramophone. It was playing a song that seemed to be titled, 'When They Sound the Last 'All Clear'.'

Her mother raised her eyebrows and shook her head, and they both laughed.

'I don't think we're going to get too far today, do you?' said Lizzie.

'Let's give it a try,' sighed Jenny. 'But I think you could be right.'

The door was already unlocked, and after a few 'Coo-ees', they went inside and made their way to the parlour. Elizabeth was standing on a straight-backed chair, singing along, and dusting a picture rail.

'Did you know the front door is open?' asked Jenny.

'Oh yes, dear. I'm expecting the vicar to come and collect the Red Cross food parcel that I've made up for the prisoners of war.'

Lizzie saw an old brown carton on the table. It was stamped with the insignia of the Order of St John under a big red cross.

'Good grief!' exclaimed her mother. 'This is a collector's dream!'

Elizabeth insisted on making tea, but there was to be little or no talk about the family tree today. To her, the Battle of Britain was raging in the skies overhead, and Elizabeth would talk of nothing but the war effort.

They had barely finished their cups of tea when the old lady was ushering them to the door. 'See if you can get me some dried eggs, dear, and perhaps you'd drop my parcel off at the vicar's house to save him collecting it? Now, off you go. TTFN!'

The door shut behind them.

'What's TTFN, Mum?' asked Lizzie.

'Ta-ta for now,' explained her mother, 'It's a way of saying goodbye.' She looked down at the box in her arms. 'Oh well, I'd better take this and check that she hasn't put anything perishable in here, and find a way of smuggling the rest back into her store cupboard.' She placed the box on the back seat of the car and they returned home.

Jenny made them both a hot chocolate, and Lizzie carefully opened the box.

'Mum! This isn't food at all!' she called out.

Her mother came over and looked.

There were no cans of tinned peaches or condensed milk. No cocoa or toffees. Instead, bundles of letters and cards, all tied up with ribbon. There were embroidered handkerchiefs and worn velvet ring boxes. In a cellophane envelope lay a bunch of faded dried flowers and some tiny silver-coloured horseshoes. A heavy, tarnished silver photo frame held a wedding photograph of a smart young man in what must have been a fashionable suit, and a shy, pretty, eighteen-year-old Elizabeth, in a long, white satin gown with a huge bouquet that seemed to be all dark foliage and roses.

'Oh no! The silly old thing! This is her precious memento box. She used to keep it under the bed. She'd get it out occasionally and show me treasured bits and pieces. Well, thank goodness *we* took it! Heaven knows who she thought she was giving it to, but at least it won't finish up in a charity shop or in a skip.'

She was just about to close it up when Lizzie spotted something on the wedding photo. 'Wait, Mum, what's that?'

Sticking out from the back of the frame was a piece of paper. Her mother removed it and found a letter, wrapped around another photograph. Lizzie found herself looking at Elizabeth, standing next to the dark-haired young woman, both smiling lovingly at whoever was taking the picture.

Lizzie took it, turned it over and read, *Me and Eleanor, taken by Frederick before he left England.*

Jenny was staring at the folded letter, then said, 'This isn't ours to read, darling. I'm going to show your daddy and then I think we should return it to Elizabeth. I believe it's the answer to the mystery, but it belongs with Elizabeth, not us.'

. . .

Liz got up, walked to the window and stared out into the bleak, cold garden. She had been grateful that her father wasn't of the same opinion as her mother. He believed they should know the truth, but agreed that Elizabeth should not be told that they had found the letter and read it.

And so they had discovered that Frederick had written to Elizabeth, shortly before he had been sent to the front line, begging her forgiveness but telling her that he had fallen in love with Eleanor. Should he be spared and come home after the war, he wrote, he would be asking her for a divorce.

Liz could recall clearly how sorry they had all felt for Great Aunt Elizabeth. Her mother had shed tears, saying that it would seem that Elizabeth's mind just couldn't accept that terrible rejection — she must have completely wiped it from her memory and continued to wait for Frederick to come back to her. And she had waited, and waited.

A glance at her watch told her she had ten more minutes. Liz hurried to the desk, flicked through the photo album and removed all the pictures with the unnamed girl in them. Then she took the larger family photo and a pair of scissors. This time she cut a line that removed all trace of the dark hair and the shoulder of the mystery woman. She then trimmed around the whole photo so one edge didn't look different to the others, and slipped it back into the album. She took one last skim through the whole book, but nothing of Eleanor remained. Liz placed the album back on the shelf.

Of course, if that was all there was to it, a heart-rending story of a lost love, she would never have worried. But it didn't end there. Maybe if she had never chosen the police force for a career, it would have all been forgotten, but she *had* become a police officer, and then a detective, a very good one. Perhaps it was a kind of serendipity — it was because of the family tree that she found her lifelong vocation. The searching for answers and finding out the truth had captured her young imagination, and she knew exactly what she wanted to do when she left school.

Now she was retired and living comfortably in the house left to her by Great Aunt Elizabeth, there being no other surviving relative. Her aunt had lived to receive her telegram from the Queen, although she was devastated that the palace should have got it so wrong. According to Elizabeth, it should have been from His Majesty King George VI.

It had taken years of saving and hard work to make the place what it was now, but Liz had married fairly young, and her husband was a man who was not afraid of getting his hands dirty to build a dream home for his wife and child. Together they tamed the garden and resurrected the parts of the house that had been so badly neglected. Her darling Tony had been a partner at a building contractors, which was wonderful when it came to working on Linden House, but he took his position very seriously, and worked all hours to fulfil the company's contracts. In retrospect, he should probably have relaxed a little more and allowed his builders to shoulder more responsibility, because he died in his sixties.

It was a year after his death, while they were tackling a project that had long been put off, that Liz and her daughter discovered the body in the old air raid shelter at the bottom of the garden. Hardly a body, it was a partially mummified skeleton, and as soon as Liz had seen the dark hair still clinging to patches of parchment-like tissue, she had known she was looking at Eleanor.

As a detective inspector, she had managed to keep the discovery relatively quiet. Forensics dated it as having been there since the time of the Second World War, and from the head injuries and the debris heaped around her, it was decided that she had been seeking cover during an air raid and was killed when a blast hit the shelter. Liz knew that several bombs had fallen in the area when enemy planes had been making for the nearby port but misjudged their targets. A brief investigation showed no suspicious local activity at that time, and no missing persons seemed to have been reported. Case closed.

Liz destroyed the heavy meat tenderiser that she had found next to the corpse, the one with the matching handle to the knives that had always sat at the back of the scrubbed butcher's block in Elizabeth's kitchen. She had always believed there was more to Elizabeth's mental state than her husband telling her he was leaving, and over the years, before the old lady died, she had noticed too many anomalies in the things she said, and too many flashes of pure anger, or maybe it had been hatred, if anyone mentioned her cousin Eleanor.

In the end, and after a lot of soul-searching, she and Harriet had decided to let sleeping dogs lie. After all, Eleanor's family were all long dead, so what good would it do?

The doorbell chime brought her back to the present. She hurried to greet her granddaughters.

'My darlings!' she called out, holding her arms out to the two excited girls who rushed to hug her. They all went into her parlour. They loved that room, especially now, with a Christmas tree all decorated with old-fashioned decorations, and surrounded by so many old relics of long ago. Alice loved the old wireless, while Pippa was fascinated by the polished wood mantle clock that chimed every quarter of an hour.

'Now, Alice,' she said after they were settled. 'Your project! I would love to help you, especially as I did one myself many years ago. I've got lots of names and information, and old photographs too, but, please, don't get too excited, angel. It's all a bit boring really, with no famous people, no dark secrets or mysteries.' She looked at the mild disappointment on the child's face and added, 'Now, your daddy's family might be really exciting! Concentrate on *his* ancestors, Alice dear, and who knows, you might even find a sinister mystery woman!'

***

Joy Ellis, a bestselling crime thriller writer, was born in Kent but spent most of her working life in London and Surrey. She currently lives in a village in the Lincolnshire Fens with her partner, Jacqueline, four Springer spaniels and one little rescue Breton spaniel. Now writing full-time, Joy believes her choice of genre is a no-brainer as her partner is a highly decorated retired police officer.

You Let Me In
by Keri Beevis

'Hi, can I help you?'

Rachel stared through the gap in the door at the man standing outside, glad the chain prevented it from opening further. She didn't know him; it was after dark, and she was home alone. And well, you could never be too careful.

Especially at the moment.

'Sorry to bother you, but my car's broken down. I don't suppose you have a phone that I could use?' He held up his mobile and offered her a pleading smile. 'I can't get any signal out here.'

That would be true. The village was in a dead zone. Something they hadn't even considered asking about before they bought the house. Still she questioned the rationality of letting a stranger into her home.

He seemed affable enough and from what she could see in the porch light, he had friendly eyes. But looks could be deceiving. He was young, leanly built, and although wearing an overcoat, wasn't really dressed for the weather. No gloves, hat or scarf.

If he had been driving though, and hadn't expected to get out of the car...

It had been snowing heavily for much of the day and the falling flakes were sticking to his hair, his cheeks red with the cold. What had he been doing out here? They weren't on a main road and the house was set back down a long driveway.

She and David had both placed privacy high on their list when moving.

'We don't have a landline,' she told the man at the door, making her decision. 'I'm sorry.'

She didn't want him in her house. He might be genuine, but it wasn't worth the risk.

It wasn't a lie. There was no home phone. Of course they did have wifi, but she wasn't going to mention that.

'I see.' He looked resigned. 'Okay, well, sorry to have troubled you.'

As he turned to walk away, she started to close the door, a little irritated when he paused.

'Can you tell me where your nearest neighbour is?'

'Um, you want to follow the road to the left. It leads into the village. I'm sure someone will be able to help you.'

'How far is that?'

'Just over half a mile.'

He looked a little daunted and guilt pricked at her conscience.

'Okay, well, thank you.'

Stop being so paranoid. Help the poor man.

Rachel tried to ignore the nagging voice.

It wasn't wise letting someone she didn't know into the house. What if his broken-down car story was a ruse?

Yes, but what if he is telling the truth?

It really was bitterly cold outside and the snow falling in

thick icy flakes; the imprints left by the man's shoes covered almost instantly. Once he was back on the road, there would be no shelter from the wind as it whipped across the open fields.

What if something happened to him and she hadn't helped him?

Okay, enough.

'Wait!'

He paused and though it wasn't easy to tell as the snow globe raged around him, she thought there was a hopeful expression on his face.

'We have wifi. You can connect using that if you have wifi calling.'

It was too late to retract the words now and he didn't need to be asked twice, hurrying back towards the house.

Please let me have done the right thing.

Her stomach churning, she released the safety chain from the door and eased it open, inviting him into the sanctuary of her home.

'You are an angel,' he grinned at her as he stepped over the threshold, and there was something in his expression that had her worrying whether she had made the wrong decision.

'Nice place you have here,' he commented, looking around as he ran a hand through his sodden hair. 'Very cosy.'

Was he scoping her house out, trying to figure out if she was here alone and what the layout was? Maybe he planned to rob her. Rachel hadn't actually considered that and while she hoped not, she guessed it was preferable to the other sinister motives her overactive imagination had conjured.

Up close he was younger than she had initially thought. Mid to possibly late twenties.

Again she questioned what he had been doing out this way, though didn't voice it out loud. Instead she gave him the password to the wifi, wanting him to make the call and be out of her hair as quickly as possible.

'Thank you again. I really appreciate this,' he told her, phone pressed to his ear. She watched him wander across the room towards the big Christmas tree that was decorated in gold and red, pausing as his call was connected, and she listened to the one-sided conversation.

He was speaking with a recovery company, and her tension eased a little after he asked her for her address.

They would come and fix his car and he would no longer be a concern to her.

Or was he planning on waiting here for them?

She was doing her good citizen bit, but once he had finished the call she wanted him gone.

Back out into the cold to wait in his broken car.

If she let him stay he could be here for hours.

By which time David will be home and you will feel safe.

Except David had a work meeting. He had promised he would try not to be too late, but there was no guarantee and his meetings often overran. Plus Rachel had asked him to stop off at the supermarket on his way back, which would delay him further.

Meanwhile she would be stuck here with a man she didn't know and who could possibly have a dark agenda.

It wasn't her fault he had broken down. She had tried to help him. And it was understandable she was nervous about him being here.

Four women. She could picture their faces from the news.

'The recovery van will be here as soon as possible, but they said because it's treacherous out, it could take a while. Thank you for this. I appreciate you letting me stay.'

Rachel opened and closed her mouth. She hadn't offered

for him to stay. He had presumed. But what the hell was she supposed to do now? Kick him out?

She had been edging towards the door, ready to open it for him, but he had caught her off guard, so instead she wrung her hands, wishing like hell David would surprise her by arriving home early.

Given what a workaholic her husband was, she knew the chances of that happening were slim to none.

She shouldn't begrudge him though. He was doing this for them, for the home where they planned to raise a family. This had been their dream, but the mortgage payments were high.

Was that dream now about to be taken away from her thanks to one foolish decision?

Four women. She knew all of their names. Vicky Bell, Kirsty Heappey, Sarah McDowell and Debora Raber.

'I don't suppose I could use your loo, could I? I've been on the road for hours.'

Automatic good manners kicked in. 'Um, yes, of course.'

This was good. While he was in the loo, she would call David, tell him about her predicament and how uncomfortable she was feeling here alone in the house with this man.

She led him down the hall, though kept her head half turned so she was aware of his movements, hating that he was making her so nervous in her own home. 'It's just down here.'

'Thanks. This place is huge. You don't live here alone, do you?'

What? Why did he want to know that? Her heart thumped as she answered. 'No, I live here with my husband.'

'Oh, okay. Is he home?'

'He's on his way.'

'I see.'

Was it her imagination or did her answer seem to amuse him?

'Well, it's crazy weather out there. I think they're forecasting another five inches of snow tonight. I hope he doesn't get held up.'

He left her with that thought, closing the cloakroom door, and Rachel hurried through to the kitchen where her mobile was charging, snatching it up.

She tapped in David's name, moving through to the conservatory as she waited for the call to connect, not wanting the stranger to hear her on the phone.

When it didn't ring she looked at the screen, swallowing when she realised the wifi signal had dropped out.

No, no, no. It did this sometimes, but not now, please. Not when she had precious seconds to make the call.

She tried again, still getting no service, and it was then an awful thought occurred to her.

If the wifi was down then how had the man managed to call the recovery company?

Had he really spoken to them?

The sound of the chain flushing had her nearly dropping the phone. She quickly slipped it into her pocket, smoothed shaking fingers over her hair and tried to steady her nerves before he rejoined her.

There was no point in asking him to leave. If he was really an innocent stranded motorist, that would make her cruel; while if he intended to harm her, he wasn't going to leave now, no matter how firmly she asked him.

As she stepped back into the kitchen, she spotted the knife she had been using to chop the vegetables. It was small, but sharp. If she had to use it as a weapon, could she?

The man wandered into the kitchen as she was debating, taking the decision away from her as he leant back against the counter, blocking her view of the knife. He stared around the room in apparent awe. 'Wow, this is a nice kitchen. Exposed beams, Aga. Very nice set up.'

'We like it.' Rachel was aware her tone was a little stiff, but he was making her so uncomfortable.

'Have you lived here long?'

'We moved in earlier this year.'

'So it's your first Christmas in your new home. Nice.'

It was and Rachel had spared no expense, wanting the place to look like a festive greeting card. Both hers and David's parents were coming to stay over Christmas and she wanted everything to be perfect. They had a real tree, the open fireplace, and a huge wreath on the front door. When it had started snowing earlier it had seemed like the final touch. Now though she wished the snow would go. It had brought this stranger into her house and might delay David getting home.

The man was silent for a moment as he studied her and she suspected he was picking up on her unease. 'I'm sorry. I guess I should introduce myself. I'm Matthew.'

'Rachel.'

'Thank you for letting me into your home. I hope I didn't scare you, showing up in the dark like that when you're home all alone.'

He held her gaze as he spoke and she wondered if he was trying to gauge her reaction, see if he was scaring her.

He was. Her legs were trembling and her stomach knotting. She was trying her best to hold it together though.

He pushed away from the counter and for a moment she thought he was going to make a move towards her, but instead he turned to study the kitchen again and this time she saw his eyes sweep over the knife.

She spoke quickly. 'Would you like something to drink? Tea or coffee?' Was relieved when he glanced back at her. That was good. She had his attention again.

She needed to keep him occupied, buy some time until David arrived home.

It was her husband she was counting on now, as she was pretty certain the recovery van wasn't coming.

'Coffee would be great. Thanks.'

'How far away did you break down?' She asked the question as she filled the kettle, put it on to boil, trying to keep her tone casual and friendly, not sound as if she was prying.

If he was suspicious of her reasons for asking, he didn't show it, taking a seat at the table. She hadn't invited him to and thought that was a bit presumptuous, but then she guessed that if she had been thinking straight and was a gracious host, she would have already offered.

At least sitting at the table put him further away from the knife.

'Not far from the end of your drive actually. Thank God you were home.'

When Rachel didn't respond to that, instead busying herself with mugs, milk and coffee, grateful to have something else to focus on, he continued.

'I'll be honest. I didn't think you were going to let me in. I had already thought about the wifi when you said you didn't have a home phone, but I wasn't going to push it. I mean, I get it. You're a lone woman, and your house is in the middle of nowhere. You don't know who I am. Just some random guy claiming to have broken down. If you'd have asked me to go, I would have. It had to be your decision to let me in. I'm glad you did.'

Rachel's spine stiffened. Was he a mind reader or were her reactions that transparent?

Either way, she suspected he was playing some kind of twisted game with her.

Her hand shook as she put his mug down on the table.

'Thank you. Are you not going to sit?'

She hovered for a moment, her own mug still in her hand, hating how closely he was watching her. She didn't want to sit down with him and put herself in a more vulnerable position.

'No, I should get on with making dinner.'

That was good. Going back to the chopping board would give her access to the knife.

'Of course. I interrupted you,' he commented as she crossed the room.

The only problem was, she realised, dicing the peppers and onions meant her back was to him. Even now the knife was in her hand, she didn't feel comfortable at all.

What if he crept up behind her?

She twisted the chopping board so she could stand at an angle, hoping he would think she was doing it out of politeness so she could still talk to him.

'Do you live locally?' she asked, trying to make an effort.

'Taverham.'

Which was a suburb north of Norwich. What was he doing this far south? Perhaps he had been on business. Although he wasn't wearing a suit, his dark trousers and jumper were smart.

'Do you work out this way?'

'Just today. I was on a hunt for the right opportunity. This whole snowstorm threw a spanner in the works, but I guess it worked out okay in the end.'

'Sorry?'

'It worked out okay because I found you.'

Rachel's stomach dropped. Her whole body tensing. 'What do you mean?' The words came out croaky.

'You were home. You let me in.'

'I did.' And she was bitterly regretting it.

'You have no idea how grateful I am. Not many women would let a stranger into their home, especially not with everything going on in the news. It's scary when it's happening right on your doorstep.'

The women. He was going to taunt her with the women he had killed.

'And of course, the police have no leads. No idea who he is.'

He trailed off, seeming a little distracted and Rachel realised he was looking at the knife she was clutching tightly in her hand. He drew his eyes up to meet hers and for the briefest moment she was certain they could read each other's thoughts, both of them aware of the charade they were playing out.

Vicky Bell had been abducted while walking home; her body found in woodland the following day. Kirsty Heappey had been attacked in her flat six weeks later. Sarah McDowell and Debora Raber were also taken from their homes. In each case there was no sign of forced entry. The police believed they had invited their killer in.

It had to be your decision to let me in. I'm glad you did.

All four women had been brutally tortured then strangled. All of them were brunette and in their thirties.

Just like Rachel.

'What time did you say your husband is getting home?'

'Could be any moment now.'

The man, Matthew (if that was really his name), seemed to consider that as he sipped at his coffee. Without warning, he pushed back his chair and got up, and Rachel took an involuntary step back, her bum hitting the counter. Her grip tightened on the knife as she watched him, her coil wound tightly, terrified he might suddenly pounce and attack her.

How had it been for the other women? Had there been any warning of what he was going to do or had he caught them off guard?

When he moved past her to look out of the kitchen window, she actually considered running. Out of the door and into the snowstorm, or upstairs and into the bathroom where she could lock the door.

Which one offered more hope?

She knew the truth was neither. She was trapped here with Matthew and could only watch him closely until he tried to make his move.

'I hate to say it, Rachel, but he might not make it home. Have you seen how bad it is out there?'

No. He was playing games with her. Trying to scare her.

David would come home. He had to.

'I'm sure he'll be fine. His car is equipped for this kind of weather.'

When they had first moved to the country, David had insisted on buying a new car, wanting something that was more suitable for the terrain and had a bigger boot for his golf clubs.

The new vehicle had been expensive, but he worked hard, and his golf weekends were his only chance to blow off steam. Rachel couldn't begrudge him that, especially when he had let her go crazy with the house design.

'Was it the AA?'

'What?'

'Who you called?'

For a moment Matthew seemed to have forgotten his story, but he quickly recovered. 'No, the RAC.' He wandered back across the kitchen, this time stopping in front of her. 'So what are you cooking?'

Rachel hadn't missed that he had conveniently switched the subject again. 'A chilli.'

'Want a hand?'

He had removed his overcoat before he sat down and he now rolled up the sleeves of his jumper, seeming to assume she would say yes. 'I might as well make myself useful while I'm here.'

87

Rachel almost didn't hear him; her focus on the scratches on his arms.

Where had they come from?

She remembered from the news that the killer's latest victim, Debora Raber, had put up one hell of a struggle.

'Oh these?' he told her, seeing her looking and seeming amused. 'Have you ever tried giving a cat a pill?'

Really? He expected her to believe that? It was almost as if he was showing them off.

Taunting her.

'So, dinner. Can I help? I'm good at slicing things.'

His dark eyes burned into hers, the ghost of a smile playing on his lips, and for a moment Rachel wasn't sure she could breathe, let alone speak.

'No! I mean, thank you, but I can manage,' she said, finally finding her voice.

'Fair enough.'

He said it affably enough, but made no attempt to back up, still far too close for her comfort.

This near she was aware of how much bigger he was than her, his fitted jumper silhouetting wide shoulders and a muscular torso.

She would never be able to fight him off.

'Look, Rachel, I–' He never got to finish his sentence, the sound of a key in the front door drawing both of their attention to the hallway.

David!

As her husband stepped inside the house, stamping snow off his shoes onto the doormat, she wanted to cry in relief.

'You're home.'

He seemed pleased at her delight to see him, shrugging off his coat and hanging it up on one of the pegs. 'We decided to postpone the meeting,' he told her. 'The weather is terrible.'

Glancing at Matthew he nodded. 'Hello. I didn't realise we had company. David,' he introduced himself, shaking Matthew's hand.

'This is Matthew,' Rachel told him. 'His car has broken down just up the road and he's waiting for the RAC.'

'Oh no. Not a good area to have a breakdown, and in this weather too. Good job Rachel was home.'

'Yes, I was lucky.'

Was it her imagination or did Matthew seem a little subdued now David was here?

'I'm surprised I didn't see your car on the road,' David commented to him as he handed Rachel a shopping bag. 'Though it's coming down so heavy out there I was probably too focused on seeing where was I going.'

So David hadn't seen Matthew's car. It had all been a lie.

She just wanted this stranger out of her house now.

'Your RAC man might struggle getting to you. Has Rachel invited you to stay and have some dinner with us?'

What? No!

'I'm sure Matthew needs to be on his way, David.'

'We can't just throw him out in the cold, honey. And he'll need a hot meal for when he has to go back out there again. What do you say, Matthew?'

'Well, if you're sure you don't mind.'

'Not at all.'

'And you don't mind either, Rachel?' Matthew asked, seeming to want her approval.

Rachel scowled at her husband. Sometimes he was too bloody friendly for his own good. She could hardly say no now though. 'It's fine.'

Dinner, but then he was to go.

She looked inside the bag of groceries she had asked her

husband to pick up, so she could get on with making the chilli. 'David, you forgot the kidney beans.'

'No I didn't. I remember grabbing them off the shelf.' More interested in his new friend, David turned back to Matthew. 'Do you drink whisky, mate? I have a bottle of Johnnie Walker through in the other room.'

'I do, but I have to drive.'

'Not for a while yet. Besides, one for the road won't hurt. Come on.'

As they disappeared through to the living room, Rachel emptied the bag, putting the groceries on the counter. Definitely no kidney beans.

She found the receipt, frowning when she saw they were listed. Maybe they had fallen out of the bag and were still in the car.

She could ask David to go and check, but that would leave her in the house alone again with Matthew. Besides, when she peered in the living room, the pair of them were preoccupied talking about golf. She would go look.

Slipping on her coat and wellies, she found David's keys in his coat pocket. David would be okay alone with Matthew for a couple of minutes. The killer had only ever targeted lone women. He had never gone after a couple.

As she let herself out of the front door, an icy blast of wind hit her in the face, stealing her breath. It really was bitterly cold out and David was lucky he had made it home.

As she trudged across to the garage, feet sinking into the deep snow and the thick flakes swirling around her, she thought again about Matthew's car.

David would have seen it, surely.

Matthew said he had broken down close to the end of the driveway and she was tempted to go look. If she could prove he was lying, there was no reason for him to stay in their house.

She was still debating whether to go check, knew the heavy snow would hamper her, as she let herself into the garage. She clicked at David's car, the automatic light switching on, and she opened the passenger door. Seeing that the tin of kidney beans wasn't in the footwell, she rummaged underneath the seat, though found nothing.

They had definitely been on the receipt though.

Unless he had put the bag of shopping in the boot.

Often his golf clubs were in there, but with the recent bad weather he hadn't played for a few days and they were stored in the garage.

She had just started to pull the boot open, when her foot kicked something. Looking down, she realised it was the mystery tin of beans. Scooping it up, she slipped it in her coat pocket and went to slam the boot door shut.

Something was caught in the way, stopping it from catching.

She tried again, pulling the door fully open when it still wouldn't close.

The internal light shone on a woman's naked body.

She was covered in bloody lacerations, the skin around her throat dark with bruises, and her sightless eyes wide with terror.

As Rachel tried to register what she was seeing, a scream caught in her throat, she heard a voice calling from the house.

'Rachel? Honey, where are you?'

***

Keri Beevis is the internationally bestselling author of Dying To Tell and Deep Dark Secrets. Her other titles include Trust No One, Every Little Breath, The People Next Door and With Friends Like These. Dying To Tell reached no. 1 in the Amazon chart in Australia and was a top 25 hit in the UK, while Deep

Dark Secrets was the bestselling Bloodhound Books title of 2020. Keri lives in Norfolk, England, with her two naughty kitties, Ellie and Lola, and a plentiful supply of red wine (her writing fuel). She loves Hitchcock movies, exploring creepy places, and gets extremely competitive in local pub quizzes. She is also a self-confessed klutz.

STILL LIFE
BY MARRISSE WHITTAKER

THE BODY FELL from the high bridge over the River Thames like a broken angel, arms flapping madly as if desperate to take heavenly flight. In a split second it was as though a giant's hand had shaken up the perfect winter snow-globe scenario below. The fairy-lit, gingerbread-scented, snowflake-speckled, decorative market stalls, full of souls who had been getting into the Christmas spirit, had been flung into a tailspin.

The boy chorister's piercing scream cut through the air, 'Silent Night' now history. It shattered the warm bubble of joy to all men, like an ice pick smashing into delicate crystal, as the flying body missed the water, landing with a sickening thud behind Patsy. The screams continued apace as people raced to the spot where the fallen soul had landed.

Patsy remained frozen to the spot, paralysed with shock and horror. She was terrified to move anyway. She'd just been given another warning by Nasty Nick, her boss, for having broken her pose as a still-life, living-statue performer. Today, she was masquerading as a white marble effigy of Blessed Virgin Mary, Mother of Christ. Luckily, she had brought her own prop Jesus.

She'd rammed it into her rucksack when she had run away from home, with no intention of ever going back.

Her dad had given the doll to her on the day she was born, and it had lain next to her on her bed, every night since. Not that she actually had a bed now, but Patsy was sure her dad was still looking down on her from Heaven like a guardian angel. He'd been gone for exactly one year, having taken his last breath on Christmas Eve. Patsy shivered at the chilling memory, though he had passed peacefully.

'Bye, my little angel,' he had whispered softly as Patsy had sat on his bed clutching her doll. 'Bye, Sid Vicious,' he had then gasped. It was the name that he had given to the toy, with its odd face and wild red hair. He'd been a right joker her dad. That was the very last thing he had said. Life was funny like that, Patsy reflected sadly.

'Think she's a gonner.' Patsy heard a man from behind calling the police. She suddenly thought that she might vomit.

'Is it a woman?' Patsy couldn't hold her pose any longer. Whipping her head around, she called over her shoulder to her fellow still-life performer, Connie, posing as an Ice Queen, a few metres away.

'I think so. I can't see for sure, with everyone crowding around. Day you're having, you're lucky she didn't land on your head,' Connie joked.

'Is she dead?' Patsy glanced down towards the doll in her arms. He appeared to have bright-red blood splashed across his face. She felt dizzy and tried to steady herself. Nasty Nick would kill her if she collapsed in front of all of these people.

'What do you think?' Connie shrugged. 'Could anyone survive a drop like that?' A tall, broad figure suddenly lurched between them.

'Oi, Madonna!' Nasty Nick was standing far too close. 'Second warning today. One more wrong move and it won't just be that baby Jesus in your mitts wot ends up crucified. Got it?' Patsy reckoned that he could smell her fear as acutely as she could smell the stench of beer and sweat oozing from his pores. But she also recognised that with her being fifteen years old and on the run from home, there weren't exactly many other career options on offer.

'The kid nicked my money,' Patsy tried to argue, as an ambulance, blue lights flashing, came to a halt behind the wooden, mock-Austrian market stall. The female appeared to have landed inches from the very spot where Patsy had been dossing down at night. She shuddered at the thought.

'You're lucky you weren't arrested. You could go down for a long time, beating up that brat like you did this morning.' Nasty Nick glared at her. 'I'm guessing that you're trying to keep a low profile, don't want the fuzz knowing where you are. Am I right?'

Patsy shut her lips tight. She had no doubt that he knew the score. The last thing she wanted was him grassing her up and the police dragging her back home. But who could blame her for the tussle earlier? The thieving child might have had the looks of an angel, but definitely rocked the soul of the Devil himself. Her dad had always told her to stick up for herself. So as far as she was concerned, the kid had deserved all of the Christmas blessings that the Virgin Mary had rained down upon its golden curls, aided and abetted by baby Jesus. He'd been something of a lethal weapon and as Patsy saw it, the only way to retrieve her total morning's takings of one pound and fifty pence from the child's vice-like clutches.

'She stinks like an old sock.' The girl, having had the nerve to have been wearing angel wings on her sparkly net-petticoated dress, had sobbed loudly to her parents. Until that moment, they had been much more interested in the Glühwein stall than the fact that their preschool child had been loitering with intent, within kicking distance, Patsy had noted, of the dark deep river.

'You were mouthy with that woman as well. Don't think I've had my back turned. Now she's gone and chucked herself off the bridge. Happy are you?' Nasty Nick loomed over her, his eyes threatening.

'That's not the same person who's fallen?' Patsy gasped, before Connie cut over her shocked words.

'The woman was a nutter. She trespassed into the manger, tried to grab Patsy's wrist. All she did was shake her away, tell her to bog off and leave her be.' Connie stepped forward, as Patsy willed her sudden tears to stop falling. She hadn't *really* made that woman jump from the bridge, had she? Nasty Nick turned his evil eyes on Connie instead, but she'd been on the streets a bit longer than Patsy, dossed down with her at night. She was used to fighting her corner.

'You shut it!' Nasty Nick retorted. 'In fact, you're sacked. Get on your bike. Hop it. Go on!' he shouted at Connie. She gave him the two-finger sign in return.

'Too late, mate. I've already decided to jack your useless job in. Slave labour more like. Here...' She threw a giant icicle – one of her props – at him, like a spear. At least it made him jump back. Freddie, who manned the market stall with the sign *Cheeses of Nazareth* above it, approached as the ambulance moved off again at speed on full blues and twos.

'Everything all right here, girls?' he said. Freddie had a kindly face and was even taller and broader than Nasty Nick, who immediately slunk away into the crowd. Patsy wiped her eyes, but the tears kept trickling down.

'Is the woman dead?' Patsy whispered. *Had she killed her*?

'I think there's still a glimmer of life in her yet,' Freddie said. 'And where there's life there's hope, right?'

Patsy swallowed hard as he continued onwards to his

market stall where people were queuing up to buy fresh cheese and delicious toasties. He left one each for the girls every night when he slipped them the key to his market stall. At least they were safe and dry, even though dossing inside was against the Health and Safety rules pasted on the wall next to Patsy's sleeping bag. It was true that as a result of being surrounded by giant truckles of Gorgonzola and even a cheese called Minger, which made them giggle, both girls stank like a mountain of steaming, well-worn socks, just as that thieving kid had pointed out.

Freddie was one of the Three Wise Men that she and Connie had picked out as protectors. Ralph, on the doughnut stall would slip them sweet treats when they felt numb and dizzy from standing stock-still for so long and Tom manned the Victorian barrow-style hot chestnut stand. He always dropped off bags of leftovers at night, behind *Cheeses of Nazareth*. Never said a word, but he clearly knew what was going on. Patsy didn't even like chestnuts, but she used one bag at her feet, and another clutched tightly in her hands to stay warm.

'Has someone offered you another job?' Patsy asked Connie, her voice a whisper and not only because she was trying to keep her pose.

'I'm heading back home, to college. Got a text from Mum begging me to give it another go. She's paid for my train ticket.'

'When she put the dosh into your bank account last time, you spent it on that hostel we stayed in for two days,' Patsy said. Connie had been a good friend – the best. Maybe they could do it again, wake up in proper beds on Christmas morning?

'Yeah... but she's emailed the actual ticket this time. Maybe she's right. I mean, I've learned that it's not all beer and skittles out here in the big wide world and I had dreams of going to drama college...'

'Me too,' Patsy replied. She'd gone to acting classes after

school. That's where she had learned to be a living statue, before her whole world tipped over and shattered...

'See the headlines there?' Connie nodded to the news stand opposite her pitch. It displayed magazines with covers featuring perfect families, wearing lots of sequins and red velvet and eating Christmas dinner, surrounded by enough candles to deck out a cathedral. But it was the front-page newspaper story that stood out. 'It looks like The Christmas Market Killer has headed to our patch.' For the first time, Patsy recognised fear in Connie's eyes. 'See? That's the girl we dossed down with over by the food market.'

Patsy read the headline and felt a shiver race up her spine. *Runaway escapes smelly market strangler by the skin of her teeth. Police are searching for a man driving a white van.* The photo of a bruised and battered girl with bloodshot eyes and garish purple marks around her neck, stared out of the paper.

'Oh my God.' Patsy nodded in horrified agreement. Of course, she had been aware of a murderer featuring in the news during Christmases past, who seemed to target vulnerable homeless kids, striking near festive markets around the country. But in her other life the news had hardly registered. If she had thought about it at all, she would have decided that such things happened to other teenage girls, who lived a different life, far away from her own happy family.

'The train leaves in a couple of hours.' Connie smiled. 'We'll keep in touch, yeah?' She rested her hand on Patsy's arm. 'Maybe you should go home too?'

'Your home?' Pasty's heart leapt with the idea, but Connie shook her head sadly.

'I'd love that, but you know I've already got a shitload of bridges to build with my folks...' Patsy nodded sadly.

'Yeah, of course. It was a stupid idea. Forget I said it.'

'What about going to your own place? You said your old

bed was really comfy – well, in comparison to a pile of hard cheese.' Connie giggled. Patsy couldn't quite raise a smile in response.

'Like I said, my dad is dead,' Patsy replied.

'But your mum–' Connie began to say before being cut off.

'Moved in a druggie, who cooks up skanky stuff in the jam pan.' Patsy heard her voice rise in fear and fury at the memory, as she thought of the huge pan that she and her mum and dad had gotten out every Christmas to make strawberry champagne glitter jam. They'd hand the jars of preserve out at the Christmas fair on the village green, to people who needed a bit of sparkle in their lives.

Her dad, brave Captain George Lloyd, always looked handsome and dashing, cutting a swathe through all those bog-standard people, dressed in his dapper army uniform, as everyone looked on in admiration. She bet those angels were swooning big time, up in Heaven. 'My mum's probably dead now too,' Patsy added, trying to rub the bright-red smear off baby Jesus's face.

'Well, you could go to the police station. I mean, they might put you somewhere safe–'

'Safe? You've seen some of the other kids the cops have picked up. They'd kill their own mother for a few quid. I might end up dossing down next to one of them.' Patsy felt bile rise in her throat at the very thought.

'It's just that the Three Wise Men are closing shop. Christmas stops here. The huts are going to be towed away first thing in the morning. No more *Cheeses of Nazareth* to offer shelter. No more free meals...'

'Yeah, well, have a nice Christmas.' Patsy turned away rather than show the tears smarting her eyes. Connie put her arm around her friend.

'Come on, Patsy,' she coaxed, 'we've both got to move on.

We can't just go on standing still in this one spot forever. *Everything* comes to an end sometime. If we try to take little steps forward maybe things really *will* start to get better in the new year.'

'Yeah and pigs might fly,' Patsy replied, trying to wipe a vision of the woman winging it through the air from the high bridge from her mind. She didn't want to move forward, that would take her further from the past, when her beloved dad and happy mum had made her feel that she could take on the world. Now it felt as though her life had come to a dead end.

The fairy lights of the Christmas market huts went off one by one. Patsy had watched Connie walk away along the Thames footpath, stopping every few steps to wave, until her straining eyes had finally lost her friend to the shadows and now falling snow. It felt a little like the death of a loved one all over again. Patsy realised for the first time that it was possible to feel real grief for a living person, as well as those souls who had headed from planet Earth for good.

She had managed to wipe off most of her white statue make-up in the cold trickle of water from the one working tap in the public toilets, using her sleeve as a flannel – the cubicles were out of paper tissue. The *Cheeses of Nazareth* stall was currently still standing so Patsy headed around the back, sleeping bag rolled under her arm. She was aware that she had absolutely no protection from the snow which was now falling quite heavily, nor the Christmas Market Killer, should that white-van man be lurking somewhere near, but as it stood, this was the safest spot she could think of. Or maybe she was like those migratory lemmings her dad had once told her about. Perhaps she did have a death wish. It wasn't like Connie hadn't spelled out the dangers she would be facing, once she was totally alone.

'I mean, the killer could have been amongst us all of the time, working on the stalls,' Connie had warned, looking seriously freaked out, or perhaps desperate to find an excuse to go home, tail between her legs, without losing face. 'It might even be one of the Three Wise Men,' she had added. But Patsy decided that she would rather take her chances. In her mind there was absolutely no point in heading back to the place she had left.

As she tried to hunker down a metre away from the back of the shed, Sid Vicious tucked safely in her pocket, the dark waters of the Thames grew choppy as gusts of wind lifted the snow into pocket blizzards. Patsy pulled her woolly hat down low. No hot chestnuts now to keep her fingers from freezing, no comforting smells of mulled wine, spicy gingerbread, and cinnamon candles to offer a cosy Christmas scenario. 'Cheese gives you nightmares,' her dad used to say, but Patsy had found that not to be true. She felt that the real night terrors were just about to begin.

She looked up to the bridge, from where the lady had launched into that spectacular tumble. Patsy just knew that she was now dead. She was also certain in her mind that if she hadn't been so dismissive towards the distraught woman earlier, then she wouldn't have done such a shocking thing. She deserved to fall asleep and roll into the dark depths of the river or get pounced upon by the Christmas Market Killer.

A glint of gold suddenly caught her eye, only inches away from her feet, almost covered in snow. She reached out and touched it, realised that it was a locket, lying in a pool of red, right where the woman had landed. Patsy swallowed hard before grabbing it and wiping the red stickiness off on her sleeve. She clicked it open. It showed a smiling woman and man with a tiny child between them. They looked happy. Patsy remembered when her family had felt just like that.

'Hey, there you are.' Freddie suddenly appeared alongside her, holding a hot cheese toastie in his hand. 'I saved this one for you.' He offered the sandwich. Patsy shook her head.

'I'm not hungry.'

'You know that the Christmas market's over? I've just loaded all the cheese up into the van.'

'I can tell. You smell even worse than I do.' Patsy tried to make a joke. She didn't even want to consider that Freddie could be the Christmas Market Killer, whatever anxieties on the subject Connie might have voiced – even if Freddie *did* have a white van and couldn't help smelling of strong cheese. Was *that* the odour that the girl who had been attacked had been referring to? Freddie didn't laugh.

'You can't stay out here all night, Patsy. It's freezing. Isn't it time to go back to your folks, like Connie?' Patsy saw Freddie glance over his shoulder. There wasn't another soul about.

'I'll be okay.' Patsy rolled the heavy locket between her fingers, deciding that if she got seriously freaked out, she could offer it to someone in return for a place to stay for the night. Her dad would call that using her initiative, after all, and she remembered that he had said that gold always holds its value.

'What's that you've got in your hand?' Freddie caught hold of the locket before Patsy had a chance to tighten her grip. He clicked on the torch on his mobile as he opened the engraved heart and stared at the photo inside for a moment, before looking back at Patsy.

'That's the woman, isn't it? The one who jumped off the bridge?' He raised a dark bushy eyebrow in query. Patsy shrugged.

'I didn't see her.' She looked down, ashamed. Freddie was looking at her like he was a mind reader.

'Maybe we should go and give it back to her,' he suggested.

'Connie said she's sure to be dead,' Patsy whispered. 'So it's no use to her now.'

'But what if she isn't? This looks precious. No doubt it would make her Christmas to get it back. Might give her a bit of hope.'

Patsy shrugged. 'We don't even know where they took her away to.'

'St Thomas' Hospital is just along the river there,' Freddie answered. 'I think we should go now. Come on.' Freddie pulled Patsy upright and almost marched her towards his white van.

'We could walk...' Patsy started to say. If he let go of her arm she intended to leg it. She'd just have to leave her sleeping bag behind. What if Connie had been right about the Christmas Market Killer?

'It's quicker to drive and my guess is she will be waiting with open arms for this. Don't worry, you'll be safe with me.' Patsy fell into panic mode. She wanted to cry out and run away as fast as she could, but Freddie had a grip like someone who knew how to handle a body and there was no one within screaming distance to hear or care about her predicament.

'You could just give it to her yourself,' Patsy pleaded, as she was swiftly deposited in the van, door locked, as Freddie slid behind the driver's wheel. Patsy identified the smell as Stinking Bishop. Her dad had once told her that it was the smelliest cheese on earth.

'My guess is that it would make her day, if you were the one to give it to her,' Freddie answered as he sped away. Patsy doubted his words. Even if he didn't intend to murder her, the woman probably did, after the row she'd had with her earlier.

'If you don't let me out, I'm going to tell the police,' Patsy ventured.

'Knock yourself out,' Freddie snorted as in a matter of

minutes he turned off the road. But instead of stopping at the brightly lit main entrance of the hospital, he drove past and around the back, towards an area in deep shadow, stopping by a door marked Mortuary.

The corridor that Freddie lead Patsy into was dark and foreboding. If Freddie had been telling the truth about returning the locket, then why hadn't he taken her to the reception desk?

'Any idea where the bridge jumper ended up? Not in there I hope,' she heard him ask another man, as she passed the mortuary door. She felt nauseous. Did he have an accomplice?

'Ward ten,' the other man answered. 'Nurses are doing a carol service up there. Maybe that will cheer her up a bit.'

Freddie pushed a door open and they emerged into a brightly lit seating area. Patsy wrenched her arm free and took off like a scud missile. She reached a staircase and took the stairs two at a time, skidding to a halt on the third floor, hearing Freddie's footsteps running behind her. Along the corridor a group of nurses were standing at the entrance to ward ten, hymn sheets in hand, singing 'God Rest Ye Merry Gentlemen'. Patsy burst through them and into the ward. The woman sat propped up on pillows, her arm in a cast and sporting bruises, looking as white as the sheets, but otherwise in one piece.

'I've brought your locket back.' Patsy held out the chain as the woman looked up, tears filling her eyes.

'Oh, Patsy love...' She trailed off as Patsy climbed on the bed and hugged her tightly.

'I'm so sorry, Mum,' Patsy sobbed. 'I didn't mean for you to throw yourself off the bridge.'

Her mum rubbed her back, just as she'd always done at

times of stress. She had rubbed Patsy's back all night long exactly a year ago on that dark snowy night when her dad had left them both.

'Is that what you thought?' Patsy's mum smiled, shaking her head. 'That's not the way it was, Patsy. The workman on the bridge went off for a tea break and I snuck into the open access bit to take a photo of you. Your dad would have been so proud at how good you were at being that living statue. Then I just seemed to go dizzy and suddenly toppled over...'

Patsy didn't know if she was telling the truth or not. It hadn't been easy for her mum either, this past year. 'I was holding a jar of strawberry and champagne glitter jam in my hand. Thought it would act as a carrot on a stick when I showed it to you.' She sighed, remembering the scene. 'But I must have dropped it when I fell...' She trailed off, looking sheepishly at Patsy, who pulled her doll out of her pocket.

'I know, it splashed all over Sid Vicious.' Patsy nodded, tears tracking white pathways down her grubby face.

'He's had a makeover I see. No more ginger hair now he's playing Jesus.' Patsy's mother took her hand, a wide grin lighting her face. 'Someone must be watching over us. It was lucky that I landed on that huge tray of Camembert stored behind the market stall.' She glanced up. Freddie stood in the doorway. 'Going to introduce me to your new friend?' she asked. Patsy waved Freddie in. She must have been crazy thinking that he might be a murderer.

'She's the double of you.' Freddie shook hands with Patsy's mum as Patsy made introductions. 'Could see the likeness the minute that I clocked the photo in the locket,' he added. 'Don't worry, I've been keeping an eye on her. She's a good kid.' He winked at Patsy. 'Lost my dear wife three years ago. I know how it can affect you.'

'I'm sorry to hear that.' Patsy's mum patted Freddie's hand.

'You never get over it, but believe me, you do grow used to it in time. Truth is, I'll always carry a little piece of her here in my heart.'

'I bet you didn't move a druggie into the house though,' Patsy said to Freddie, her salty tears not enough to dampen the spark of hurt that had triggered her slamming the door on her past. Patsy's mum rolled her eyes good-naturedly.

'Patsy, your dad was right; you are such a drama queen. Jack wasn't boiling up drugs in the jam pot. He was making a herbal remedy. His Mind and Soul group claims it helps to heal grief. It just gave me heartburn.' She chuckled. 'He's not staying over anymore, love. You were right, it was way too soon. Maybe I was just frightened of being alone.' She sighed. 'I've got a family-sized turkey for dinner tomorrow. Some old habits still die hard,' she lamented.

'You could join us.' Patsy suddenly turned to Freddie. 'I mean, if you've got nothing better on. To say thank you.'

'That's a wonderful idea,' Patsy's mum agreed. 'You would be very welcome.'

'I've got a load of cheese to offload and much of it is squashed.' He winked at Patsy's mum. 'So it's not a bad idea. Looks like I'll be getting Christmas Day off...'

Patsy looked behind her. Freddie had been distracted by a uniformed police officer now standing outside the door, beckoning him. His face was suddenly serious as he crossed towards the stern-faced man. Patsy wondered if he was about to be arrested, but after a whispered conversation, Freddie slapped the officer on the back, turned and rejoined them.

'Trouble?' Patsy's mum asked.

'Not anymore,' Freddie answered. 'Your old boss Nick has just been arrested on suspicion of the Christmas market crimes. My team of detectives have been working undercover, watching his every move. Tom and Ralph are good men,' he added, flashing his identity card which read *DCI Freddie Robinson*. Patsy suddenly realised that she had been surrounded by Good Samaritans all of the time. She had simply been blinkered to it.

'Let's go home,' she said. This extra shock was all too much to take in right now. She suddenly had a desperate urge to sleep in her old bed, as the choir of nurses launched into a rousing rendition of 'Away in a Manger'.

'If your mum's fit enough to go, we can all squeeze in the van,' Freddie offered. And so they did.

As Patsy shook the snow globe and watched the glittery fallout, she knew that she would keep it forever.

'Thanks. I love it!' Patsy grinned at Freddie. He shrugged.

'I meant to give it to you yesterday,' he answered.

'It even has little market huts inside, like *Cheeses of Nazareth*.' Patsy shook the globe again, filling the scene with sparkly snow. Freddie would leave it until another day before he broke the news that Nasty Nick had been caught whilst trying to break into the back of the cheese hut, dressed up and equipped for dark deeds, hoping that Patsy was spending her last night inside and all alone.

'You know, Patsy, making new friends doesn't mean that you are being disloyal to those who you still grieve for,' Freddie advised, as they finished tucking into the turkey and eyed up the pile of squashed cheese in the middle of the table. Patsy nodded. She understood. She couldn't ever get her dad back, but this still felt good.

'Before she passed away, my wife made me realise that life is a privilege that some people lose way too soon. So out of respect for those we have loved and lost, we have a duty to live life to the full, rather than just remain stuck forever in a bubble of sadness. Better instead to keep their spirit alive in every new thing that you do.'

Patsy suddenly felt compelled to raise a toast, as her dad had always done. She decided to carry on the tradition.

'To new friends,' she announced, 'as well as the old ones, up there. You will continue to live on, in our hearts, forever. But it's time to move forward.' Patsy watched her mum and Freddie exchange glances as they clinked their glasses together. 'Because for us, there's still life.

***

Marrisse Whittaker has been creating characters all her working life, travelling far and wide, first as a TV and Film Make-Up Artist, where she may have been called upon to construct a corpse, age an actor by a hundred years or make a real-life raddled rock star look desirable. Her first published book with Bloodhound Books, The Magpie, was shortlisted for The Lindisfarne Prize for Outstanding Debut Crime Fiction. Marrisse lives by the sea in rural Northumberland in the UK, inventing stories of murder and mayhem, whilst wandering through the dramatic surf and turf landscape right on her doorstep.

MERRY F***ING CHRISTMAS

by Rob Sinclair (writing as CJ Stone)

THE HEELS *of my shoes click-clack on the hard but sodden tarmac, a constant rhythm that somehow regulates with my thudding heart and my heavy breaths, getting quicker all the time.*

Can I go even faster?

In the darkness I stumble. Why? A tiny pebble on the path perhaps. Or did I simply turn my ankle? I'm walking too fast on these shoes. I'm a little drunk too. Not so drunk as to be out of my mind. I don't do that. But drunk enough to think it was a good idea to walk home.

Thoughts flash in my mind. Me, abashedly telling my friends I'll be fine. I've got my phone. It's only a mile. It's not even that late.

And what other choice do I have anyway?

Only a few days ago the heavens opened and we had the worst rain I've ever seen, or could even imagine. Roads all around the usually trickling River Reeve were suddenly covered in swirling water, which eventually took out the only vehicular bridge from Reeve town centre to my house across the usually serene gorge. A twenty minute or so journey home by foot. A probably fifty minute or more car journey around open countryside to find a suitable route and the next usable bridge.

Maybe I should have just stayed home tonight.

Instead, I walked out, crossing the bridge over the still raging torrent of water below, using the footpath alongside the still working railway line.

And then I chose to walk back home too. I've done so countless times before.

But it shouldn't be this quiet. It shouldn't be this isolated. Solitary.

A rumble behind me. Distant. I glance over my shoulder. I can't see it yet, but I know it's approaching. The noise gets louder. I can feel the vibrations rising up through the ground.

Another look behind me. I see the lights of the train, a couple of hundred yards away.

That's not all I see. A darkened figure, on the path behind me. Twenty yards? Close.

I try to speed up but other than breaking into a jog, I'm already walking as quickly as I can.

The train approaches so fast. The noise fills my head. I feel the air moving behind me.

It's only the train. It's the train. The train.

I shudder, tense when the huge hulk thunders past, sending cold air blasting into my face. I look up. See the windows – lit up – blurring as the train whizzes by. I see figures on board but can make out no features.

Can they see me?

The train flies away in front of me. With its departure I feel all the more alone, as though there was a certain safety in its presence.

I try to go faster still, chasing the train down. I can't bear to look behind me to the figure.

It's probably no one, I try to convince myself. Just someone else walking home.

The exit from the path is fifty yards ahead. A few seconds, then I'm back under street lights.

I'm going to make it. I'm going to make it.

'Hey.'

A voice. Right behind me. I don't so much turn as duck and cower.

The man grabs my wrist...

I open my eyes. Glance at myself in the mirror. See the panicked look on my face. I can't go out like this. I can't let my weaknesses show. I wait, watching as the look of terror slowly dissolves, but passivity is about the best I can achieve with any credibility. At junior school my teacher said I had an *ever-present winning smile*. Whatever that meant. Teachers always considered me a happy child. I can't find even a hint of that smile now.

Did it leave me all at once or has it been a slow slide?

I smooth down the fabric of my black blouse. I like it. It's a nice fit. Not too tight. Not too baggy. Not too revealing. More boring, really, than I'm used to. It covers my chest, both my arms. That's perhaps the most crucial aspect. I run my hand down the sleeve, to my wrist.

Pain. I feel it still. But I don't know anymore if it's only in my mind.

I've done all I can to prepare. Mentally. Physically. With a sharp intake of something close to embarrassment, I head out of the house.

· · ·

I walk. I have to. Six weeks on from the floods and the little cluster of streets where I live, affectionately known as Hilltop because of its prominent position, is still cut off from Reeve, from my friends, from my job too. The bridge repairs began in earnest two days after the floods first subsided, and although a temporary pass was opened a couple of weeks after that while the main rebuild took place, a heavy snowstorm, followed by icy conditions led to a bus smashing into the works one night. The crash caused significant damage and further delayed any prospect of life returning to normal for the Hilltoppers, particularly as we remained in the coldest of cold snaps I could ever remember.

Six weeks. Outside of daylight hours, I've hardly left the house in that time. Tonight I'm determined to finally make an effort. Christmas is only two days away. I *want* to be excited by that. Tonight should help. No, tonight *will* help.

The bar is fine. Familiar. We've been here countless times, although in a town as small as Reeve there really aren't that many other choices. It's not some highly fashionable place like the trendy cocktail bars you see in bigger towns and cities, but it's relaxed enough - though on a weekend night so close to Christmas, it's rammed. There's music playing but it's quiet for now, yet the hubbub from the chatter is bordering on raucous and I know as the night goes on it'll only get worse and worse, and as much as I try to ignore the silly morose voice in my head that never stops bleating, my anxiousness is on a constant rise.

How long before it's acceptable for me to make my excuses and leave?

'I think you did the right thing,' Maeve says, getting my attention. I'd been miles away.

Kate and Helen are at the bar. It's horrible to think but I felt awkward within seconds of them leaving me and Maeve alone. Not that I don't like Maeve. I *love* her. We were best friends for so long. But we aren't kids anymore and our friendship hasn't quite grown with us. I know she still cares, even if she doesn't really get *me*. This me. Not ten-year-old me.

'You don't have to talk about it if you don't want to,' she adds when I say nothing.

A strange thing to say really.

'I was speaking to him the other night, though, and–'

'You were speaking to Keenan? Where?'

She looks flustered, but perhaps only because of my accusatory tone.

'We... bumped into each other. Just in town.'

'Yeah?'

'Yeah.'

'Okay, and what did he have to say for himself?'

'Why are you talking to me like that?'

I shake my head and look away. Am I being too hard on her?

Maeve reaches out and puts her hand on mine on the table.

'Babe, he's hurting too. He looks like a lost little boy when he talks about you.'

She laughs and just a little bit of my agitation disappears, but only a little bit, because I don't buy that they 'bumped' into each other. Why? History.

'He's a good guy,' Maeve says.

'I don't really want to talk about it. Not tonight. Please?'

She gives a meek smile, just as Kate and Helen return to the table with a tray full of drinks: a bottle of Prosecco, four flutes, and four shot glasses filled with something dark.

'Let's get this party started!' Helen calls as she picks up her shot glass and holds it aloft. The rest of us follow suit and on the count of three we down the thick, perfumed liquor. I swallow in one gulp but the strength of alcohol, and the insipid taste, makes me gag and retch.

'Bloody hell, Helen, are you trying to poison us?' Maeve says, face screwed up. Half of her shot remains in the glass.

Kate pours the wine. Helen looks over her shoulder, back to the bar, a couple of times.

'First time I've seen those lads in here,' she says.

She doesn't need to say anything more to help me identify the group of three, as I already noticed the brief exchange between the men and my friends at the bar.

'Apparently they're from London, into finance or something, but are working here,' Kate says.

'Bollocks,' I say. 'What would they be doing in Reeve?'

Helen and Kate both glare at me as though I've offended them.

'They actually seem really nice,' Kate says. 'Especially compared to the usual idiots around here.'

'Really nice,' Helen repeats. 'And single.'

'But you're not,' I say to her.

'But *you* are,' she replies with a cheeky wink, and I can't help but smile despite myself.

'And so am I,' Kate adds, looking back over to the three. Or gazing, really. The tallest and most handsome of the three catches her looking and smiles back before Kate abruptly turns to us again.

Helen and Maeve burst out laughing. I keep my eyes on Kate. Even in the darkened room I know her cheeks are burning. She's smitten.

'Why don't you two go and chat to them?' Maeve says.

'Because we're not desperate,' I reply.

'Speak for yourself,' Kate says, eliciting another laugh from Helen.

I look back to the men. It was a real struggle even to get me out here tonight, the last thing on my mind is flirting with some random guys.

'Oh shit,' Helen says, and I follow her line of sight to the entrance where two men have walked in.

I groan. Keenan, of course, with his best friend, Ben.

I glare at Maeve, and the way she shrinks kind of answers my unasked question. Did she tell Keenan I was coming out tonight?

Keenan does a bad job of not looking at us as he and Ben walk to the bar, standing right next to the three Londoners and pretty much blocking them from our view. Poor Kate.

'Just ignore them,' Kate says.

'I intend to,' I say, before taking a big swig of wine.

'Bastard,' Helen adds for good measure.

Maeve doesn't say anything.

'I can't believe they're here,' Kate says. 'What are the chances?'

In a town as small as Reeve, probably quite high really, even without any sneaky intervention.

'We can go somewhere else,' Kate suggests to me.

'No. We're not having our night spoiled because of them.'

All three of my friends stare at me for a few moments, as though weighing up whether to say something in response or not. None of them do and thankfully, with a bit of help from a tag-team effort by Kate and Helen, we move the conversation on.

For a while everything feels like it's going to plan, even if I do keep one eye on Keenan, now sitting in the opposite corner of the room, and even if Kate does still have one eye on the guys at the bar. Soon they're the drunkest and rowdiest of anyone in the place, singing along to the cheesy Christmas songs – the music a notch louder now than earlier – as though they're doing late-night karaoke.

'We need some more drinks,' I say, looking at the empty glasses. 'My round I think.'

'I'll help,' Kate says, practically jumping out of her seat.

We head to the bar. I put the order in. Another bottle, another round of shots. Although I really wanted to make the effort of coming out tonight, I hadn't intended on getting drunk, but now I'm here, now that Keenan is here too... perhaps there's a certain appeal to the numbness that I hope will follow the drinks.

'What's your name?' the man to my left asks. The handsome one. Even more so now I'm up close. If he had glasses on he'd be a Clark Kent type, with rugged angular features but soft eyes. Kate is talking and laughing with his two friends. So apparently this guy isn't the one she's after.

'Why do you want to know?' I ask.

'Because you're the prettiest girl in here.'

I roll my eyes. 'That is lame.'

'Prettiest girl in the whole town, from what I've seen.'

'Try harder.' Though I'm smiling as I say it.

'My name's Joel.'

He holds out his hand. I hesitate, but then shake it.

'And yours is...'

'A secret,' I say to him. 'Sorry.'

I nudge Kate and pick up the drinks and turn to head back to the table, the smile still on my face, at least until I catch sight of Keenan glaring over.

'They are soooo nice!' Kate says as we sit down. She sounds like an overexcited schoolgirl, but then it's good to see her enthused – she's had a tough time herself with love the last couple of years. 'You like the tall one, don't you?'

'Joel?'

'You got his name! Quick work.'

'He seems fine. But not tonight.'

'This is their last night here before Christmas,' Kate

continues. 'But they're back in January. They'll be here for a few months, apparently.'

'All the more reason not to rush into things tonight then,' Maeve says, a little snottily really.

At least her comment seems to distract Kate, and we're soon back into a relaxed chit-chat for a while, even if I'm sure the music is even louder than before now and I pause from the conversation for a few minutes when The Pogues come on. My favourite Christmas song, although it sounds a lot more sad and a lot more regretful now than in the past.

'I'm bursting for the loo,' Helen says, rising up. 'Anyone else?'

'Yeah,' I say. I've been desperate for ages but hadn't wanted to make the move, and risk inviting any attention from Keenan or Joel as I passed, but at least I have company now.

I look nowhere but at the sign on the toilet door as we head across the bar. Once inside we move into adjacent cubicles.

'I'm really glad you came out tonight,' Helen says.

'Thanks. Me too.'

'I know everything with Keenan was... shitty. But... is everything else okay with you?'

'How do you mean?'

'It's only... the last few weeks. I don't know. I'm just worried for you.'

I close my eyes as a well of emotion builds up, but doing so only sends horrible images from that painful night flashing through my mind.

Would that ever stop?

I haven't told anyone what had happened out on the path by the railway. I hate myself for that, but I can't. The shame I feel makes it impossible. Led to me and Keenan splitting for good, I think, even if we'd had problems already. Has led me to alienating myself from my friends, from everything good in my life...

Not anymore.

'Thanks,' I say. 'Thanks for not pushing me too hard. For understanding.'

Helen laughs. 'I don't really understand at all. But I'm here for you, whenever you want to talk. About anything at all.'

We flush the toilets in unison. As we wash our hands, Helen's phone vibrates and chirps with an incoming call.

'It's Louis,' she says, putting the phone down on the sink without answering, but a moment later it's dancing on the porcelain.

'Take it,' I say, catching her eye in the mirror. 'It might be important.'

I carry on out as she answers. I hadn't intended to, but I find my gaze drawn to the corner of the bar. Ben, sitting at the table. No Keenan.

'Hey.'

I cringe at the sound of his voice. I stop and turn, and Keenan is standing right there, empty-handed. I'd at least expected him to have two newly poured beers in his hands as cover for him just happening to bump into me.

'What do you want?' I say, folding my arms.

'A bit less attitude would be a start.' He smiles at his own words but they weren't particularly friendly. 'This is our song, isn't it?'

Mariah Carey.

'No, it's not.'

'Well, our Christmas song at least. Don't you remember that night at–'

'Sod off, Kee,' I say, about to turn away from him, but he grabs my wrist and I wince. Real pain or just the memory? I'm not sure.

'Please?'

I shrug him off and turn back to face him.

'Please, what?'

'Can we not even be civil? Can we not even have a conversation?'

'About what?'

'Oh come on, you don't need to do this.'

'I just want to have a good night with my friends. Please leave me alone.'

I turn away from him again, but once more he grabs my arm and I notice Kate and Maeve looking over with concern.

'Let go of her, Keenan,' Helen blasts as she storms over.

'Oh, piss off, will you?' he says to that as I pull from his grip once more.

And that should have been it. With Helen by my side – who'd always hated Keenan, by the way – I expected us to walk off, back to our table to enjoy our drinks.

'Everything okay?' Joel asks.

I slump. Keenan's face immediately switches to anger.

'Who are you?'

'Her date,' Joel says, wrapping his arm around me.

I really wish he hadn't. Perhaps he thinks he's being chivalrous. Perhaps he's read the situation entirely correctly and realised Keenan is pestering me. But I don't want this kind of intervention, *his touch*, even if it's entirely innocent.

Is it?

'Get off me!' I scream, a reflexive reaction. I duck and turn and swing my arm and the slap catches Joel perfectly on his cheek, the force enough to make my hand sting. He reels back, shock on his face rather than anything else. But at the same time...

The half-filled pint glass in Joel's hand goes flying and the sticky amber liquid sloshes out of the top and right over–

'Helen!' I shout in dismay.

'What the hell?' Joel says to me, face full of rage. He looks like he might come for me.

'You touch her and I'll tear your head off,' Keenan says, stepping forward.

'Would you both just STOP!' I scream, and for a couple of seconds I'm sure the music has stopped too and it feels like every single person in the bar is watching and listening.

'Both of you, get lost,' I say to them before I try to put my arm around Helen's shoulder, but she squirms from my grip and marches back to our table.

I follow her, note the look of shock on Maeve and Kate's faces. I daren't look at the faces of everyone else around us.

'I'm so sorry,' I say to Helen.

She sits down and wipes at her top.

'It's... I'm soaked.'

She cries.

'Let's go to the bathroom. We'll get you cleaned up.'

'No. I'll get Louis to pick me up. I can't...' She looks around. 'I'm so embarrassed.'

'You don't have to leave,' Kate says. 'Please.'

'I just want to go home.'

A bit of an extreme reaction? I really don't know. Perhaps something happened on that phone call with Louis?

We can't change her mind and minutes later only three of us remain, and the mood struggles to pick up. Despite me whacking Joel, I can tell Kate is still interested in talking to his friends some more. As the drinks go down, Maeve seems up for it too, and before long they've persuaded me to stand up and have a dance, as others have around the bar, even though there's no dance floor. Band Aid. I do love that song. Joel and his friends edge toward us and Kate begins to grind with the stocky one she's had her eye on.

Ben and Keenan remain in the corner, ever watchful, a glower on Keenan's face. I know if I stay, and the closer Joel and his friends get, then round two is inevitable.

So I call time. On my night at least.

It's not as though it's that early anyway. Half eleven. I hadn't really intended to stay any later. I wait until Joel has disappeared off on his phone and his mates are at the bar.

'You're sure you'll be okay?' Kate asks, looking from me to Joel's friends, as though making it clear where her interests lie.

'I'm fine. I'll get a taxi. And I've got my phone.'

Although it only has five per cent battery left.

'It was really good to see you,' Maeve says.

'You too.'

I hug them both and we have a drawn-out goodbye.

'Merry Christmas,' I finally say to them, before I head for the door.

I shiver as soon as I step outside. The temperature has dropped several degrees in the few hours I've been in the bar. I duck my head down into the thick furry neck of my coat and look around. Quiet. More so than I expected. Yes, it's a cold winter's night, but it's also only two days before Christmas, only one night of revelry left before the big day. I'm about to move when I'm sure I see someone lurking in the alley across the street. I stare there for a few seconds. It's not as if I'm brave enough to go and take a closer look, so instead I turn and head off to one of the town's two taxi ranks, a couple of hundred yards away.

Three other people waiting. No taxis. I stand in the queue, still shivering. Try to stop myself from checking my phone. I need to conserve the battery.

Ten minutes later I'm head of the queue, a man and woman now wait behind me too. Five minutes later and my taxi finally pulls up. The driver winds the window down.

'St Mary's Lane, please.'

The doubt in his eyes is almost instantaneous.

'Hilltop?'

'Yes.'

'Sorry, love. I'm not going all the way over there tonight.'

'I'll pay.'

'No. Sorry. I can't do it. I'll be out all night.'

'If you're not getting in, can we?' asks the man behind me. Or, more like states really.

'Where you off to?' the taxi driver calls out to him.

'Foster Street.'

'Jump in.'

Seconds later the taxi pulls away with the man and woman in the back.

'Bastards.'

Another ten minutes before the next car pulls up.

'St Mary's Lane.'

'Hilltop?'

I can already sense where this is going.

'Yes. Please? I really need to get back.'

He shakes his head, but at least looks a little sympathetic, I think.

'That'll be my night done, and it'll take me a couple of hours to get home from there.'

'How much?'

'I can't meter it. Like I said, my return journey–'

'Please, how much?'

'Hundred.'

I only have thirty.

'Can I pay by card?'

'Sorry. But there's a cashpoint around the corner.'

'Wait there.'

I rush off. No one waiting at the cashpoint. A good sign? No. No one is waiting because it's out of order.

'Shit.'

As I turn I see a group of three women climb into the taxi. I watch it pull away then stand there feeling lost. Midnight has already come and gone. Hardly anything left open in our small town. Will there be any more taxis at all?

I take out my phone to call Kate. The battery's dead.

'No,' I say, fighting back the urge to scream or cry or something.

I could go to the bar? No, Keenan would still be there. I don't need the hassle.

'Fine,' I say out loud, to myself, before sucking in a big lungful of icy air, and setting off for home.

Cold. Dark. Eerie. In the past I liked this walk home. The views from the top of the bridge, looking across the valley to the east, are spectacular. In the daytime. With a bit of sunshine.

After midnight, the route is pitch black and sinister. Not even a train coming in either direction to distract and break up my whirring thoughts.

I look over my shoulder every other step as I walk. I see nothing. How can I? With no moonlight even, I wouldn't see if someone was right there.

Why have I done this? There must have been another option. I could have stayed with one of them. Keenan, Joel? No, I don't want to think about them.

A noise behind me. I stop and spin around. No one there.

Or is there?

'Hello?' I say.

I stand completely still. Don't even breathe. Can hear nothing but the rustle of branches in the wind and the distant cry of a night-time creature.

No, something else too. Footsteps?

This can't be happening again. Please... not after last time.

My body trembles. I'm ready to turn and bolt, whether someone is following me or not. I only hope my shaky legs will allow me.

But then the figure somehow comes into view from the blackness and I freeze.

'Kee! What the hell?'

'What are you doing?' he says, stopping a couple of steps from me.

'I'm going home. What are *you* doing here?'

'I followed you. I wanted to make sure you're okay.'

'I'm okay. So you can go now.'

'No,' he says.

He doesn't budge. I don't know what to say.

'That guy was watching you. The guy from the bar.'

The figure I thought I'd seen in the alley?

'But it's you who's followed me here,' I say. 'Leave me alone.'

I turn to walk away, but he pulls on my coat to halt me. I spin around, ready to swipe at him, but he's too quick and too strong and he wraps his arms around me to pin my arms to my sides, and pushes his head to the side of mine.

'Stop,' he says, calm, but his breaths are heavy and he stinks of beer. 'Stop fighting. I'm not going to hurt you.'

'You *are* hurting me!' I say as I writhe.

'Stop!' he says, more angrily.

I do. He doesn't let go.

'I miss you,' he says. 'I miss you so much.'

I squirm a little more but he holds on tight. Then I feel his touch on my neck. His lips. A light kiss. To start with. And then one hand gropes my bottom. I cringe. I feel sick.

'Please come back to me, babe.'

'No!' I roar and in a sudden burst of strength I pull out of his grip and punch him hard in the chest and step back.

Run? No. I don't know why, but I stand my ground.

He shakes his head, his eyes pinched with anger.

'It's over, Keenan.'

'You reckon?'

'Yes!'

'I would have done anything for you,' he says. 'But you toyed with me. Strung me along. Like you're still doing now.'

'I didn't. I'm not!'

'Yes you are. You enjoy it. Manipulating me. Seeing me hurting.'

'What are you talking about?'

'You're poison.'

He's so mad, and his words genuinely sting. If only he knew the truth... but I can never tell him. Not now.

'I hate you,' he says.

And then he comes for me.

I don't know what to do. I don't know what *he'll* do. I'm too confused, too bewildered. After the last time... how can I be in this position again?

Have I brought it all on myself?

Keenan lunges for me. Not to hit me, to grab me. I try to fight him off. I lift my knee into his groin. He groans. The hit takes some of his strength. I reach forward and clamp my jaw onto his shoulder but all I get is a mouthful of thick overcoat.

He swings me around. I stumble, about to fall. Somehow I manage to take hold of his coat sleeve and as I spin I haul my leg out. My foot collides with his ankle, takes his standing leg. I yank on his sleeve and he lurches toward me, teetering.

I side-step and let go of his sleeve and he falls from my sight, crying in surprise as he tumbles and crashes down the verge, into the woods below.

I stand in shock for a few moments.

What have I done?

I can't see him down there, but I can hear him. Moaning. He's hurt.

I drop to my backside and clamber down the verge into the woods. I somehow find him in the darkness. Notice the thin light from his dirtied phone screen on the ground. I pick the phone up and shine the torchlight on him. He's lying in a heap on the soggy ground, his leg twisted horribly, the bright white of bone protruding, his trouser leg glistening red all around it.

'Help me,' he says.

I stare down at him.

'What would you have done to me?' I ask.

He doesn't say anything, but the look in his eyes...

'What would you have done to me?' I ask again. 'How far would you have gone?'

'Please,' is all he says.

Not good enough.

I look around and pick up the biggest rock I can find. I put his phone in my pocket. I don't need to see. I hold the rock in the air then bring it down with as much venom as I can, right where I know Keenan's head is.

Crunch.

I use my instincts after that, moving slowly through the dark woods, every step an effort across the heavy ground, towing Keenan's limp body with me, but it isn't that far to go.

I reach the concrete shell, buried in the hillside. A disused bunker, I think. Nobody ever comes down here. The padlock on the grate door remains in place but is so badly rusted it's fallen apart.

I pull the door open then drag Keenan inside.

I let go of him and take his phone out again. I shine the torch down, onto Keenan's bloodied face. His left eye is all mangled, his cheek torn apart, his bottom lip protruding strangely. But his right eye is open, and staring at me. He's awake, sucking in small breaths through his battered mouth somehow.

I kneel down to him. Move the torchlight across the small, concrete-walled space. Damp. Dank. Cold. Green and black slime lines the walls and ceiling. I find what I'm looking for on the floor. The other figure. The other face. White. Lifeless now. But the images it conjures…

I cringe to try and take the memories away. The memories of that night, up on the path. When he'd grabbed me… when he'd…

'No,' I say out loud.

I don't want to take myself back to that night. Not ever.

And I hadn't wanted to bring myself back here ever either. I would never have done so had it not been for Keenan.

'P… Please,' Keenan says. 'H… H… Help… me.'

He wants my help?

'You got it.'

I pick up the stone by his head and crash it down onto his skull.

He doesn't say anything after that.

I straighten up, the torchlight just wide enough to frame both bodies at once.

'Merry fucking Christmas,' I say. 'To both of you.'

Then I turn and walk away.

***

CJ Stone is a pseudonym of Rob Sinclair, author of multiple bestselling thrillers; most notably the James Ryker series, and the Sleeper 13 series. His books have sold more than a million copies worldwide. Having made his name writing breakneck thrillers featuring globe-trotting spies, ruthless assassins and continent-spanning conspiracies, CJ Stone came about as a result of Rob's desire to diversify into other areas of thriller writing, in particular psychological suspense and domestic thrillers. He continues to write under his real name, with a bright and distinct future of twisty thrillers planned for CJ Stone.

ALL THEY WANT FOR CHRISTMAS

BY VALERIE KEOGH

THE LAST WEEK in November and my thoughts were already on Christmas. When my daughter rang that evening it was the first thing I brought up. 'What would you like for Christmas this year?'

'The same as I've wanted for the last three years, for you to come and spend the day with us.'

I should have anticipated the answer. Emily was nothing if not consistent. Stubborn too. More like her father, Chad, than me, although she'd be horrified if I said such a thing. Although she'd inherited her stubbornness from him, I hoped she and her brother, Michael, inherited their kind nature from me. 'You know we can't come to you for Christmas. Your father would never agree.'

We couldn't go to her, or to Michael who would also ask, and they refused to come home. Not after the catastrophe four years before. Things that go wrong, devastating as they may be at the time, are often overlaid with humour in hindsight. Not that Christmas Day though. It coloured the relationship between my children and Chad in indelible shades of black and I knew by *you*, Emily meant me and not her father. She would probably have put up with him had we gone. Michael, on the other hand, would make it clear the invitation was for me alone. He hadn't spoken to Chad since that Christmas.

'I suppose he's already started, has he?'

I could hear the sneering criticism in Emily's voice but couldn't bring myself to complain. 'You know he has. Switch-on will be December the first. He'd already started by the time I got out of bed.' And couldn't have a shower or make myself a cup of tea. Not until he came in at lunchtime and switched the electricity back on so *he* could have a cuppa with his lunch. I didn't say any of this to Emily although she'd know the way it would be. The way it always was.

It had been my fault, but I never could have realised the implication of what I did. Chad and I were married six months. We'd stretched ourselves painfully to buy our first house together in an estate in Woking near where we both worked. It was near to family and friends too and we'd pictured family get-togethers and parties. Unfortunately, we couldn't afford either. Both our salaries were needed in those early days to pay the mortgage. Only Chad's extra part-time job, two evenings a week, allowed us enough for food and the odd beer in our local.

We'd discussed Christmas, agreeing that we wouldn't waste the money on useless gifts simply for the sake of it. But then I saw the snowman. Three foot high. Flashing lights and cheeky smile. It made me laugh and I knew Chad would love to see it sitting outside our house when he arrived home tired after yet another long day.

My mother had given me a cheque for Christmas. I had planned to put it toward food. Instead, I handed over a ridiculous sum of money for an outside decoration we could only use for a few days every year.

I thought Chad would be a little annoyed, but hoped it would cheer him up, relieve a little of the burden our huge mortgage had laid on both our shoulders. With the snowman unpacked and sitting in front of our living room window, I plugged an extension cable into a hallway socket, opened the window and fed it through. When I switched it on and the snowman lit up, I couldn't help the automatic grin. It was wonderfully delightful.

I stood at the window, waiting. His evening job was local, so he walked home, and I saw him as he turned the corner. Under the street light, I could see his face, puzzlement changing to disbelief, then straight to amazed glee. He ran the last few feet and stood in front of our house, laughing.

And I was inside, laughing.

How could I have known, then, I'd unleashed a monster.

The following year, both of us had had promotions, interest rates had come down and suddenly our mortgage didn't feel so crippling. Chad was able to give up his part-time job, and we even had sufficient funds to have the occasional party.

At the end of November, Chad took the snowman down from the attic, checked it was in working order and on the first of December, despite my complaint it was way too early, he had it sitting outside. I had to smile at his enthusiasm, my smile broadening when I got home from work the following week to find a luminous reindeer standing beside the snowman.

My smile dimmed slightly by the time a second reindeer joined the first.

Over the next three years, our family expanded. Emily arriving first, Michael a year later. Our Christmas lights collection had grown faster, added to by a six-foot red and white chimney, another smaller snowman, three wall-affixed stars, two penguins and three elves. Some had flashing lights, some were static, but all glowed brightly from December first until the evening of January sixth – the latest Chad felt able to leave them up. He took them down, checked them over and packed them away. At first, they went into the attic, but with so many more to store it became impractical. The alternative was to shift our one car onto the driveway and use the garage.

I'm not sure when it changed from being fun to an ordeal.

It might have been the year when Emily was six. She was watching some children's Christmas movie whose name has long faded from memory. Minutes from the end, the TV went off – no warning. Chad had switched off the electricity to make some changes to the illuminated display. I pleaded with him to wait until the movie was over, but he wouldn't listen. It took me a long time to console our distraught daughter.

Or maybe it was the many times meals were delayed... or ruined... because he switched off the electricity despite my asking, time and time again, that he'd tell me in advance. No. He'd look out the window, see one of his precious figures on the blink and everything, and everyone, went out of his head.

'It's getting a bit over the top, isn't it?' our next-door neighbour, Tony, said, staring at the newest figures Chad had attached along the length of the roof ridge.

Loyalty made me smile and shake my head. 'It's Christmas. I don't think you can ever have enough lights.'

'Hmmm. Well, you're running out of space for any more.'

I hadn't the heart to tell him about the life-size Santa that was waiting to be attached to the chimney.

'It's too big,' I'd said when it had arrived the previous day. I was five-six, the Santa was an inch or two taller and I was imagining it standing in the last spare gap in the garden between the reindeers and the snowmen.

'Nonsense, it has to be big enough for people to be able to see it from the ground.'

I looked at him in horror. 'You're not putting that on the roof!'

He ignored me.

I'm not sure when he'd started to do that either. 'He's off in a world of his own.' I'd explain his behaviour away as if Chad were some sort of deep intellectual thinker lost in philosophical thought instead of a rude bastard who couldn't be bothered to answer me. It had become a habit, over the years, to cover for him. For his sake, or mine, or the children's. I was never really too sure.

When the children were older they saw through it all, but their attempts to make things better for me only succeeded in making things worse all around. I felt a combination of relief and sorrow when, in their late teens, both moved out.

They came home for Christmas, of course, even when Chad's illuminations became not just the talk of our small town, but the county. I pleaded with Emily and Michael to say nothing, not even when Chad switched off the electricity and none of us could have a shower, or a hot drink. Once, Michael, fuming, took Chad's car keys and headed off, returning thirty minutes later with takeaway coffees and warm muffins. The three of us sat around the kitchen table and scoffed the lot.

From early December, people came from all over to have a look. The children staring with open-mouthed delight, their parents no doubt wondering how much our electricity bill was, and probably thanking their lucky stars they didn't live next door.

Tony, who did, quickly progressed from asking nicely if Chad would rein in his display to demanding the council took action. He'd possibly have taken matters into his own hands and tried to sabotage the display, but Chad was wise to any such move – CCTV cameras were positioned to capture footage of anyone who entered within a few feet of the display. Tony was angry, but he wasn't stupid. The council did their best and sent out inspectors to assess the fire risk and danger to passers-by from tumbling figures.

Chad took great delight in entertaining the inspectors, proudly showing off his top-of-the-range electrical connections, the stability of each figure. He even insisted on taking one up a ladder to show him how he'd secured the elves and the Santa on the roof. 'I make safety my priority,' he said to them. 'No shortcuts, ever.'

After his appeal to the council failed, Tony took a further step and went to a solicitor to plead the display was causing him stress and interfering with the enjoyment of his home.

Chad laughed when he got the letter. 'They're in *my* garden, on *my* roof!'

I knew there was no point in saying it was *our* house.

Although it was in both our names, Chad lived by the theory that he who paid the mortgage owned the house. It didn't make any difference; he wasn't going anywhere. It wasn't other women who tempted my darling husband, it was yet another piece to squeeze into his display.

The only concession Chad made in reply to the solicitor's letter was to turn the display off at nine rather than eleven. 'Makes sense, most people come to see it much earlier.'

They did, blocking the road, our neighbours' driveways, the constant stream of traffic annoying everyone. 'Not my fault,' he'd say when they complained. 'I don't ask them to come, do I?'

But come they did in the weeks before Christmas and on the day itself. Then afterwards, the excitement would die down and the road would return to normal. Everyone felt relieved it was over for another year, apart from Chad, of course, who missed the admiring glances, the laughter and pointing fingers of the children. Reluctantly on the sixth, he'd start the big removal, taking a week off work to get it all done.

That final family Christmas four years before, Emily had brought her new fiancé, and Michael a woman he'd been seeing for a while. I'd spent the previous week polishing and cleaning, stocking up the cupboards with all kinds of delicacies. I even went into M&S and bought new bed linen for their beds. Everything was all ready for their arrival when Chad arrived home from work early on the twenty-fourth. He didn't have to do anything when they arrived a little later, just play the charming host, the loving father.

But neither were roles he was interested in playing.

Luckily for the success of Christmas Eve, his display didn't as much as flicker out of sync. He did, of course, run out to check every hour or so and insisted on giving Emily's fiancé and Michael's girlfriend a lengthy tour. It was icy cold, both too polite to cut him short. Anyway, it gave me time to spend alone with my children. It was the best part of the Christmas. The only good part.

Overnight, a wind picked up. Chad had, as he always did, carefully installed each figure of his display ensuring they could withstand whatever the weather could fling at them, but he'd never predicted the savage gale that hit us that night.

I was a light sleeper. Always had been and more so since the children were born, waking at their slightest cry when they were babies, and later, waking at the creak of the stairway as they came up to bed, or at the squeak of the hinges on the front door when they'd come home after a late night. When they'd both left, I'd wake and think of them, wondering if they were safe.

Chad slept through everything. I could have woken him, especially when I heard an ominous crashing sound from outside. I could have... instead, I lay there wondering what impact it would have on the Christmas Day celebrations.

The wind was still swirling around the house, whistling through the poorly fitting wooden-framed windows, shrieking through Chad's display. I watched his eyes open, quickly shutting mine as if I too had slept through the noise.

His cry of disbelief was lost as a louder gust rattled the windows. He jumped from the bed, pulled on a rag-tag mix of the nearest clothes to hand. I hid my smile as he pulled my pink fleece over his shirt as he ran out the door.

My smile faded as the sound of the front door slamming hit me with a loud blow of reality. Chad would turn off the electricity if any of his display needed fixing. He wouldn't give any consideration to the needs of the day, our family, or guests.

Climbing from the bed, I peered through a gap in the curtains to assess the situation. It didn't take an expert to know it was bad. The Santa that had been secured so tightly to the chimney was lying, up close and friendly, with the snowman. And I recognised one of the elves as being another of the roof inhabitants.

Dressing in the new outfit I'd bought for the day, determined to impress my children and their partners, I headed downstairs. The doors of the other bedrooms were still shut tight; I said a quiet prayer they'd stay that way for an hour or two longer.

'Is it going to take long to fix?' I asked, standing in the front doorway, watching as Chad manoeuvred the Santa upright.

He shot me a vicious look without replying.

I stepped outside, shivering as the icy wind swirled around me. 'I need to know, Chad, we have visitors, don't forget. I'd planned to do a big fry-up for breakfast.'

Chad was checking the damage to the Santa. 'I'll be done when I'm done.'

There was no point in standing out in the cold arguing with him. Especially since, with the electricity off, there'd be no heating either. At least I could do something about that. Ten minutes later, I put a match to the fire and sat back on my haunches. I'd been looking forward to this day for weeks and now it looked as if it was going to be spoiled. Tears were wasted on Chad, as was anger or entreaty. He'd simply do what he wanted regardless of anyone else's needs.

Four years had passed but I can still clearly remember Michael's face when he came downstairs, his face screwed up into a line of angry frustration.

'He's done it again, hasn't he?'

'He'll be finished in a little while.' The lie blithely tripped off my tongue as it had so often before. But Michael wasn't a child, and he wasn't fooled.

'He's bloody well going to finish now!'

Pleading with Michael was as much a waste of time as pleading with his father. When I stood between him and the front door, he did as his father would have done and pushed me out of the way. Not unkindly, not with the total disregard for my feelings his father would have used, but out of his way, nevertheless, determined on his course of action.

'What's going on?'

I turned to see Michael's girlfriend, Casey. Her hair was mussed, her face prettier without the make-up she'd been wearing the previous night. 'The wind.' I waved a hand in the air. 'It blew Santa down from the roof. Chad is trying to fix it.'

'Oh.'

I almost smiled. Michael obviously hadn't filled her in on his father's obsession and she seemed oblivious to the ramifications of Chad spending time fixing his display. 'It means we've no electricity. No electric showers. No heating. No breakfast.'

'No coffee!' Now that reality hit her, she looked aghast.

Thinking of the big turkey sitting in the fridge, I was going to comment that coffee was the least of my problems when yells from outside made me hurry to open the front door.

What I'd dreaded would happen for years, had happened. The two men... my son and my husband... were wrestling with one another, each of their faces twisted in determined anger. Chad's no doubt heightened by the elf lying crushed under their feet.

Leaving Casey with her hand over her mouth, her eyes wide in horror, I rushed out and tried to get between them.

If Casey had stayed with her hand over her mouth, things might have ended more easily. But she didn't. Trying to help...

and inadvertently making it much worse... she ran upstairs and shouted for Emily.

Chad and Michael were still on the ground, grunting and growling, when Emily and her fiancé, Angus, came bowling down the stairs, Emily wrapped in a robe, he wearing only jeans. As Emily shouted for her father and brother to stop, Angus dived in, trying to tear them apart. Unfortunately, Chad didn't take kindly to his intersession and let swing with his fist. It was a lucky shot for him, a dreadfully unlucky one for Angus who stumbled backwards, blood gushing from his nose. It dribbled dramatically down his chin, the blood loss looking considerably more impressive when Emily rushed to his side. Within seconds, her white robe was streaked with red.

Blood. Santa lying face down. Two men still wrestling and growling in the middle of crushed elves. The Christmas scene had turned into a horror show.

It was Casey who finally brought it all to an end. Nobody had noticed her disappearing from the melee, nor had we noticed her return until suddenly she was there with a basin of water. Her aim was sure, the water flying in a sheet over Chad and Michael's heads.

And that was the end of our Christmas Day.

Fifteen minutes later, Emily gave me a hug. 'I'll ring you from the hospital after Angus gets seen by the doctor, okay?'

I held her to me. I remembered her baby smell, her first tooth, first babbled word. Now she smelled of expensive perfume and when I pulled back to look at her face, her eyes were filled with sadness. 'You're sure you want to drive home afterwards. You could come back here.'

She leaned into me again, pressing her lips to my cheek. 'I

don't think that's a good idea, Mum. I'm sorry. We just want to get Angus' nose looked at, see if it's broken, then get home.'

I stood and waved them off. Maybe Chad did too, I don't know, he was on the roof trying to get Santa back into place.

I was glad he was still up there when Michael and his girlfriend arrived downstairs ten minutes later. They were carrying their bags, so I didn't need to ask if they were going to stay. 'I'm sorry,' I whispered into my son's ear as he gave me a hug.

'Why do you stay with him, Mum?' he whispered back. 'You know you'd be welcome to come and live with me.'

I could have lied, said I loved Chad, but my son would see the lie. It would diminish me in his eyes and one parent failing him was enough. 'Old habits are hard to break.' I patted his cheek, thinking for the millionth time, how blessed I was to have two such wonderful children. 'Don't worry about me, we rattle along together all right most of the year.'

I could see he was going to argue so gave him a gentle push. 'Go home, try and have some happiness today.' I tilted my head to where Casey stood. 'I like her, hang on to her, okay?'

He hugged me again. 'I'm planning to.'

'I'm sorry it's been such a disaster,' I said to her, reaching a hand out to take hers and pull her close for a quick kiss on the cheek. 'Take care of Michael for me.'

Casey smiled and nodded. 'That I'll do.' Her smile faded and she gave my hand a squeeze. 'You ever need someone to talk to, we're there for you, okay.'

'I'll be fine,' I reassured her. 'Drive carefully. Let me know when you're home safe.'

I stood waving till their car was gone from sight.

From our roof I could hear sounds of hammering. I looked around the mess of damaged Christmas figures that littered the lawn. It would take Chad all day to restore order. Possibly all the following day too. I could have helped tidy up, but I knew he wouldn't thank me for interfering, so I headed inside.

In the kitchen, I opened the fridge and stared at the huge free-range turkey I'd splashed out on. I'd had to move food around to make room for it. It wouldn't get cooked that day. I took out a packet of smoked salmon and made myself a sandwich before remembering I'd no hot water to make myself a cup of tea.

I thought about taking the kettle next door, asking Tony if I could boil it there but I couldn't bear the pity I'd see on his face. It was bad enough to see it on the faces of my children and their partners.

Instead of tea, I took a bottle of wine with me and settled on the sofa in front of the fire. I ate my sandwich and worked my way through the wine, lost in thought. Only when the fire burned low did I move, getting up and shovelling more coal onto the embers.

It was almost dark when I realised the Christmas gifts were still under the tree. I'd imagined us all sitting around to open them after dinner, mulled wine in our hands, smiles on our faces. They'd go in the post now. I'd bought nice chocolates for Casey. Pulling the gift from under the tree, I tore off the wrapping, opened the box and ate them all.

Four years before. It was the last time Michael or Emily were home for Christmas and I missed them each year. That year, with Emily's little girl, Abby, almost two, and Michael and Casey's two boys one and three, it was going to be even harder. What I wouldn't give to have them all there for the day – to have the house filled with the sound of children: theirs, mine.

'Emily and Michael aren't coming for Christmas Day,' I

said that night as Chad sat ploughing through his dinner, head down, total concentration on his food. Probably thinking of all he had to do to get his display ready for the December first switch-on. 'They asked if I'd go to them.'

He scraped his plate with his knife. 'Is there more?'

I got to my feet, took his plate and dished up another spoonful of the stew. It had been in the slow cooker all afternoon, the meat deliciously tender. Not that Chad would notice or compliment me. 'Here you go.'

I sat again, played with the smaller portion I'd given myself. 'Did you hear what I said?'

He looked up in surprise at my raised voice. 'What?'

'Michael and Emily won't be here for Christmas this year.'

He shrugged. 'They've not come for years. Too busy with their own lives now. Just as well, don't want three crying babies disturbing our peace.'

'It would have been nice. Christmas is for families.'

'You should go and stay with them. I'm sure they'd put you up.' He scraped his plate again and pushed it away.

'I couldn't leave you!' I smiled at the thought.

'Why not?' He got to his feet and stood looking down at me. 'It's not as if you do anything apart from cooking. I have to stay for the display, you can go wherever you like.'

I waited for him to laugh, to say he was joking, but his expression didn't change. All these years I'd believed deep down he cared for me, just didn't show it. What a fool I'd been. All those wasted years.

I threw the remainder of my meal into the bin and put all the plates and cutlery into the dishwasher, working on autopilot, lost in my thoughts. A cup of tea would have been nice, I could have cupped my hands around its warmth and hoped it would melt the numbness creeping over me. But just as I reached for the kettle, the lights went out.

No warning. I heard the front door slam, minutes later the clunk as the garage door was pulled open. In the darkness, I moved through to the living room and pulled the curtains back to peer out in time to see him put the ladder against the house. That stupid Santa and those elves. It would take him at least two hours. I glanced at the fireplace. I should light it, with the heat off, it would quickly grow chilly.

But I didn't move. I stood and watched as Chad manoeuvred Santa up the ladder, the LED in his beanie hat lighting the way. It would take him a long time to get the figure secured to the chimney, then more time attaching him to the electrical supply. I stood in the darkness, chilled inside and out.

When I saw him come down, then minutes later go back up, I knew he was going to work on the electrics. He could have waited until this stage to turn off the electricity and if he'd any thought for me, he would have done.

Why had I never considered this before? Why had I been such a fool?

I dropped the curtain and went into the hallway. The fuse box was in a cabinet to the left of the front door. Chad had left the door hanging open.

He was usually so careful, officer. He'd only planned to secure Santa to the chimney. He's paranoid about it falling off as it did a few years ago, so he spends a long time making sure. He hadn't planned to touch the electrics, not with the power on, but he must have forgotten. He was so obsessed with his illuminations.

It sounded believable, didn't it? I reached for the mains switch and pressed it down.

That year, I'd give my children exactly what they wanted for Christmas.

***

Valerie Keogh lives in Wiltshire with her husband and a huge black cat, Fatty Arbuckle. She grew up reading Agatha Christie and initially wrote crime novels - she now writes psychological thrillers. She has a BA in English and an MA in American Literature. The Little Lies was shortlisted for the Crime Fiction Lovers Award 2021.

PART TWO

HOLLY JOLLY CHRISTMAS

The Robin's Call

by Beverley Harvey

The last time my mother left the house, a carpet of cherry blossom petals lay browning in the cul-de-sac where she lived, and her sixty-fifth birthday had yet to come. And when it did, during the last week in May, there was no big family gathering, no balloons or celebratory champagne, just a strained patient visit that took place in my mother's airless conservatory.

'Mum, why don't we walk to the pub and sit in the beer garden. It's such a beautiful day,' my sister, Laura, urged, after our gifts had been opened with an air of indifference and we'd consumed wedges of the chocolate cake I'd lovingly baked.

'No thank you, I'm fine in here,' my mother answered, her mouth set and miserable.

I'd tried next. 'Well, at least have a glass of wine. It's your birthday – surely that's worth a toast?'

But the shutters had come down, and we'd left an hour later; me crying in the passenger seat of Laura's car, while she drove the thirty-minute route back to south London, her expression grim.

Mum – Maggie to her friends, back in the days when she

had friends – hadn't always been so reclusive. But a sequence of upsets that had started with our dad dying suddenly of an undiagnosed heart condition, followed by Laura's announcement that she was gay and engaged to a nurse called Hannah, and the final straw, Mum getting her purse snatched in Sainsbury's one Saturday afternoon, had led to her emotional collapse.

She'd phoned the police from a back office in the supermarket before going home, shutting her front door and deciding that *outside* was not a place she wanted to be.

At first, nobody had taken this new-found agoraphobia seriously. Certainly not me, tearing around London necking cocktails after work with my thirty-something girlfriends. And not Laura, busy embracing a whole new scene now that she and Hannah were officially loved-up, out and proud.

Not even Janet, Mum's best friend of twenty-odd years, who lived in the next street and who soon missed her company on walks, shopping trips and rare days out in the countryside.

'She'll come round, Katie, love. You'll see,' Janet had said kindly. 'What with losing your dad, your sister's news, and getting her pursed nicked... well, it's taken its toll and knocked her confidence. Give her time.'

I didn't bother to contradict her; to pick her up on lumping the death of Mum's soulmate and my sister finding true love at the age of thirty-eight into the same category – let alone the fact that Laura and Hannah were desperate to foster a child and were making real progress.

I'd tried to talk to Mum about it; to make her see that Laura finding love for the first time with *anyone* could only be happy news. But she'd clammed up, saying she couldn't think about it now – couldn't take it in – not after losing Dad. Instead, she wore her grief like armour and kept everyone at bay.

Then in the first week of July, a chink of hope appeared

when Mum agreed to see a counsellor and bereavement specialist. With great trepidation and military-style planning, Laura and I propelled her through the rusty rituals of showering, dressing and walking the few metres from her own front door to Laura's waiting Volvo, before escorting her through the door of Patricia Webb's therapy room. We'd collected her an hour and a half later, as nervous and expectant as parents meeting a teenager from her first dance.

It was to be a one-time only event: arms folded and tight-lipped in the car going home, Mum's whole demeanour had been glacial, as she dropped the bomb that *no way* would she be seeing Patricia or any other counsellor in the future.

The summer months cooled, the leaves fell and turned brown and still she remained indoors. Where it's *safe*, she said.

There was little incentive for her to leave the house. No job to turn up for; no dog to walk; her groceries were delivered to her door; clothes too – not that she needed much these days, barely changing her shapeless jeans and loose tops from one week to the next. Her hair – always a pretty shade of strawberry blonde – grew long and frayed, white roots creeping down her scalp.

I'd mentioned it once – the hair thing – and she'd looked at me non-plussed. 'Your dad's in the cemetery and you want me to get my hair done?' Ashamed and speechless, I'd slunk away.

Time ticked by.

Now the trees were bare, and the pavements sparkled with frost. Fairy lights twinkled up and down her cul-de-sac. Christmas cards, put through her letter box – neighbourly acts of goodwill – languished unopened on the hall table.

Insane with worry, Laura and I continued our thankless visits during which Mum never smiled, or asked for news, although we had plenty – our work lives full of commitments and deadlines, our diaries rammed with social events.

In early December, the subject of Christmas was raised, aired – and promptly swept under the carpet.

'I'm not doing Christmas this year,' Mum said, as if she were declining an extra pint of milk.

'Mum, you don't have to *do* anything. Laura and I will come to you, you can meet Hannah if you like, she's lovely. We can get a real tree, decorate the house – I'll even have a stab at roasting a turkey – how hard can it be? Just say *yes* and leave it all to us.'

A shake of the head, a pursing of the lips followed: 'I'll be fine on my own, just me and my memories,' Mum said, shutting the conversation down and turning her face away.

'God, she's stubborn! It's a shame she can't put as much energy into restarting her life as she does into being an obstinate old cow,' Laura fumed later, her anger boiling over. 'Well, let her rot in that house if she wants to. I'm not putting up with any more emotional blackmail or passive-aggressive nonsense and neither should you, Katie.'

'You don't mean that – she's grieving. And I know we miss Dad terribly too, but it's different for us; he was Mum's entire world, wasn't he?'

Laura bit her lip. 'Sorry. It's just that... it feels like we've lost *both* our parents, and this will be our first Christmas without them.'

I hugged my sister, felt her bird-like body heave in my arms. 'Laura, we can't give up on her. She'll get better. It's just going to take longer than anyone expected, that's all.'

Then, on a dull mid-December day, as we were running out of hope and ideas, Laura got the email she'd been waiting for.

I'm in the coffee room at work, waiting for the kettle to boil when my mobile vibrates in my pocket. The screen lights up: LAURA CALLING.

At once, I'm on high alert; personal calls are frowned upon in the office and my sister knows this. 'Hi, are you okay?' I whisper, closing the door of the tiny kitchenette.

Laura has no time for pleasantries. 'Katie, it's happened. We're getting a baby... a toddler. He's called Daniel, he's two, and he'll be with us for Christmas.' Her voice catches with emotion and when I speak, mine does too.

'Oh, Laura, I'm so chuffed for you. That's incredible. All the months of red tape – being assessed and investigated – and now you and Hannah are going to be parents. How long have you got Daniel for?'

'We don't know. Could be weeks, could be months. That's the nature of fostering and we were warned to expect it. It doesn't matter – I can't wait to get him home, give him a stable, loving, happy Christmas. Katie, I wept when I read his file; poor little chap has been through so much in his short life already.'

There's a brief exchange about timings and logistics; how Laura will work from home to provide full-time childcare, while Hannah will reduce her hours at the hospital.

I nibble my thumbnail. 'Laura, have you told Mum?'

There's a brief pause on the line.

'No. I'm not sure I want to. She's barely registered Hannah, let alone the fact that we've been planning to foster. I think I can safely say she's not interested.'

'Love, don't hate her for it. She's not herself, is she?' My tone brightens. 'I on the other hand am exactly my usual nosey self and I can't wait to meet the little fella. How soon can I come over?' Behind me, a door opens and closes; there's a clank of crockery. 'Laura, I've got to go – I'll call you tonight from home. Bye.'

That evening, I pass on drinks with colleagues, head home and get off the underground a stop before my usual one. Instead, I walk an extra mile to my flat via leafy suburban streets all lit up for Christmas. It reminds me of being nine or ten; of our parents taking Laura and me to see the lights in the West End. I can almost feel the tingle of icy wind on our cheeks as we sat upstairs on an open-top bus, eyes wide and shining, spellbound by the exotic shop windows – another world, full of magic and sparkle.

Now the festive lights blur as I blink back tears and hurry home to my flat.

Later, mollified by pasta and a glass of Shiraz, I call my sister and am warmed by her excitement and optimism. Neither of us mentions Mum. After all, it is not my place, not my job to share her news.

I picture my mother, marooned by grief and stubbornness, spending Christmas in a dark dusty house, with only ghosts and memories for company. It is my last waking thought that night.

Two days before Christmas, relieved to have finished work until New Year, I head out into the grey dankness, and straight to my favourite department store. There, I take the escalator up to the kids' department where I buy cute outfits befitting a two-year-old before doing a lap of the toy section. With mounting excitement, I blow the budget, seizing soft toys, wooden blocks and Disney characters that sing or squeak, giddy at the thought of meeting my sister's first foster child and sharing in her joy.

Once home, I light a candle and revel in the warm scents of cinnamon, clove, and clementine. Then I put on Christmas carols while I wrap my stash of gifts.

It's noon on Christmas Eve when I knock on my sister's door. Hannah answers.

'Hey, merry Christmas, Katie. Come in. Laura and Daniel are in the living room.'

'Sorry I'm a bit early,' I say, leaning in to hug my future sister-in-law, 'I'm just so excited for you all.'

Beaming, I follow her to the back of the house and find Laura, hair askew and still in cosy PJs, a brown-haired little boy with the bluest eyes I've ever seen snuggled on her lap. He jumps as I approach, his face crumpling with uncertainty.

I hang back, still clutching my holdall and the bag of presents. 'Happy Christmas, Daniel,' I croon softly, then to Laura. 'He's beautiful. How's it going?'

There's a brief rundown of Daniel's arrival, the practicalities of his first forty-eight hours in his new home. My sister looks tired but happy and I marvel at her serenity.

'You're a natural, Laura. Can I hold him?' I take a tentative step towards them.

Laura smiles. 'Maybe just sit beside us for now, he's had a lot to take in already.'

'Of course. Tell you what, why don't I give you both some space? I'll put my presents under the tree, then give Hannah a hand with lunch.'

The kitchen is a vision of organised chaos. On the range, there's a pan of home-made soup for now, while on the worktops, Daniel's baby cups, bowls and special food vie for space with an abundance of Christmas fare. I open the fridge; it's full to bursting point, a fat turkey at its centre.

Laughing, I turn to Hannah. 'Wow, so much food! Are you nervous about doing Christmas dinner tomorrow? I mean, it's a lot of work and now with Daniel and everything...'

Hannah grins. 'Yeah, it'll be fun. You and I can manage the bulk of the cooking and Laura can be backup while Dan's napping. I'm sure the three of us can muddle through.'

The afternoon passes pleasantly while we watch and play with the baby. After dark, Hannah opens a bottle of sparkling wine and puts out nibbles. Laura declines the wine: the novel responsibility of new parenthood weighing on her for the first time. Christmas songs play on the smart speaker while Laura dances with Daniel in her arms, the jiggling movement makes him gurgle and laugh.

She's dressed him in one of my presents: dark blue pyjamas, dotted with snowflakes, the motif of a red-breasted robin filling his little barrel chest. 'Baard,' Daniel shouts, prodding himself with his index finger.

'Bird! Yes, that's right, you clever darling boy,' Laura swoons, hugging him tightly.

I raise my voice over the music. 'Remember how Dad loved robins? He used to say that they carried messages from loved ones who'd passed away.'

Sadness flashes into my sister's eyes as she holds my gaze. 'Yes, I remember.'

I reach for my mobile phone. 'Let's give Mum a call. Please? I think it's important and we'll regret it if we don't.'

She glances at Hannah who nods. 'Go on, hon. Katie's right. You need to FaceTime Maggie. I know she's been distant, but at least you won't feel guilty if you give it your best shot.'

We turn the music down and there's tension in the room while we wait for Mum to pick up. When her face fills the screen, I can see at once she's been crying.

'Hi, Mum, it's me,' I begin, stating the obvious. 'Look, there are some people here who want to say hello and happy Christmas.'

A look of horror passes over her face, a hand straying to her hair which is limp and unwashed. 'You look fine, Mum,' I say, beckoning to Laura and Hannah.

Laura leans in, her face tight to the screen. 'Hi, Mum. How are you? I want you to meet Hannah – please, it's time. Say hello,' she urges, waving the phone in Hannah's direction.

Hannah beams into the handset. 'Hi, Maggie, I've heard so much about you. I can't wait to get together when you're up to it,' she says kindly.

'I'd like that,' Mum says, her chin wobbling visibly.

I retrieve my mobile. 'Mum, there's someone else you need to meet.' I wink at my sister, who's hovering at my side, the baby in her arms. 'Remember we talked about Laura and Hannah fostering a little one? Well, it happened! This is Daniel.'

Right on cue, Daniel smiles and gurgles, the epitome of sweetness. 'Baard!' he says, touching a drool-covered finger to his chest, delighted with his new party trick.

My mother gasps. 'Ahh, what a little *angel*,' she breathes, her eyes misting. 'Look at that little face.'

Unable to stop the tears from falling, she reaches for a tissue.

'Mum, please don't cry. Come and join us for Christmas tomorrow and you can meet him properly. All you've got to do is turn up. We've got loads of food – and we could do with your advice to be honest. At least say you'll think about it.' A pleading tone has crept into my voice, but a part of me already knows it's hopeless.

Mum shakes her head. 'I don't think so. I haven't left the house since April. It's been too long... I can't, I just... I've got to go.'

'I'll come and get you, first thing.' It's my last desperate pitch before Mum ends the call.

A deflated silence fills the room. 'We tried,' Laura says, 'we all tried.'

Maggie wakes with a start, her heart thumping hard, the fragment of a dream just out of reach. She sits up and remembers it's Christmas Day. A day she will spend alone – thanks to the fear, anxiety and (if she admits it to herself) the stubbornness she's allowed to get out of control in the last six months.

She sighs, puts on her dressing gown and slippers, and goes downstairs to make tea.

Waiting for the kettle to boil, she eyes the box of mince pies left on her doorstep along with a poinsettia and a bottle of pink Prosecco two days earlier. Festive tokens of friendship left by Janet when Maggie had refused to open the door even a crack. What must Janet think of her?

After breakfasting on toast and two of the mince pies (which are far nicer than she remembers) Maggie showers and dresses in pale grey trousers and a red sweater. For reasons she can't fathom, she sprays perfume on her wrists and dabs blusher on her cheeks.

She puts the radio on; soon the melancholy sound of *Carols from King's College* fills the room, bringing tears to her eyes.

'For goodness' sake, Maggie,' she says aloud. Such sadness, such self-pity. Why has she done this to herself? She crosses to the bureau, its surface crowded with family photographs, and notes with shame that they would all benefit from a duster and polish. She picks up a photo of Jim, holds it to her heart and closes her eyes.

What would he think of her spending Christmas Day alone

– away from their girls? Maggie replaces the photo, makes another cup of tea, and takes it to the conservatory.

Outside, the sun is trying to shine and the lawn glitters with frost. A platoon of tiny sparrows land on the winter ghost of a hydrangea, before taking flight. A fat robin lands on the fence, then swoops down to the patio, hopping so close to her window, she can see its feathers ruffle on the chilled air. She smiles despite herself, remembering how Jim loved his birds – especially cheeky, friendly robin redbreasts like this little fella. She'd laughed at his superstitions; he'd thought they carried messages from people who'd died.

What if he'd been right all along? Embarrassed by her own silliness, Maggie gets up from her armchair and taps lightly on the window. To her amazement, the little bird doesn't startle or fly away, instead it hops closer, its scarlet chest puffed out with pride.

She recalls the previous night; the difficult tearful conversation with her girls. The kindness and goodwill in the room, the glow of contentment on Laura's cheeks, pink as the robin's breast on baby Daniel's pyjamas – yet here she is, alone. Missing it all.

Maggie watches the robin as it continues to hop around her patio. Feeling her chest constrict, she picks up the phone, calls Laura's number, but is diverted to voicemail. Undeterred, she tries Katie who answers on the second ring.

'Mum, happy Christmas. How are you?' Katie's voice is shrill and breathless; Maggie imagines her running for the phone whilst cooking or helping with Daniel. Michael Bublé croons good-naturedly in the background and she can hear laughter and sing-songy baby talk. Her heart swells.

'Happy Christmas to you all, Katie, love. I've been thinking… about all sorts… but mainly about your dad. And I was wondering, if the offer still stands… if I could—'

A cheer erupts from Katie then: 'Laura! Mum's coming for Christmas. Yes, *really*!' There's the background buzz of approval.

Smiling, Maggie ends the call and returns to the conservatory. There is no sign of the robin. She opens the back door, struggles a moment with its stiff bolts, and lets in a blast of cold air.

'*Merry Christmas, Jim,*' she whispers, stepping outside and turning her face to the weak sunshine.

***

Beverley Harvey was born in Yorkshire and currently lives in rural Kent with her partner and their adorable terrier. When not writing, you'll find her reading, walking the dog or listening to rock music. Throughout Beverley's many years spent working in advertising and PR, she'd always wanted to write fiction. In 2015 a creative writing course inspired her debut novel, Seeking Eden, which was published in 2017. The sequel, Eden Interrupted, soon followed. Beverley has also written two standalone psychological thrillers.

DANCER

BY JOHN HARKIN

IT WAS COMING ON CHRISTMAS. All the big department stores had done a wonderful job of their displays; leaping reindeer, industrious elves, and large, red, jolly Santas dominated the festive window tableaux. The twinkling Christmas lights strung high across the main shopping thoroughfares brightened the darkening late-afternoon sky. Glasgow city centre was heaving with Christmas shoppers.

Adam Eslick cooried inside his goose-down parka and trudged through the snowy pavements. He loved the idea of a white Christmas, but the snow was turning to a greyish slush, not the most favourable conditions for a winter wonderland.

He spotted Marina, the smiling young blonde Bulgarian woman, who sold the *Big Issue* from her pitch at the edge of the vast shopping complex, close to where he worked at the city's main jewellery arcade. Marina looked frozen despite her old grey heavy overcoat, woollen hat, and fingerless mittens.

'Hello, Adam,' she said in her heavily accented English.

'Hi, Marina. You must be frozen my poor love.'

'I'm okay, I'm really well wrapped up and I've nearly sold out.'

'Well, I'll take another one off your hands.' He paid ten pounds, well above the cover price, for the Christmas special edition. He always bought his *Big Issue* magazine from Marina. He knew she lived in a hostel for vulnerable women. It was a far cry from her days living on the cold, dangerous city streets. Her little microbusiness enterprise had offered sanctuary and given her hope for a better future in a new country.

'Merry Christmas and thank you, Adam,' she said with her wide beautiful smile.

'Happy Christmas to you too, Marina.' Adam gave her a little hug.

A simple act of kindness, Adam thought.

Adam was back at work for the first time in two weeks following a holiday in Tenerife with his partner, Sean. Anywhere warm to escape the damp, frozen horrors of a west of Scotland winter. But it was good to be home in time for Christmas. The shop would be very busy in the run-up to the big day with items of jewellery an ever-popular gift. His store was late-night opening and he'd popped out to buy some dinner.

His encounter with Marina reminded him that he needed to check up on Hamish. Hamish was a homeless man, who usually pitched at the mouth of an access lane to a large disused department store with his black-and-white dog, Dancer. His spot was set back from the pavement and offered decent shelter and protection from the wind and the rain and the snow.

On catching up with the shop gossip on Adam's first day back, word was that Dancer had gone. Not seen by anyone for over a week, with explanations ranging from the dog had died or had been removed by animal welfare inspectors. Either way, thought Adam, old Hamish would be devastated by the loss of his faithful companion. He'd check it out for himself.

One of the other shop assistants thought Hamish was overly belligerent. Adam had no time for aggressive street beggars, but Hamish was never abusive, and he'd never seen him do any actual begging. He was a bit of a local character, chatting to various passers-by, especially the regulars who stopped to feed titbits to Dancer. The little dog was part collie, part terrier and had a striking white flash on an otherwise jet-black muzzle. Adam had fallen in love with those asymmetric ears – one pointed, the other floppy, and those giant doggie brown eyes. Dancer had been trained to perform for snacks and would offer a paw, or stand on his hind legs, for a rewarding morsel. Adam had got into the habit of buying a carton of soup or a steak bake for Hamish when he nipped out on his lunch break. The old man would take a couple of bites of his pasty and offer the rest to his dog. Adam would break off a scrap of bacon or cold meat from his own roll and feed it to a grateful Dancer, who'd perform a hind-legged pirouette in appreciation.

Adam braced himself against the freezing wind and bitter cold of the December afternoon and made his way through the city centre towards Hamish's pitch. Tenerife seemed like a lifetime ago. *Geeze*, he thought as the winter's chill enveloped him, burning his cheeks, and nipping his eyes. *How can people like Hamish survive living rough in this climate?* West of Scotland winters can take your breath away. Extreme cold is one thing but the insidious damp creeps into your bones, like a sneak thief in the night, robbing your body of its last warmth. Adam was glad of his parka.

There was no trace of Dancer. So it was true. When he saw the state of Hamish, Adam was shocked. It had only been a fortnight, but the deterioration was obvious. The old man was squatted on his pile of cardboard with an empty space where Dancer used to lie.

His shoes, or what was left of his shoes, seemed to have melded into Hamish's bare feet, with no socks visible and putrefied flesh gaping through the holes. Hamish was huddled inside his familiar, faded, crimson-red motorcycle jacket, layered over a vivid red-and-white fleeced workwear shirt in dress Stewart tartan. He wore shabby corduroy trousers over frayed and greying long johns, visible at his bare ankles. Hamish's long snowy-grey hair and his untamed bushy white beard were as wild as ever and as familiar as his rosy cheeks, but there was a noticeable sadness in the man's eyes. Hamish smiled as Adam approached and handed him a carton of chicken soup.

'Where's Dancer?' Adam asked.

'The animal welfare inspector took him off me. Said he was malnourished but that's nonsense. He ate more than I did. I think they forced the issue because I challenged them and threatened to set him on the inspector. But you know Dancer, he wouldn't attack anyone.'

'Get this soup down you. It must be murder in these temperatures. Can you get Dancer back?'

'He's in the cat and dog home. They won't give him back to me, but you could get him for me. Or you could take him in at your house.' The old man's eyes were tearing up. 'You'd be a familiar face and I hate to think of him with strangers.'

'My partner isn't as dog friendly as me,' Adam said. 'If you can't get him back then I'd think about taking him, he's a beautiful dog. I'll try to help if I can.' It would be another act of kindness to reunite this poor wretched creature with his devoted pet. It was clear just how much he was missing his animal companion.

'They'd take him away again,' Hamish said softly. 'I'd rather he was with people who cared for him properly, let him run in the park. The state of me and my old bones, I can hardly move these days.'

'I'll make enquiries at the dog shelter.'

'You could do me a big favour. I'm selling this for fifty pounds.' Hamish scooped a leather cord from under his shirt and held out a gold ring looped onto the end with a clasp. 'It's worth fifty quid, see.' Hamish unhooked the clasp to allow Adam to examine it.

'You keep the ring. I'll give you thirty pounds so you can buy some new socks and shoes for your poor feet.' Adam was more concerned about Hamish's wellbeing. 'Can you not get booked into a hostel, even for this cold snap?'

'I'm not a fan of hostels,' Hamish replied. 'They would never take Dancer.'

'But that's not an issue now,' Adam said as he examined the ring. It was a beautiful example of Celtic jewellery; white and yellow gold, threaded in a filigree of silver knots in a golden outer band. 'You don't wear it?' Adam asked.

'My fingers are too thin. It falls off, so I keep it around my neck.' Hamish held out his long, bony fingers to prove his point. Adam looked at his gnarled, emaciated hands and the filthy, broken state of his fingernails. A manicure would be the least of Hamish's worries, thought Adam, but between the state of his hands and feet, he really needed a hot bath and a good scrub.

'I've got no money on me so let me go to a cashpoint and lift £100. The ring's worth more than you're asking.' Adam suspected the ring was worth two or three times what he was offering but he wasn't ripping anyone off with his price. The poor man, this must be the last thing of value he owned. Adam slipped off his gloves and tried on the ring. It fitted nicely on his left-hand ring finger. Maybe it could make a fitting wedding band for him or Sean when they got around to the happy event they were planning.

'You can wear it if you like,' Hamish said. 'Get it valued at the jewellers if you don't trust me.'

'I trust you, Hamish. I'll be back shortly with your money.' Adam liked the fit and feel of the ring. Wedding thoughts aside, it could make a lovely Christmas gift for Sean and celebrate his Irish roots.

Adam kept his gloves off to operate the bank cashpoint terminal. As he waited for his cash transaction to finish, he looked again at the beautiful object on his finger. Removing the ring to closer inspect the fine tracery of the trinity knots, the hallmark confirmed 18-carat gold. He was getting a real bargain, but was he ripping Hamish off? There were several traders in the arcade that dealt in pre-owned jewellery. They could assess the ring; even the value of the gold melted down would fetch a tidy sum. The old man asked for fifty pounds, he was paying double. Adam was no Christmas Scrooge. Everyone likes a bargain.

As he rotated the ring for further inspection, Adam noticed that it was inscribed along the inside edge of the gold band: *Morag and Hamish – 23 May 1987.*

The sudden realisation that this must be a wedding ring left Adam feeling a bit overwhelmed. Is Morag still alive? Did they have any children? Should this ring not be in their family? Adam felt a sense of shame and remorse over his actions; he could not own this ring. He would return it to Hamish and donate fifty pounds so the man could get some new socks and shoes. Maybe he could make some enquiries and try and get him admitted to a hostel. Could he do something about getting Dancer back? He was sure that Sean would be persuaded by such a beautiful, clever dog. Their flat was right on the edge of the city's Queen's Park. It would be great to give Dancer a taste of a more expansive outdoor life. No more dancing for his dinner. He would make a great running partner when he and Sean went on their park outings.

Adam stopped in the precinct and joined a growing throng of shoppers who'd braved the bitter cold to listen to the Salvation Army band. Resplendent in their navy and maroon, the band were playing 'Hark the Herald Angels Sing'. It was a beautiful noise and a lovely tune to entertain the shoppers, lifting the gloom of a freezing afternoon, and spreading the Christmas message. The big brass tuba shimmered under the gleam of the coloured Christmas lights. Or was it a euphonium? Adam could never remember the difference. He lingered longer as the band played 'Silent Night' and then 'Away in a Manger', before remembering that he had a ring to return and some money to gift to old Hamish. He loved the ring, but it wouldn't be right for Sean or him, not with another couple's name engraved. He could maybe recreate the Celtic design for Sean's wedding ring but that would have to wait. Hopefully Hamish could buy some shoes and socks for his poor feet and maybe find a shelter for Christmas.

As Adam returned the few blocks to Hamish's pitch, he saw a commotion on the edge of the pavement and an ambulance parked at the kerb. He quickened his pace and got to the scene as Hamish was being stretchered into the back of the emergency vehicle. He rushed forward to speak to the medics. 'What happened?'

'Do you know this man?' asked the female paramedic at the foot of the stretcher.

'I know his name is Hamish. I think his surname is McCormack and he's originally from the Dennistoun area, but he's a homeless man. I speak to him most days. Is he conscious?' Adam asked. As he entered the ambulance cabin, he noticed that in addition to the vast array of medical equipment; screens, meters and cabling, the crew had lined the roof with red and silver tinsel.

'I'm afraid he's gone. It looks like Hamish has had a massive heart attack,' said the paramedic. 'Do you know if there's any family?'

Adam was shocked. He'd never seen a dead body before and although Hamish could not be described as a close friend, he'd felt a strong acquaintance with this old homeless character and his little canine companion. Adam gathered his thoughts quickly and discreetly removed the ring from his finger and with his back between him and the paramedic looped it back onto the clasp on the leather cord, showing her the engraving. 'I think this is his wife and the date of his marriage. I'm not sure about her or any family but it's all I can tell you.'

'That's a nice ring, thanks. It'll be somewhere for the police to start their enquiries. He's no other identification on him.'

It was just another simple act of kindness.

'I need to take him to hospital now, thanks.'

Adam took that as his cue to leave and just before he jumped off the step, he glanced back at the sad and sorry sight of Hamish lying in the ambulance. The dead man's snowy-grey hair and bushy white beard contrasted starkly with his ruddy cheeks; no doubt burned into his face by severe Scottish winters and a homeless lifestyle. The ring, restored around Hamish's neck, caught the glare from the strip light in the ambulance roof and sparkled a sad farewell.

It was the second week in January before the funeral could take place. It gave Adam time to track down the arrangements. A daughter, Maggie McCormack had been traced and the family had a lair at the vast Linn Cemetery in the city's south side.

There would be no pauper's funeral for old Hamish. It also allowed Adam time to rescue Dancer from the dog pound. As Adam had hoped, it was love at first sight between Sean and Dancer. The little dog had aced his audition and was enjoying his new home adjacent to the big park.

High on the cold and windswept cemetery hill, a handful of mourners gathered at the graveside. The skeletal leaf-shorn trees and a gloomy late-afternoon sky added to the desolate scene. Adam had brought Dancer along but kept him on his lead. He chatted with Marina, who was wearing a smart new black coat and was without her usual knitted hat. The gravestone showed that Hamish's wife, Morag, had predeceased him by seven years. Maggie McCormack recognised Dancer and introduced herself to Adam.

'Dad would be glad someone took in Dancer.' She ruffled under the dog's neck. 'Did you know the old chancer?'

'I used to stop and chat on my lunch break. Shared some food with Hamish and Dancer. So you knew he was on the streets?'

'Aye, I used to work in the city centre. Got him into a couple of shelters but he would never stick it. He used to find somewhere a bit warmer for the winter but not this year. I think the cold done him in. He was only sixty-seven. Could have gone a bit longer. He was a hardy old soul.' She bit her lip and pushed an errant strand of brown hair off her face. That's when Adam spotted the ring.

'Is that your dad's wedding ring?' Adam asked.

'Yes, why?' asked a puzzled Maggie.

'He tried to sell it to me for fifty pounds on the day he died. I told him it was worth more than that and he should hold on to it.'

'Are you sure it was this ring?' Maggie held her hand up for inspection.

'I think so.' Adam hesitated. 'Inscribed for Morag and Hamish on their wedding date. Is that it?'

'You would have been buying this actual ring then.' Maggie shook her head with a rueful smile. 'I'm amazed he still had it.'

Adam wore a confused expression.

'The old rascal used to sell fakes of this ring. He got a pal to copy it and he'd offer it around the pubs for thirty pounds or fifty pounds for a quick sale to pay a debt. It was quite an elaborate con with a sob story to match. He had to move about a lot when people found out they'd been scammed. But that was before he was homeless.'

'I work in a jeweller's shop,' Adam said as he adjusted his parka collar against the biting wind. 'I hate to think I'd have been taken in.'

'Poor soul. That ring and his dog were all he had left in the world. He must have known his health was failing if he was selling his actual wedding ring.' Maggie started to sob. 'He must have really loved her.'

'I see she's been dead seven years.'

'Aye, but she left him two years before that for another man. That's what started his decline and why I'm surprised he kept the ring.'

'But you'll be happy it came back to you?' Adam felt vindicated.

'Yes. It's all I have now, that and a few pictures of them together when I was young.'

When the celebrant finished her eulogy, the undertaker offered the mourners a wooden box filled with soil for the internment. Adam followed Maggie and Marina and kneaded the damp clay between his fingers before scattering it over the coffin. Everything turns to dust in the end, he thought, as he patted a very well-behaved Dancer. The little dog had stood quietly by his side for the entire ceremony. Adam wondered if he knew what was going on.

It was a mournful end to a strange Christmas season; there was the sadness of Hamish's passing but he had taken great comfort from rescuing the old man's dog. He and Sean were now experiencing the joy of having the wonderful Dancer in their lives.

Comfort and joy. A lovely Christmas surprise.

***

John Harkin was born and raised in Glasgow where he still resides with his wife. They have an adult son. He's a former shipbuilder, police officer and business consultant. His debut novel, *The Fear of Falling*, was published by Bloodhound Books in January 2022. As a former police commander and hostage negotiator, John's writing draws upon his police experience. Serving in uniform, CID, and firearms teams, and with experience of policing armed sieges and major incidents, he can tap into a rich seam of material for writing crime fiction. Away from writing, his other passions are reading, music and football. He is a season ticket holder at Celtic FC.

THE MINCE PIE
OF DOOM

BY LAURA STEWART

STRANGE TO THINK it was a mince pie that ended my marriage.

That almost seven years of matrimony could crumble just as easily as the packet had promised the pastry would do. A mince pie is such an insignificant thing...as insignificant as my husband's view of his marriage vows turned out to be.

I suppose, if I'm being *completely* honest, it wasn't just Mark's infidelity that was the problem, it was also his spineless, craven, weak-willed personality along with his interfering dragon of a mother that all helped to end the marriage. Sometimes it's just easier to blame the mince pie.

But tonight I'm having to talk about 'it'. There's no escape. I'm sitting in my local pub with my two best friends: Cabernet Sauvignon and Rebecca. It's Christmas Eve, just one day away from the two-year anniversary of Mince Pie Gate. Rebecca wants to talk and to check I'm moving on and being *mindful*. Rebecca is an explorer of feelings.

I would prefer to smother them under a vat of red wine, snog someone completely unsuitable under the little piece of plastic mistletoe the bar have hung up at the front door, head home in the wee small hours of the morning and spend most of Christmas Day in a hung-over fug, eating my way through selection boxes whilst watching whatever shit film BBC1 put on in their prime-time slot. Each to our own.

'You should see a counsellor,' Rebecca says.

'I see *you*.'

'You should speak to someone who can help you move on and give you closure.'

Rebecca is big on words like 'closure' and anything she can stick a 'self' in front of.

'You need some self-care and self-actualising,' she says.

See?

'Well, *you* need some self-awareness to realise I'm fine,' I retort.

'You do know that FINE stands for Fucked up, Insecure, Neurotic and Emotional?'

Rebecca can also be a self-satisfied smug know-it-all.

'You still have a lot of emotions to unpack.'

'I don't.'

'If you were to book on an EasyJet flight you'd have to pay a fortune for excess baggage!' She stands up. 'We need another bottle,' she says, sploshing the remains of the first one in the bottom of our glasses then heading over to the crowded bar.

I sit back, nursing my wine as the folk at the table next to me begin singing along to The Pogues' *Fairytale of New York*. Why does Rebecca have to go and ruin a completely happy period of denial and evasion by bringing up dormant emotions? Dredging up memories of Mark has a domino-knocking reaction, and makes me remember his mother.

Penelope. Or Pepper, as the *girls* in her tennis club call her. First a politician's daughter, then a politician's wife, she then channelled all her efforts into making it her son's career too, to make it a three-generation hat trick of power, with No.10 as the end goal. Pepper's jolly hockey sticks and flower arranging persona mask a backbone of pure titanium and an inner drive Genghis Khan would have envied.

Argh! I take another sip of wine and hope it pushes away all these memories but they start bouncing up to the surface like a bag of oranges that has been freed from under a rock on the ocean bed and the events of two years ago come back.

Since arriving late on Christmas Eve, Pepper had stalked around the house like a velociraptor in a Barbour gilet and tweeds, head moving from side to side, beady eyes on alert, leaving a heady cloud of her signature scent, L'air du Temps, in her wake that always made my nostrils burn.

I'd spent all Christmas Eve tidying, cleaning and scrubbing so I could pass whatever invisible tests she'd decide to judge me on that year. I do remember thinking I'd won, as there was nothing this woman could pick apart.

Dinner had gone as well as could be expected but it was when I'd produced the plate of mince pies in the post dinner, pre-cheese and port lull, that it all went wrong. Pepper eyed the little pieces of pastry nestled within their silver foil cases, a haughty smile playing around her puckered coral-lipsticked lips.

'Did you make these?' she asked, knowing full well I never had been, and in all likelihood never would be, a baker.

'Nope.'

Pepper picked one up and looked it over, almost as if she expected a supermarket label to be branded on the pastry.

'They're not Waitrose, are they?'

Everyone at the table knew the question was loaded.

'Nope, Tesco's,' I said lightly.

Pepper replaced the little foil casing back on the plate. 'That's a pity, you get a nice mince pie with Waitrose,' she said and sniffed.

I'd had no idea there was even a hierarchy in mince pie outlets.

Then she went for the jugular.

'It was a lovely mince pie you and your old friend, Lucinda, brought me last weekend,' Pepper said to her son, pushing at the paper hat that hadn't dared budge from when she'd sat it on her carefully styled bouffant hair hours earlier.

'Mummy!' Mark looked at his mother aghast.

I know, yes, as a grown man he still called her Mummy. Alarm bells should have deafened me within the first week of getting to know Mark. I'm an idiot. Rebecca no doubt has a dossier made entitled 'where it all went wrong; a case study'.

Pepper had ploughed on. 'It's so nice you're back in touch with each other. I always had high hopes you'd get together.'

I know I must have sat there looking like an idiot, a fixed smile on my face, paper hat from my cracker slipping down over my eyes as my brain went into overdrive. The previous week Mark had his work do. He'd stayed away the Friday and then said he and a couple of work buddies would stay the Saturday night in the hotel too. He'd returned early evening on the Sunday, subdued, citing a killer hangover as the cause. He'd never mentioned he'd visited his mother, especially not with his ex-girlfriend in tow.

Mark blinked stupidly for a moment or two before saying, 'We bumped into each other in town. She and Mummy always got on. I thought it would be nice to...' He'd trailed off, knowing no spin could really make this look good.

'It was no trouble. I'm always prepared for visitors.' Pepper waved her arm dismissively, the diamonds on her new tennis bracelet glinting as the light from the candles caught them. I still sat there, holding the stem of my wine glass, smiling.

'It wasn't planned,' Mark said weakly, looking at his mother, no doubt hoping for backup, but Pepper just smiled.

'Of course it was, silly, you told me two weeks ago you'd both be coming. I needed time to dust off my good china and polish up the silverware.'

I'd no idea Pepper *had* good china, never mind having ever been allowed to use it!

'And sweet Lucinda brought me mince pies. Home-made, you know. Cooked the mincemeat last year and left it in the jar to mature.'

I always knew Lucinda was playing the long game.

Mark pulled at his green paper hat. 'I can explain...' he'd said, but we all knew he couldn't, not really.

Then Mark's father laughed as he waved the joke from his Christmas cracker about. Never one to willingly wear his hearing aid, he often didn't pick up the vibe of a room. He looked up at everyone expectantly. 'Knock Knock...' he said as he continued to laugh.

'Who's there?' I'd asked, dutifully.

'Arthur!'

'Arthur who?'

'Arthur any mince pies left?' He laughed again, pointing at the plate of mince pies just in case clarification was needed. He clearly hadn't put his glasses on either, for even with mine and Mark's look of horror, he continued laughing.

The rest of Christmas went by torturously slowly. Clearly Pepper wanted to stay for the grand finale fireworks but Mark ushered her out the door not long after Mince Pie Gate. A lot of silence followed then half sentences from Mark that started badly and fell away. He'd clearly bought into the game of split-up bingo, using all the tried-and-tested excuses. 'It's not you, it's me...', 'We're too different...', 'It would never work...', 'Have to focus on politics...', 'I'm feeling stifled...'

I watched him pack a bag and then he left.

Then I walked into the dining room. He hadn't even helped

with the washing up. I'd sat back down at the table, poured myself a glass full of port and downed it in one. Then scoffed all six mince pies and promptly threw up in the bin.

I sigh as Wizzard's 'I Wish It Could Be Christmas Everyday', blares out and I down the last of my wine as Rebecca returns to our table and proceeds to top up our glasses.

'I got us a raffle ticket,' she says.

'What's the prize?' I ask.

'No idea,' she says with a grin and chinks her glass against mine. 'Are you OK? You look glum?'

'I started to mentally unpick my emotional baggage when you were at the bar.'

'That's good.'

'No, it's *not*. All I seemed to have found is the equivalent of a big bag of dirty washing. A two-year-old bag of festering dirty laundry.'

She leans over and pats my hand. Annoying as her one-woman mission to analyse me is, she's still my best mate and has stuck by me through the great dividing of the friends, which came after announcing the divorce.

There were clearly two camps: Camp Me and Camp Mark. I obviously had all my old university and pre-Mark friends firmly on side. Most of these friends came up with such glorious insights in that they'd never liked him, never thought he was good enough for me, and although chalk and cheese sometimes work, most long-term marriages don't last when such polar opposites.

And we were opposites, obsessively tidy Mark was boarding-school educated and on a political trajectory. I was a repeat messer-upper, local comp educated and floated about as a drama teacher. Although these differences were glaringly obvious in hindsight, I really wished my friends had aired their opinions seven years earlier when I was about to marry him.

It was the 'couple' friends that surprised me. The couples we'd befriended when we'd also been a couple and had moved to the area. I assumed I'd get these ones as Mark had been the one to move away. But after an initial rallying round and supportive group gatherings, I began to feel the cold eyes of suspicion fall on me. It was clearly a truth universally acknowledged that, in a small rural village, a woman who was in the throes of divorcing her husband was clearly on the lookout for someone else's.

No matter how often I declared I was off all men, most probably for life, more of these friends and neighbours became absent from my life, holding on to their husband's arm as they passed me in the street, as if I was about to pounce on their menfolk and straddle them outside the Co-Op. I had contemplated taking out an advert in the local paper, but hesitated because the editor in charge of advertising was fairly good looking and seen as a bit of a ladies' man, and I really didn't have the energy to have to explain myself in case that set more tongues wagging.

I did wonder about moving but I liked my house. It was close to my work and after all the dust had settled I still had some good friends nearby who looked further than at the space my wedding band had once been on my finger.

'Look! They're doing the raffle!' Rebecca says, breaking me out of my self-indulgent bout of navel-gazing.

Numbers are called and cheers erupt. Then Rebecca gives a whoop and waves our ticket in the air. 'That's us!' she calls out. The raffle guy, wearing a jauntily-angled Santa hat and tinsel draped round his neck comes over and, wishing us a very merry Christmas, hands us our prize.

A packet of mince pies.

❄

The walk back to my house is cold and takes far longer than it should due to the amount of wine I've had, icy weather and the stupidly inappropriate high-heeled open-toed shoes I'm wearing. Rebecca lives in the other direction and we promise to message each other when we get back to our respective homes. Such is the safety lot of a single woman.

I am teetering up my driveway when I notice a car sitting alongside mine. It is a sleek looking silver thing that probably cost more than my first flat.

The door opens and my nostrils are instantly assaulted by a cloud of L'Air du Temps and I have to stop myself from hitting the ground as a wave of PTSD washes over me.

Then the driver appears. Pepper; The Ghost of Christmas Past in a pair of Dubarry Duncannon boots and a Deerhunter shooting jacket.

Having no words to say that could adequately sum up the emotional trauma I feel, I simply open the door and let her follow me into my house. With nothing better to do I switch on the kettle.

'Tea?' I say over my shoulder.

'Please.'

I while away another couple of minutes making the tea as my mind goes into overdrive. Is this Rebecca's doing? Has she arranged for my ex mother-in-law to come here as part of my therapy? In a kill or cure way?

I add milk to the mugs and slide one over to Pepper then I remember the raffle prize in my bag. I fetch the box of mince pies, open them and put them in the middle of the table.

'Don't worry, they're from Waitrose,' I say, noticing the label as I fold up the box and pop it in the recycling bin. I know it is a low dig, but I figure years of her not-so-silent disapproval allows me one moment to exact some sarcasm. I clutch my tea and wait.

'Firstly, I would like to apologise. I realise I've done you a disservice over the years.'

I am very glad to be leaning against the kitchen worktop as it stops me keeling over. I momentarily wonder if someone slipped a roofie into the wine and this is causing me to hallucinate but I feel quite fine in every other way, if a bit tipsy.

I have no idea what to say to this, but luckily Pepper fills the gaping void of stunned silence.

'I know I wasn't always supportive of you and Mark. I'll be honest, I thought he could do better. I didn't think you'd help his career. A drama teacher isn't really...well, it would have been different if you taught a STEM subject. You didn't seem to grasp what it takes to be a politician's wife.'

Her idea of an apology falls quite short.

'He wasn't a politician when I was married to him.'

'Yes, but that was always the goal.'

'I'm sure Lucinda's a much better prospect,' I say, as I blow on my tea.

'Ah, you heard,' Pepper says, more as a matter of statement than a question. Yes, the jungle drums have already done their job and I've known about their engagement for a couple of months.

'I'm starting to have doubts about Lucinda. I don't feel she's quite right for Mark.'

How on earth can mincemeat-making, Roedean-educated Lucinda, who does something impressive but forgettable in the city, not be right for Mark?

'Have you told Mark this?'

'I haven't seen Mark for a few weeks.'

I try to hide my surprise. Mark had always been on the phone to his mother. Even on our honeymoon he called her as soon as we got to our hotel, before we'd even unpacked.

And *still* the alarm bells hadn't rung! Dear God, I was an idiot.

I smile into my tea. Pepper is desperate for Mark to have a suitable partner for his (and Pepper's) political aspirations. Pepper wants someone as well educated/ travelled/ cultured and high-reaching as her son. Someone *Tatler* would approve of. Lucinda is perfect. In fact, Lucinda is so suitable a partner for Mark, it's as if she's been created in Pepper's own image.

Ah! And I finally understand. With a new version of Pepper on the scene there is no room for the original model. No doubt Lucinda isn't putting up with Pepper's interference. And pushed to the kerb, Pepper realises the quiet, easy-going, malleable drama teacher is by far the best person for Pepper, and therefore Mark.

Ah, to have been privy to the stand-off between the two women! Pistols at dawn would have had nothing on the lacrosse sticks after afternoon tea of those two!

'I believe my son still has feelings for you.'

Goddam! That word again; *feelings*.

I manage to not spray my mouthful of tea all over the table.

Mark's feelings for me evaporated as soon as his mummy told them to, and I'm sure in some twisted Oedipus way, Mark is more than happy with his new model of wife-mummy.

'The ship has sailed on that relationship,' I say.

Pepper sighs and helps herself to a mince pie. 'I'm sure he could be persuaded,' she says, then takes a bite.

'Hmm, the thing is, I don't want him back.'

She looks at me in bewilderment. Clearly this thought has never crossed her mind. She goes to speak but bewilderment quickly turns to horror as she grasps her throat and starts making a very strange noise whilst flapping her other hand in the air. I think it an odd time to be showing me the new sapphire ring on her hand – an early Christmas present? But then her face starts to turn the same shade as her ring.

Pepper is choking.

Yes, the thought of letting her choke does cross my mind but I'm a far better person than that.

And I have no idea where to bury her body!

I can't deny, walloping her on her back a few times to dislodge the offending piece of mince pie does give me a great amount of satisfaction, so I suppose I'm not *that* saintly.

Pepper sits looking dazed for a while and doesn't speak. Probably more as a result of me turning down her suggestion of getting back with her son to suit her agenda than almost choking to death. But, just to be on the safe side, I call an ambulance.

It is surprisingly quick to arrive.

And it isn't all bad.

As Pepper is wheeled into the back of the vehicle the cute paramedic chats me up and takes my phone number. Funny that when one door shuts due to dried fruit and spices cased in pastry, another one opens.

'Mince pie?' I say offering him the plate before he drives off.

He grins but shakes his head. 'Sorry, I don't like mince pies.'

'Neither do I,' I agree, tipping them into the bin.

***

Laura lives in a picturesque village just outside of Glasgow with her husband and three young daughters, along with an exuberant golden retriever, crazy black lab and two cats. After studying English Literature at Glasgow University, she attended some Creative Writing evening classes and was delighted to find herself amongst like-minded folk with a passion for writing. When not writing, Laura is usually to be found reading, with at least two books on the go at any given time. She also enjoys losing herself in art galleries and cooking up hearty meals to be enjoyed well into the evening with good wine and good friends. One day she hopes to add bees, ducks and a couple of alpacas to her menagerie. Her cozy murder mystery, *The Murderous Affair At Stone Manor*, is published by Bloodhound Books.

ONE NIGHT WITH NICK

BY NATASHA BOYDELL

THEIR EYES MET across a crowded room. All around them fairy lights twinkled, casting a warm, almost magical glow as the light reflected off the glassy baubles hanging from the Christmas tree. A gentle, festive ballad played softly in the background and the scent of cinnamon and clove lingered in the air. For a few heady seconds, as their eyes locked, her world stood still. The man in front of her was a stranger, yet it felt as though she'd known him for all her life. She smiled playfully, a little coquettishly, and began to move towards him.

She was distracted by a commotion to her left and she reluctantly forced her gaze away from his blue eyes to see what the cause was. Her eyes widened in horror.

'Sam, you *cannot* do wee-wee in the middle of a toy shop!'

'But, Mummy, I really need to go.'

'Pull your trousers up right now, young man!'

With flaming cheeks, Harriet grabbed her son's hand and turned away from the handsome stranger, dashing to reach the department store toilets before a critical incident was declared. As they weaved around hordes of overexcited children and stepped over discarded toys and crushed, half-eaten snacks, she tried to swallow her frustration. After forty-five minutes of waiting to see Santa Claus, they had finally reached the front of the queue. Now they'd probably have to start all over again at the back and she wasn't sure they had enough time, which meant that, once again, she would have to witness the disappointment on Sam's face.

They reached the loos in the nick of time. Harriet locked them into a cubicle and looked down at her son sternly.

'You're four years old now, Sam. You're big enough to know better than that.'

'Sorry, Mummy.' He looked crestfallen. 'I didn't want to miss Santa. Do we have to go home now?'

Harriet's irritation with her son was quickly replaced with guilt. 'Sorry, little man, but I have to be at work in a couple of hours. I don't think we have time to queue again.'

Sam's lip wobbled and his eyes filled with tears. 'Please, Mummy! Please!'

Oh, for god's sake. Why was everything so damn hard all the time? Even a simple trip to see Father Christmas, which she thought would be a nice treat, was turning into a disaster. Just like the rest of her life.

Harriet considered her options. Another hour in the queue, five minutes with Santa, fifteen minutes to get back to the car and half an hour to drive home. There was no way she could make it in time for work, and if she lost her job they'd have more to worry about than missing Santa. But although common sense was warning her to give up and go home, she couldn't bring herself to let Sam down. The boy had already had enough heartbreak in his short life.

She sighed with resignation. 'Come on, wash your hands and we'll see what we can do.'

His face lit up like a Christmas tree. 'Thank you, Mummy! Oh, thank you!'

She took his tiny hand into her own and led him back towards the entrance of the grotto, which was being policed by a bored-looking elf.

'Hi there,' she said, plastering on her best smile. 'We were just about to meet Santa but then my son needed to go to the toilet urgently. Any chance we could go to the front of the queue again?'

'Sorry,' the elf said, looking anything but. 'No queue jumpers.'

'Well, technically, we're not queue jumpers as we were already in the queue,' Harriet argued.

The elf looked at her with a vacant expression and pointed at a sign, which said: 'no Q jumpers.'

Harriet gripped Sam's hand tightly, anger bubbling up inside her. It was one thing to mess with her, but quite another to mess with her boy.

'Look, you power-hungry, prepubescent little elf...' she began through gritted teeth, but before she had the opportunity to launch into a full-scale character assassination, she was interrupted.

'I remember this boy,' a deep male voice said. 'Let him through.'

The elf shrugged, moving aside to let them pass, and Harriet found herself looking into the captivating blue eyes of Santa Claus for the second time that afternoon. Her stomach gave an involuntary flip at the sight of him, and she instinctively patted her hair.

'Thank you so much,' she said, feeling shy, as though she was the young child and not the responsible adult.

'Not at all,' Santa said, holding her gaze for a fraction too long, before turning his attention to Sam. 'Now, my dear boy, what's your name?'

With Sam talking ten to the dozen about what he wanted for Christmas, Harriet couldn't tear her eyes away from the stranger. Which was odd because he was wearing a heavily padded red suit and she could barely see his face under that bushy white beard. He was not the epitome of a male pin-up. And in any event, she hadn't fancied anyone in years. Perhaps it was the relief of not letting her son down that was making her so giddy? No, it was more than that. There was something about this man. She couldn't quite put her finger on it; even though he was dressed like an old man in a fat suit, he was giving her the feels.

Crikey, she fancied Santa. She really did need to get out more. It was so absurd that she was almost overcome with giggles, and she had to turn away for a minute to recover. When she looked back, covering her mouth with her hand to keep the laughter safely inside, he was watching her intently.

Seconds later, the elf reappeared. 'Time's up,' he said impatiently. 'Come on, let's go.'

Sam gripped tightly to his present and gave Santa a hug. 'I love you, Santa,' he said.

'Merry Christmas, Sam,' Santa replied, and then turned to Harriet. 'Merry Christmas.'

She smiled back goofily. 'Merry Christmas.'

As they left, she risked one last glance back, but Santa was already talking to another child. The hysteria that had been growing inside her exploded out in an undignified snort.

'Why are you laughing, Mummy?' Sam asked. 'Did I miss a joke?'

'I'm just getting into the Christmas spirit,' she said, looking at her son fondly. Perhaps the trip to the shopping centre hadn't been such a bust after all. Her brief flirtation with Father

Christmas was the funniest thing to have happened to her in ages. 'Come on, sweetheart, let's go home.'

As they exited the car park, the song *Driving Home for Christmas* came on the radio and Harriet's festive glow disappeared as quickly as it had arrived. She hurriedly switched stations, but it was too late to stop the melancholy from descending on her, as it did every time she heard that stupid song. Two years ago, her fiancé – and Sam's dad – Michael, was supposed to be driving home for Christmas. He'd text her to say that he'd finished his business trip and would be back that evening. But somewhere along the way he'd had a change of heart because he never arrived. Now he lived with his secretary and saw Sam once a month, and as much as Harriet tried to make the most of Christmas for her son's sake, she loathed it.

'Mummy, what's this?' Sam was waving a piece of paper at her from the back seat.

'I can't look, sweetheart, I'm driving,' she replied. 'Where did you find it?'

'It was stuck to my present. It has numbers and letters on it. Zero, seven, seven...' Sam tried to read the note but while he knew his numbers, he hadn't grasped words yet.

'It's probably a receipt,' Harriet said. 'I'll look when we get home.'

As soon as they had pulled up outside their house, Sam thrust the paper under her nose and she turned the interior light on so that she could read it.

Glad you came back. Here's my phone number. Drinks tomorrow tonight?

'What does it say?' Sam asked.

'It's Santa,' Harriet replied in disbelief. 'He's asked me out.'

'Wow! That's cool, Mummy! I wonder if you'll meet Rudolph. Can I come?'

'I'm not going to go,' Harriet said, screwing up the note. It was one thing to have a silly crush on a shopping centre Santa, but it was quite another to go out with him.

'Why not?' Sam was incredulous as to why anyone would turn down such an opportunity.

'Well, I don't really know him, do I. And anyway, I prefer having dinner with you.' Harriet smiled and planted a kiss on her son's cheek.

'Mummy,' Sam said solemnly. 'I think you should go.'

'Why?'

'Because Santa made you smile today, and you never smile anymore.'

His words were like a dagger through her heart. She had tried so hard to protect him from the fallout of her acrimonious split with Michael; the anger, the recriminations, the resentment, her ongoing fear of how they would manage financially, but she clearly hadn't done enough. He may be a little boy, but he knew enough to understand that his mummy was sad and broken, and the realisation of this filled her with shame.

'Promise me you'll go out with Santa, Mummy.'

She nodded. 'All right. I'll go. Come on, let's get inside.'

Harriet's mum, Linda, was in the kitchen with a cup of tea and a crossword puzzle. She looked after Sam while Harriet worked night shifts as an office cleaner. If it wasn't for her, Harriet had no idea how she would have managed over the last couple of years.

'How was Santa?' Linda asked.

'Brilliant! He gave me a present! And he asked Mummy out!' Sam announced proudly.

Linda shook her head. 'I've heard everything now. Come on then, Sam, let's get you some dinner and leave Mummy to get ready for work.'

'Mum,' Harriet asked tentatively. 'Any chance you can stay tomorrow evening as well?'

Linda raised her eyebrows. 'Is this so you can go out with Santa?'

'Maybe.' Harriet laughed nervously.

'Well, he's a busy man at this time of year, love, so if he's cleared some space in his schedule to take you out then you really ought to go.' Linda winked at Sam, who grinned back.

'Thanks, Mum. I owe you. Again.'

As she dashed upstairs to get changed, Harriet pulled out her phone and typed out a text before she could change her mind.

Sounds lovely. Will you pick me up in your sleigh? Harriet x

Cringing at her own joke, she threw the phone down on to her bed. Opening the wardrobe to find her uniform, she tried not to think about the fact that this time tomorrow, she would be getting ready to go on her first date in a decade with a man whose real name she didn't know.

Harriet smoothed down her hair with a sweaty palm and glanced down at her cleavage to make sure she wasn't flashing her bra. She looked across the table at the empty chair. Her hands were shaking, she felt sick, and she was bitterly regretting agreeing to this stupid date. This was what came of following the advice of a four-year-old.

For all she knew, seeking out bored, lonely mums and asking them out might be a regular occurrence for Sexy Santa – as her mother had dubbed him – but agreeing to it was a big deal for her. When Michael had abandoned them, he had not only left her struggling financially, but he had also taken her last shred of self-confidence with him too. For two years she'd been battling to stay afloat, taking night work because she couldn't afford nursery fees and it was the only time that her mum could look after Sam. Now her son had started school Harriet knew she should look for a better paid job with more sociable hours, but she was afraid of putting herself out there. She hated herself for giving up, yet couldn't muster the motivation to do anything about it. The truth was, it was easier to hide in the day-to-day chaos of life than it was to confront it.

As for her appearance, it had been so long since she'd bought any clothes, the outfit she was wearing was the same one she'd worn for her first date with Michael ten years ago. It was a miracle it still fit her. Although, judging by the way her bust was threatening to spill out of it, the word *fit* was a loose description. She hadn't had her hair done or, until that evening, shaved her legs in months, and the idea of her being attractive to a man was a joke.

On top of all that, she had no idea what Sexy Santa – or whatever his name was – looked like in his civvies, and was terrified that either she wouldn't recognise him or that he would be an ogre of epic proportions and she'd be stuck with him all evening.

Feeling overwhelmed, she reached for her coat and decided to make a quick getaway before it was too late, berating herself for thinking that anything good could ever happen to her. With her eyes fixed on the floor, she hurried across the bar and pushed the door open, hurtling out on to the pavement and crashing straight into someone who was on their way in. The impact made her precariously held breasts wobble like bowlfuls of jelly.

'I'm so sorry,' she said.

She looked up and realised with shock that she recognised those blue eyes. His dark hair and beard had flecks of grey and he had the kind of weathered yet wise face that hinted of a life well-lived. He was, unmistakeably, Sexy Santa.

'Leaving already?' he asked.

Harriet was mortified. 'Oh no, I've just popped outside for a smoke,' she said, thinking on the spot.

'Okay,' he replied, leaning up against the wall and waiting for her to light up.

Except, she didn't have any cigarettes. Because she didn't smoke. She made a show of rummaging around in her purse.

'Oh no, I seem to have forgotten them,' she said feebly.

He observed her, amused. Then said, 'Let's go for a walk.' He turned and started striding down the street.

She floundered, uncertain what to do, and then broke into a jog until she had caught up with him.

'I'm sorry,' she said once she reached him.

'You don't need to say sorry.'

'Sorry. I just haven't been out with anyone for a really long time.'

'Nor have I.'

'Really?'

He chuckled. 'You seem surprised.'

'You asked a stranger out by attaching your phone number to her son's Christmas present, which implies that you're not lacking in the confidence department.'

'Fair point,' he agreed. 'The truth is that I'm too busy. I travel a lot.'

'Well yes. You've got to deliver the toys to fast asleep girls and fast asleep boys.'

'Quite.' He added, 'You should be aware than I'm only in town for a few more days.'

'Oh, right.'

She was deflated, without knowing why. It wasn't like she was planning on marrying him. It was only supposed to be a bit of fun for her too. Yet, knowing his intention stung anyway. Was he a predator, seeking out desperate single mums as prey for one-night stands because he knew they were an easy target? Should she tell him to stick it and go home?

'When I saw you at the shopping centre yesterday, you looked like you had the weight of the world on your shoulders,' he said, stopping and putting a hand gently on her shoulder. 'And I thought, a woman as beautiful as you should never be so sad.'

'Corny but effective,' she said with a wry smile.

'But if you'd rather go home now, I understand. With my nomadic lifestyle I'm hardly a keeper.'

'What do you do for a living? When you're not being Santa?' she asked, intrigued.

'I work in international distribution. What about you?'

'I used to be a PA, many moons ago.'

'Not anymore?'

'Nope.'

'Why not?'

'It's a long story.'

'We have time.'

As they walked through the city, past late-night shoppers and rowdy Christmas party goers, she found herself telling him everything: how she had quit her job when she had Sam, the breakdown of her relationship with Michael, her struggle since. He listened attentively, making her feel like she was the only person in the world. He was so easy to talk to that once she started, she couldn't stop. It all came out: her hopes, her fears, her dreams. There was something oddly liberating about knowing she would probably never see him again.

When she was done talking, she looked at him. 'Bet you wish you'd never asked now.'

He smiled. 'I think you are remarkable.'

'I'm not sure anyone's ever put my name and the word *remarkable* in the same sentence before.'

'Maybe they have, but you didn't hear it.'

'I doubt it.'

He sighed. 'You need to stop putting yourself down all the time, Harriet. It really won't get you anywhere. How can you expect others to believe in you if you don't believe in yourself?'

'Through the power of osmosis?'

'It's time to grab life by the horns again. You've been existing, not living, for too long. This is the perfect time of year to make a change and start afresh. You deserve to be happy.'

'Thank you, erm, Santa. Christ, I don't even know your real name.'

'Nicholas. Everyone calls me Nick for short.'

'Of course they do.'

They were standing in front of a hotel. 'There's a bar in here,' he said. 'Shall we have a drink?'

They had been walking for an hour and she could no longer feel her toes. She looked longingly at the warm, softly lit hotel lobby and nodded. 'Yes, okay.'

They found a sofa by the window, and she waited for him to order their drinks at the bar. When he returned, he sat down next to her, resting his thigh against hers and she felt a jolt of electricity from the contact. He smelled just like the grotto, of clove and other winter spices.

'Have you ever been married, Nick? Is there a Mrs Claus waiting for you at home somewhere?'

'No.'

'I bet you have a girl in every town.'

He laughed. 'Maybe.'

'You're not a man of many words, are you?'

'I'm not interesting. Not like you. Tell me about Sam.'

She talked and he listened. She asked him questions and he

told her about the places he'd been, and the things he'd seen, without really revealing anything about himself. One drink became two, then three. With each one she felt herself relaxing into the evening. But it wasn't the alcohol, it was the company. She'd forgotten how wonderful a good conversation felt.

When she finally looked at the time, it was midnight. 'I'd better go,' she said, searching around for her bag.

'I'll find you a taxi,' he replied, standing up. 'Unless...'

Her heart was already pounding in anticipation of what he was going to suggest. 'Unless what?'

'Unless you'd like to stay the night?'

'Here? With you?'

'Yes. Only if you want to, Harriet.' His face was serious, but his eyes were twinkling.

She quickly considered the prospect of spending the night with Nick. She was thirty-nine years old and she'd never had a one-night stand in her life. He was incredibly sexy, but she would never see him again. If she knew that, did it matter? No, it didn't. Yes, it did. She was a mother, she had responsibilities. But her mum was staying over and Sam would be fast asleep. She should do it. No, she shouldn't. She looked at him, long and hard.

'Yes,' she whispered.

Harriet buttoned up her shirt and looked over at the bed. Nick was asleep and the digital clock on the bedside table was showing five in the morning. She leaned over and kissed him gently, but he didn't stir. She watched him for a bit and then slipped quietly out of the door.

Outside, most of the city was still asleep. Looking around at the empty roads, she began to panic. She had to get home before Sam woke up so he didn't know she'd been out all night. As if on cue, a taxi appeared. She flagged it down and climbed in.

'Good morning,' the driver said.

She smiled unashamedly. 'Good evening.'

She'd been up most of the night, yet she felt like she'd slept for twelve hours. How long had it been since she'd felt so alive? Since someone had made her laugh, made her feel valued, desired, beautiful? In the cold darkness of the winter's morning, the grey world she had been living in suddenly seemed full of colour. She wasn't even disappointed that she wouldn't see Nick again. As she stared out of the window, she considered that maybe it wasn't Nick who was the main beneficiary of their no-strings one night together, but her.

She got home just in time to shower and change before Sam drifted into her room, rubbing his eyes sleepily. By the time they got to the kitchen, Linda had a pot of coffee brewing.

'Good night, was it?' Linda asked, fixing Harriet with a knowing look.

'Yes thanks, Mum.'

'How was Santa?' Sam piped up, tucking into his cereal. 'Did he take you for a ride?'

'Something like that,' Harriet replied, stifling a laugh.

Linda was doing the same. 'And will you be seeing Santa again?' she asked.

'I don't think so. He's very busy with work at this time of year.'

'I'll bet he is.'

'Leave off, Mum, I had fun. More fun than I've had in a really long time.'

'I'm sure you did.' Looking over to make sure Sam wasn't listening, Linda added in a whisper, 'I hope he jingled your bells.'

Harriet's phone pinged and she pulled it out to read the message.

You are remarkable, Harriet.

She smiled. Then pocketed her phone and went to sit down next to her son.

The department store had used the same Christmas decorations as last year, yet the grotto looked completely different. It was brightly lit and sterile. There was no scent of cinnamon in the air and the festive banger blaring out of the stereo was slightly too loud.

Sam didn't care. He was jiggling around with anticipation as they waited in line to see Santa, and Harriet prayed that they wouldn't have a repeat of wee-gate. This year, she was almost as excited as her son. It was silly to think Nick would be there, yet she couldn't help but hope anyway. She craned her neck around the queue, trying to sneak a glimpse of the man in red.

'Are you excited to meet Santa?' she asked Sam.

'So excited!'

She thought about how much her son had changed since last Christmas. He had emerged from the cocoon of his infancy, transformed into a smart, funny and confident little man. His perpetual look of worry had vanished and rarely returned. He laughed all the time. So did she. She smiled at the elf who was eying her up and smoothed down her suit. She'd picked Sam up straight after work and hadn't had time to change. She had started applying for jobs in the new year and a few months later was offered a role as a PA at a film production company. She adored her job and the stability and financial security that it afforded her. But most of all, she adored being able to read Sam a bed-time story every night.

They were nearly at the front. She tapped her foot impatiently. She still thought about Nick from time to time. Their night together felt like a dream now, and sometimes she wasn't sure if it had happened at all. Perhaps if she saw him one last time, she would know for sure.

'You can go in now,' the elf said, giving her an appreciative once over as he ushered them through.

'Come on, Sam,' she said, putting an arm around her son.

As they walked into the grotto, she closed her eyes and took a deep breath. When she opened them again, she found herself staring into the tired, brown eyes of a pensioner.

'Ho, ho, ho, Merry Christmas,' the man said in a monotone. 'What's your name?'

Deep down, she had known it wouldn't be him, yet she couldn't hide her disappointment. She thought about the way he had made her feel last year, the sense of anticipation and excitement that he had ignited in her. The feeling that anything was possible. She had wanted to experience it one more time. But it wasn't to be. Wherever Nick was in the world, it wasn't at Brent Cross Shopping Centre. She watched Sam chat with Santa, then she took a quick photo before the elf came to fetch them. Sam gave Santa a cheery wave goodbye but didn't offer him a hug this time.

'Did you have fun, sweetheart?' Harriet asked him as they left.

'Yes, Mummy.' He looked at her conspiratorially. 'But it wasn't the real Santa.'

He may be growing up, but he was still a believer and Harriet tried to respond diplomatically.

'Perhaps the real Santa was too busy, so he asked a friend to stand in for him. You know, he can't be everywhere all the time, no matter how magic he is.'

Sam looked thoughtful. Then he shrugged. 'I guess so,' he said. 'I wish I could see the real Santa though.'

'Come on, why don't we go and get a waffle. With extra chocolate sauce?'

Sam's face lit up. 'Yeah!'

They headed towards the waffle stand and as they waited for their order, Harriet glanced down at Sam, who was still clutching on to his present from Santa.

'Aren't you going to open that?' she asked.

'Oh, yes,' he replied, tearing off the wrapping paper, which fluttered to the floor, and pulling out a box. 'I think it's a game,' he said, giving it a dubious shake.

A cheap plastic knock-off of a game, Harriet thought wryly, crouching down to pick up the wrapping paper. As she did, she noticed a slip of paper tucked inside. Frowning, she pulled it out and read it. It contained just four words. *Merry Christmas, remarkable Harriet.*

She looked around, frantically scanning the crowds for a glimpse of him, but he was nowhere to be seen. She tried to think of a logical explanation but there was none. She looked down at Sam, who was studying the game carefully. Then she looked up at the waffle man who was preparing their order. He winked at her, and she stared back at him, bemused.

Harriet thought about Christmas. Tomorrow was the end of term for Sam, and she had nearly two weeks off work. She considered the Christmas bonus she had received from work, the monthly maintenance payments that Michael was finally paying after she had summoned up the courage to call him out on his bad behaviour. She thought about Sam and how she had always longed to take him on an adventure. Then she thought about how long she had spent living in a grey world and how good it felt to see it in the full vibrancy of colour again. Finally, she thought about Nick and how he had inspired her to grasp life again. And she had an idea.

As Sam devoured his waffle, she pulled her phone out and did some research. It was crazy, it was stupid, it was highly irresponsible. It was just about do-able.

She turned to Sam. 'So, you want to see the real Santa, do you? Well then, we'll just have to go to Lapland. We leave tomorrow.'

***

Natasha Boydell is a former journalist. Her debut novel, The Missing Husband, was released in 2021 and became an Amazon Kindle Top 100 Bestseller. Her second novel, The Woman Next Door, followed the same year and her third, The Legacy of Eve, was released in 2022. Natasha lives in North London with her husband, two young daughters and two Blue Cross rescue cats.

FAIRY TALE OF MAURA
AND FINN
BY PATRICIA DIXON

CHRISTMAS EVE, PRESENT DAY

MAURA FINISHED BRUSHING her hair and checked her make-up, applying just a touch because at seventy-three the days of spending hours in front of the mirror were well and truly gone; but traditions, well, they remained and before she headed downstairs to the party, there was one more thing to do.

This year would be one of the hardest, emotions running high because it was the first Christmas without her beloved mammy, who Maura had cared for until her last breath, taken under her roof. Looking around the bedroom, just one of eight in a home that was a beauty, set in five acres of countryside it was a testament to all she'd achieved – they'd achieved, her and her husband. As she thought of him she smiled, the words of her mother carried down from heaven on that snowy night, ones Mammy used for Dadaí, *The older the fiddle the sweeter the tune.*

The old days, the old country and its traditions were special, so every year on Christmas Eve, a day that marked the start and end to many things in her life, Maura always took a moment to give thanks, look back, remember, never taking anything for granted, grateful for all she had and sad for everything and everyone she'd lost.

Pulling open the drawer of her jewellery box she took from the very back – not hidden, just kept safe – a small box. After taking a breath, because she knew how the sight of it always made her feel, she opened the lid. There, lying on a bed of dark-blue silk was a fine silver necklace and on it hung a tiny shamrock. She never wore it, the links and clasp were too fragile and she was terrified of losing it. So there it lay, a testament to all that had gone before. Tears blurred her eyes as memories flooded in, taking her back to a time and place engraved on her heart. To a man who took her hand on a cold Christmas Eve and made her a promise. One that she'd never forgotten.

ENNISKILLEN, COUNTY FERMANAGH, NORTHERN IRELAND. CHRISTMAS EVE, 1970

Maura packed away her sheet music and after waving goodbye to her friends, wrapped her scarf around her neck, still buttoning up her coat as she hurried outside into a bitterly cold afternoon. She headed straight over to where her infuriating, but impossibly good-looking boyfriend was pacing the footpath, in danger of wearing away the soles of his shoes.

Maura had spotted him half an hour earlier, mid-way through rehearsals, him waving through the misted glass and beckoning that she should come outside. While her friend Clodagh had giggled at the sight of Finn's face squished against the glass, Maura wasn't amused because she'd lost concentration and missed her solo cue and they'd all had to start again.

She'd no idea what was so important that he'd turned up there. He usually spent his Saturday afternoons in The Horse Shoe Bar, drinking Guinness, playing cards, and watching the racing on telly, and anyway, they weren't meeting until later to go to her granny's for Christmas tea. The man was so unreliable, always late, forgetful, erred towards lazy and a teeny bit selfish now and then, so she was annoyed that he'd ruined her rehearsals by also being an eejit. He knew how much performing meant to her, and yes, it was only a showcase that the local theatre company was putting on for New Year's, but to Maura her starring role was a big thing. Performing was her dream job, not working at the factory, sewing yards and yards of fabric, day in, day out.

Which was why, as she ran down the steps of the community centre, she was ready to tear a very big strip off Finn McSherry and she didn't care what his excuse was – knowing him, he'd have one.

He was lighting a cigarette, his hand arched over his face to protect the flame from the howling wind, his black overcoat flapping about his knees, a hearty gust almost taking his beloved pork-pie hat with it.

When he saw her, his face lit up and he rushed to be by her side. 'Here you are at last... did you not see me waving at you?'

'Yes, Finn McSherry, I did, and thanks to you I got a telling off from Mrs Murphy for not concentrating!'

'Never mind that now. I have something to tell you, so let's be off.' Taking her arm, Finn's sense of urgency unmistakeable, he ferried her across the road and ushered her inside Ryan's café, then steered her towards the table in the farthest corner by the window. Here, remembering the manners his mammy taught him, he pulled out a chair. After she sat, he took the one opposite, removing his hat and placing it on the table, his jet-black hair Brylcreemed perfectly into place.

Maura unwound her scarf and eyed Finn curiously, suspecting he might be in some kind of bother or, like the year before, had pawned her Christmas present to buy two cheaper ones because he'd forgotten to get one for his granda. She noticed how he was looking around the half empty café in a shifty manner and it didn't bode well.

'Finn, are you going to tell me what's going on? Or am I to guess, because I really don't have the time. I want to go home and change and do my hair for Granny's.'

He was about to speak but Mr Ryan came over to take their order – Finn deciding on two mugs of tea and a KitKat to share.

Once the old man had shuffled away, Finn leant forward, lowering his voice as his eyes bored holes into Maura's. 'I've had a win on the horses. Came in twenty-to-one. I have my winnings in here.' He tapped his breast pocket. 'Paddy down at the yard gave me the nod.'

Relieved that it was good news for once and even better, maybe he'd had time to buy her something very special before the shops closed for the holidays, Maura also realised she might finally believe in miracles. 'That's grand, Finn. How much did you win?'

Ducking his head as though one of the brothers at school was about to box his ears, Finn narrowed his eyes. 'For the love of God, keep your voice down. I don't want anyone finding out.' Again, there was a lull in conversation when Mr Ryan returned and placed two mugs of tea dangerously close to Finn's hat and after pulling a Kit-Kat from the pocket of his apron, wordlessly sauntered back to the counter.

'Almost a thousand pounds. Enough for us to make proper plans for the future, like we talked about.'

Maura's heart flipped. It was a lovely feeling, like birthdays and Christmas Days rolled into one and she hadn't felt like that in such a long time, since she was little. Then she wondered if he meant what she hoped he meant, because she'd been waiting so long for him to ask. But then again she really didn't want it to be there, in Ryan's café over stewed tea and a chocolate biscuit. Knowing that Finn could be impulsive, Maura sought to rein him in, otherwise her giddy black stallion might go out of the gates too soon.

'So where did you get the money for the bet... to win so much?'

Finn gave her that look, the one she'd seen many times before, like when he'd pawned her guitar so he could go in with some mad scheme for making poteen with his daft best friend Donal. That didn't end well and almost had them arrested by the Garda. Or when he sold his motorbike to buy tickets for England v Northern Ireland at Windsor Park in Belfast, a four-day bender that, again, almost had him and his friends arrested.

Finn sucked in his courage. 'Now don't go eating the head off me,' he paused, took a sip of tea, 'but I used my wages and my Christmas bonus.'

Maura was lost for words so simply stared while Finn looked away nervously and tipped more sugar into his mug and stirred. She truly loved the bones of her man, but he was a liability. She wondered if he'd ever change, just as one of Mammy's sayings popped into her head. *If you buy what you don't need, you might have to sell what you do.*

Grimacing as she sipped her stewed tea Maura checked the time and not having the energy for a row, pointed at the KitKat. 'Pop that in your pocket and let's get going. We can talk on the way. Come on, I think it's going to snow, and I want to be home before it starts.'

Minutes later, as daylight faded to grey and the streetlights flickered on, a fine mist of icing sugar began to fall from the sky as they walked hand in hand through Forthill Park. Maura was deep in thought and suspected Finn was working up to one of his big speeches, which usually involved a grand plan that never worked out. He dreamed big, of escaping the coal yard just like she dreamt of escaping the curtain factory but so far it seemed that they were stuck where they were, destined to follow in the footsteps of their forebears. It drove him – and secretly her – almost insane. So, when he stopped suddenly at the foot of the looming Cole Memorial, she was ready for another crazy scheme and no doubt the money in his pocket was setting the lining on fire.

'Look, I know it was a risk but this time I got it right. We can't let this chance slip through our fingers so hear me out, won't you? Don't go slapping me down before I've got the words out.' His eyes, black as jet, had never seemed so intense. Maura's heart skipped a beat. Here would do the job nicely.

In a snowy park, on that frosty Christmas Eve, Finn grabbed her hand and pulled a small black box from his pocket and as he held it towards her said, 'Let's get married.' Then he panicked and had another try. 'Sorry, sorry, I'm a bit nervous is all.' He coughed. 'Maura Ellen Kenyon, will you take me, Finn Charles McSherry, to be your husband? I'd get down on me knee, but I don't want to get me pants wet.'

Maura giggled and rolled her eyes, not really one for tears but she could feel them welling, and even though there was a big fat frog blocking her throat she squeaked out a reply, one she'd practised a hundred times as she lay in the bed next to her sleeping sister, Niamh.

'Finn Charles McSherry, I would be honoured to be your wife.' Taking the box, she opened the lid to see a perfect diamond ring.

Darting forward, standing on tiptoes, she kissed him, loving the feel of her man's arms holding her tight. Once they pulled apart and after a bit of fumbling, he placed the ring on her finger and then she told him her heart. 'I thought you were never going to ask me, but I've wanted you to for so long because I love you so much.'

He smiled, clearly pleased with himself. 'And I love you, but I haven't finished with my questions yet so, wife-to-be, let your man speak.'

They clung on to one another as Maura waited and hoped it wasn't something daft, about stag dos, or God-forbid moving in with his mammy while they saved up because that was never going to happen. She'd rather go up to the convent and live with the nuns and that was a fact, or share a bed with Niamh for the rest of her life.

'I want us to get wed as soon as we can, if your dadaí gives us permission of course, and now we have some money behind us we can go on an adventure. There's got to be something more than Enniskillen, Maura, a place where we can make all of our dreams come true. I have a feeling, right here.' He touched his chest. Finn's eyes were bright, shining with hope and it was nothing to do with the glow from the streetlight.

'What do you mean, an adventure? Mammy says marriage is an adventure on its own, so let's make do with that.'

Finn held her at arm's length, his hands gripping hers so tightly. 'We deserve more than that, Maura, we deserve a chance to be someone, be more, and we can't do that here.'

Maura's heart had done another flip, but it had landed on its bottom with a thud and was struggling to get up again. 'I don't understand...'

'I want us to go to America, to New York, make a fresh start, build a new life together and write our own fairy tale. Think about it, Maura, the opportunities we'd have. There's nothing for us here.'

She made her lips move. 'We have our families, Mammy and Dadaí, and Niamh and Granny, and our friends. I can't believe you'd want us to leave them. I couldn't. It's too sad to even think about. And it'll be hard, starting on our own. What if we're poor and starving and end up in the workhouse?'

Finn persevered. 'We won't starve or end up in the workhouse. And everyone can visit when we make it big. You make it big. You told me yourself that your dream is to be on the stage, to sing and dance and hear the crowd call your name. The bright lights of Broadway are just a boat ride away, so let's go. Grab this chance with both hands.'

Maura was stunned and could do nothing other than listen to Finn as he told her about all the things he'd heard, read in the paper, seen on television. 'You know my cousin Mick is there already and he says everything's huge: buildings, breakfasts, cars, hot dogs even! Can you imagine it?'

At this Maura tutted. 'Honestly, Finn, you're getting carried away and I need to think. Not about getting married, about going away. It's all a shock, so much to take in and we need to get going for Granny's party. Now come on.'

She tried to tug him away, but he stood his ground and began to fumble in his pocket. 'Maura, open your bag, go on, quickly.' He waited and then pulled out a thick brown envelope and stuffed it deep inside before clicking the clasp shut. 'There, that's all the money and I want you to hold on to it. So you know I mean it and I won't go spending it on something daft. And until you decide, I'll be patient, because this belongs to you, Maura.' His fist thumped his heart.

Maura swallowed down a sob because in that moment, she wanted him to be right, or not to have asked at all because it was all too terrifying, but at the same time thrilling. Ignoring the look on Finn's face, the voice of worry in her head, the thoughts of starvation and missing her family, as marshmallow flakes began to fall, Maura took his cold hand in hers.

They headed out of the park, making brand new footprints in the snow when another of her mammy's sayings came like a whisper in her ear. *Remember this, Maura darlin'. Where there's love, it's easy to halve the potato.*

NEW YORK. CHRISTMAS EVE, 1974

Maura trudged through the snow, her head bent against the wind, beret pulled low over her ears, hugging her overcoat to keep warm as she dodged her fellow New Yorkers who, like herself, must have been mad to brave the elements. She was meeting Finn who'd rang the diner where she worked part-time and left a message, to meet him at McKenna's Bar as soon as her show ended. It was important, apparently.

Seriously, did the man not know how exhausted she was, working a day shift at the diner, then racing to the theatre for an evening performance? And anyway, he had a nerve because she'd not spoken to him for days after he'd ended up in the gutter drunk *again*, and she was sick of it. Sick of him, sick of New York, sick of their grotty apartment and being on her feet literally all day to keep a roof over their heads while Finn went from one job to another, never settling at anything, and it was always someone else's fault.

The only light in her very long days were the two hours she spent at the theatre on Broadway, not in the starring role, but in the chorus where she clung to the dream of getting her big break. Lately, though, the glittering career she'd imagined as they'd boarded the boat in Belfast was becoming blurry and she was losing sight of it all. So many auditions where she'd prayed they'd say her number, ask her to step forward; the call-backs that came to nothing and the read-throughs she'd practised so hard for, only for somebody else to get picked.

Turning on to 5th Avenue she passed St Patrick's Cathedral

and spotted a bundle of rags leaning against the railings and when it moved, a head reared, and a pinched face with rosy-red cheeks looked her way. Maura's heart lurched at the sight of failure, of a fate she feared. But when the man smiled and raised a hand, holding a paper bag to conceal the bottle inside, so did she.

He called out, 'Happy Christmas,' to which Maura replied, 'And a happy Christmas to you darlin'.' After digging into her pocket, she placed a handful of coins in his and gave them a squeeze, looking into glassy eyes. 'Now you take care, and God bless.'

As she walked away, Maura took comfort in the sound of her mammy's voice echoing in her ear, brought across the Atlantic Ocean. *Now you remember this, Maura. A kind word never broke anyone's mouth.*

God, she missed home and her family so bad it was like a physical pain, and it was always worse at Christmas, remembering Granny's special tea before the carol service and midnight Mass. And then the big day itself when there were too many mouths to feed around her mammy's table but somehow they all ended up with a plate piled high. And then the dancing and singing once the table and chairs were pushed to the side of the room. Dadaí would get out his fiddle, Finn would play piano and she'd sing 'The Rare Old Mountain Dew', and everyone would join in with the chorus.

The previous day, while she'd waited her turn on a plastic chair in a very long corridor outside an audition room, Maura had done a lot of thinking. And she'd figured that emigrating to New York and starting a new life had been like her favourite chocolates, Dairy Box. A mix of dark and light. Dark and bitter when she'd missed Enniskillen and everyone there like a limb, light and delicious when the thrill of the big city lifted her up and convinced her it would be okay. Like on their first

Christmas Eve as they'd walked along Broadway, Finn had promised her that one day her name would be up there in lights, his voice full of conviction, so sure that his lucky break was just around the next corner. Maura had believed him then.

He'd met her after work and they'd walked three blocks through the snow, holding hands, him telling her about the job he'd be going for at the port. They were happy, laughing and making plans and while they waited to cross at the intersection, Finn told her he loved her. She told him the same right back and there, on 42nd Street, they kissed like their lives depended on it, before racing to McKenna's, dancing into Christmas Day.

How times had changed, and she had too. As she walked, Maura remembered that night three years before when Finn proposed and as they'd headed home, each of their steps leaving brand-new footprints in the snow, clear and crisp. Now, as she looked down at her boots, covered in brown slush, her footprints were indistinguishable from the hundreds of others that had trod the sidewalk that day. And there, as someone bumped her shoulder with no words of apology, Maura stood still, frozen on the sidewalk, just another face in a big city, amongst strangers. She realised one thing. She wanted to go home.

Pushing open the door of McKenna's Maura searched for Finn amongst the crowd that jostled and jeered as she squeezed between merrymakers. Cigarette smoke filled the air along with Irish voices that should have brought comfort and familiarity but instead it made the miles from home stretch before her. Sinatra was playing on the jukebox, exalting the wonders of the Big Apple, as she spotted Finn, sitting beside his friend Tommy, the table already covered in bottles and the ashtray full. His dark mop of curly hair bobbed as he chatted – jeez, the man never stopped – and his arms waved about as he told a tale, shirtsleeves rolled up, collar undone. When he spotted her through the crowd his smile was like the sun and just as it rose each morning, she knew also that Finn loved her like no other. She wished that were enough.

'Maura, here you are. Look, I've got you a drink. Sit while I tell you our news.' Finn guided her to her seat and, still the gentleman, pulled it out.

After a few sips and a welcome from Tommy, the words tripped from Finn's lips, all eagerness and excitement, his eyes wild. 'So, you see... this is what we've been waiting for, our big chance. Tommy's family came with the first settlers from Belfast and his uncle's house was passed down and now the land is worth a fortune.'

'But where do you fit into all this?' Maura had listened to it all and was still none the wiser.

'Me and Tommy are going in together as partners. I'm going to the bank, to ask for a loan, and so is Tommy here, so we can get ourselves some tools. Then we're going to knock down the house, develop the land and build on it. Whatever profit we make, we'll invest in more land, tools, workers.' Finn was on fire, but it was just another dream that would crash and burn like all his others.

She listened to him rattle on some more but could find no enthusiasm for his ideas, or another dram, or a song by the piano because she was tired, and it was a quarter to midnight, and she wanted to go home... so badly.

Minutes later they were on the street, the snow falling in buckets, him rushing along beside her, his long legs keeping pace with her hurry, asking what was wrong and why she'd stormed from the pub and made a show of him in front of Tommy. Her thoughts were accompanied by strains of 'Galway Bay' and across the street, a choir sang them into the holy day. Maybe it was a sign. Stopping, she waited for Finn to do the same and when he turned to face her, she told him the truth.

'I've had enough, Finn, of all of it. Of you being an eejit, a stupid lazy scumbag who gets locked up every other week, the fool who pawned my locket and never got it back. And now you've come up with this hare-brained scheme with Tommy, who also thinks that a bank manager will lend two penniless immigrants a cent, never mind a dollar.' Maura was shouting so loud and didn't care who heard, and at least her words were getting through to Finn who looked affronted, down but never out.

'Why are you being like this? What's got into you? And he might, if you'd let me have the rest of the money in the envelope then I could show the manager I had something behind me, a deposit.'

Ah, now she got it, pointing as she spoke. 'That money is going nowhere, Finn McSherry, because you promised me before we left that we'd always have enough to get the boat home, and that's what I want to do. I want to go home. I miss my family and I'm tired of living on a hope and a prayer, and waiting for a call from the theatre or for you to get a fecking job that you keep for more than a week. I'm going back to Enniskillen and that's the end of it. With or without you.'

Finn looked like he'd been punched, kicked in the teeth. His mouth was moving but no words came out, and then they did. Taking her trembling hands in his, he pulled her closer. 'Please, Maura, it's Christmas. We should be merry, not brawlin' in the street.'

She rolled her eyes and pulled her hands away, angry now. 'You can stick Christmas up your arse, Finn, because it's the end. You've let me down too many times.'

She was about to turn and stomp home, pack her things and retrieve the envelope from its hiding place when she saw Finn put his hand in his pocket and pull out a small black box. She was sure his lip wobbled slightly, and his eyes were definitely teary, but it might have been from the beer and the biting wind but as he held out the gift, never had she heard his voice sound so true.

'Here, I got you this. I did overtime. It's to make up for your locket that I'm very sorry about.' He waited while she took the box. 'And I know I get it wrong all the time and I'm always fluthered, but I swear I'll mend me ways if you give me one more chance. That's all I ask. My life, my dreams, they all contain you, Maura, so if you go, it's all for nothing.'

She opened the lid and there, lying on a bed of dark blue silk, was a silver necklace and on it hung a tiny shamrock. The sight of it blurred within seconds so unable to speak she listened instead.

'I promise I'll make it right. I'll make us rich and then fly your mammy and dadaí and Niamh and your granny, even the bloody dog over, first class every Christmas, if it'll make you happy.'

'Don't be bloody stupid, Finn, this city's colder than home in winter. Granny would be dead in a week.'

'Well, she can come in the summer; they all can, and stay forever if you like. So please don't leave me. I love you so much.' Finn waited and as he did, a smile broke across his face and he pointed to the sky. 'Well can you hear that? St Pat's bells. It's Christmas Day. Now surely that's God and all his angels sending us a sign.'

Wiping away a tear, she listened to the chimes of St Patrick's and as she looked at the little shamrock, and then up, into the face of her man, Maura made the hardest decision of her life.

CHRISTMAS EVE, PRESENT DAY

The door of her bedroom burst open and in rushed seven-year-old Shona, the face of her youngest granddaughter flushed, clashing horribly with her fiery orange hair and the green of her Irish dancing dress.

'Granny, you have to hurry. Granda is waiting and he won't let us start the party till you come down.' She was about to pull Maura's hand when she spotted the necklace in the box.

'Oh, I love that. Here, let me help you fasten it then we can go.'

And before Maura could stop her, Shona had grabbed the delicate necklace and was placing it around her grandmother's neck. 'There, now come along, we're all waiting, and I want to show you my jig. I've been practising so hard. Will you sing 'Mountain Dew', like always?'

'Of course I will. Now slow down, before you have me on my bottom.' As they ascended the stairs, Maura held back the tears, quite overcome by the feel of the shamrock against her skin and the rush of memories that it had nudged from the back of her mind. Maybe it was loss, of her mammy, the first Christmas without her that was to blame but as she reached the hall, Maura touched the leaf, for luck and love, for family and happiness and all that life had given her.

As Shona burst into the lounge and joined the rest of her cousins, Maura heard the chords of the piano strike up the opening bars of 'Galway Bay'. As she stepped into the room that was dotted with photos, a framed first night poster of a Broadway show, with her in the starring role, and the many more that followed, her man came to greet her.

'And here she is at last, my darlin' girl.' Finn took her by the waist and as she smiled into his Irish eyes, still glinting with mischief, and ran a hand through hair that was no longer black as coal, Maura smiled and remembered a night long ago. As the bells rang out, and her man waited for an answer, she'd remembered some wise words, blown on an icy Atlantic wind, the wise voice of her mammy whispering in her ear.

Always remember this, that when there's two together, it shortens the road.

Which was why Maura had given Finn McSherry one more chance, to make it right and keep his promise. And he had.

***

Patricia Dixon was born, bred and still lives in Manchester and is an international best-selling author of fifteen novels. She writes contemporary literary fiction, and her stories are often set in her home city and the Loire, both places are close to her heart and from where she gathers inspiration for her characters and tales.

PART THREE
IT'S A CHRISTMAS MIRACLE

Coming Home

by Angela Marsons

I WATCH as she exits the train station at 10.13am. The sound of 'Last Christmas' by Wham! follows her out of the automatic door. She looks thinner this year. The light-coloured jeans pucker slightly below the back pockets. Her upper half is obscured by the zipped-up winter jacket, open only enough to accommodate the woollen scarf wrapped around her neck. Her hands are clad in fingerless gloves. Her hair is shorter and greyer than last year. She has had her Christmas cut early.

She swallows deeply as the full force of London assaults her senses. The traffic speeding past, the voices, the chatter, the lights, the shoppers, the urgency.

For a moment she is overwhelmed. I know that slight furrowing of the brow. She wants to retreat back into the safety of the station. She wants to buy a magazine and hide until it's time for her return journey of two trains and a bus ride to the small Worcestershire market town where she lives.

I still keep track of the dates. Yesterday would have been the Christmas tree light switch-on in the square. The whole town would have turned out for it, whatever the weather. They would have perused the brightly lit windows awash with tinsel, baubles and fairy lights. They would have made small purchases to thank the independent shops for staying open late this one night a year. They would have listened to the brass band and inhaled the aroma of spicy mulled wine and roasted chestnuts while passing the time of day with friends and neighbours. There would have been a collective whoop of joy from both children and adults when the tree burst into multicoloured light.

She would have sung Christmas carols all the way home.

And now she is in the city. People are jostling past her, eager to reach their destination. She is bewildered by it all. She wants to leave. But she won't. It's her annual pilgrimage. My birthday.

She takes out her tourist map and begins walking. I follow.

She reaches into her bag and takes out a photo so that it's ready in her hand.

She skirts around Hyde Park Estate to reach Bayswater Road, the main carriageway running along the northern edge of Hyde Park. She takes a different route every time. Last year, she walked Edgware Road right up to Marble Arch; in and out of restaurants and cafés, grocery shops, newsagents.

She lands at the edge of Hyde Park. There is a street vendor selling his artwork. His fold-out seat is placed beside canvasses awash with colours and shapes, all leaning against the wall.

She takes out the photo and shows it to the man sitting on the seat with a money bag around his waist and a Santa hat on his head. His name is Larry and he knows me. He is seventy-three years of age and refuses to hand over the stall to his son, and he doesn't work on a Tuesday. Larry has shared a ham-and-cheese sandwich with me. Larry will tell her where I am.

The man stands, looks at the photo, shakes his head and returns to his seat.

She takes a shortcut through Hyde Park. Winter

Wonderland is just opening and customers are heading in to enjoy the stalls, fair rides and lights. She approaches one vendor after another. Each one greets her with an open smile, ready to make a sale. The photo is given a fleeting glance before being handed back. She isn't fazed by the lack of interest. She is showing a photograph that can date back no later than my seventeenth birthday. Some part of her expects no response, no recognition, but she is compelled to do it anyway. Is she showing the image of me with light brown hair that almost reached my shoulders or the one she took two days before I left where I'd adopted a shorter style? I could tell in her expression that she hated it and in truth so did I the moment the hair fell to the grey linoleum floor. But it was a statement, a declaration that I could do whatever I wanted. That I was an adult. When I told her what I was going to do she said I'd regret it. She tried to stop me but I was stubborn and pig-headed. My reflection no longer represented me. I no longer felt like myself.

She continues her journey through the Wonderland but takes no pleasure in the beauty and cheer. She is oblivious to the shrieks of joy, the laughter, the excitement and happiness of the people around her absorbing the Christmas spirit.

She leaves the park and turns left, heading towards Marble Arch. She crosses to Oxford Street and takes a seat at a small coffee shop. A waitress appears and she gives her order. It will be a latte and a toasted teacake. While waiting she doesn't take out a phone to check for messages or missed calls. She doesn't ring or text anyone. She simply watches everyone passing her by. She searches their faces, looking for me. Is she trying to remove the passage of time from the people walking past her? Is she trying to erase the effects of our twelve years apart?

She smiles and thanks the waitress who delivers her order. She opens the mini rectangle of butter and spreads it onto one half of the teacake. She already knows that is as much as she will eat.

Her gaze rests on a mother leaning down into the front of a pushchair. Her child's hands have worked free from the woollen mittens. The woman reinserts them and then kisses the bundled form as though it's an opportunity not to be missed. And then she and the baby are gone.

I watch as she finishes the half teacake and takes a sip of her latte. I wonder if she regrets giving me the benefit of her honesty. Does she wish she'd never told me that at three years my senior Gary was a bad influence on me, that I had changed when we had met? Did she regret screaming at me when I dropped out of college? Did she regret not begging me to stay when I told her that Gary and I were leaving for the bright lights of London? I hope she doesn't berate herself for that. It wouldn't have made any difference. Nothing would have stopped me from getting on that train.

She had already thrown everything at me. She had given it her best shot. When he'd been caught shoplifting she had forbidden me from seeing him. It hadn't worked. When he'd turned up at two in the morning as high as a kite demanding to be fed she had called the police. It hadn't stopped me from waiting outside the police station until he was released.

It was after that episode that Gary had said we needed a fresh start, somewhere new, somewhere exciting, somewhere with life and opportunities. We talked about getting jobs and a flat, going to clubs and restaurants, meeting interesting people. What started as a wistful conversation became a plan over the course of three whole days.

She exploded when I told her what we were doing. She screamed that Gary was a user and a thug. That he cared for no one but himself and that he was already on a bad road with stealing and drugs. My angst-ridden teenage brain could not correlate a bit of shoplifting and the occasional spliff with the picture she was trying to paint. Gary was vibrant, exciting, rebellious, dangerous and intoxicating.

She warned me that he would guide me the same way, that I would follow his lead and start using soft drugs, then harder drugs and that the picture he'd painted of a utopian life in the city was not realistic and showed his immaturity.

I had laughed in her face. She knew nothing of our plans and she was wrong on all counts.

'You'll come to your senses and you'll be back,' were the last words I heard her say as I headed out the door, and her prophecy had been half true.

I watch as she stands and takes a right onto Regent Street, heading towards her final destination.

She walks beneath The Spirit of Christmas light display. Angels straddle the road from high in the air, resplendent in their sparkling finery of cool white lights. The light of the day is fading prematurely, being consumed by the greyness that will linger until dark. The window displays appear more vivid. She doesn't notice as she passes Burberry, Hugo Boss or any of the high-end stores. Even Hamleys toy store with its projected snowflake display and luxurious red wreaths fails to capture her attention. She is focused on reaching just one place.

Eventually her feet stop moving exactly where I thought they would.

How she knows that this is the very phone box from where I called six years ago I'll never understand but somehow she does.

Does she expect to see me there?

Does she know what I wanted to say when I made that silent call?

Could she sense that I wanted to tell her she was right all along?

As I stood in the phone box with tears streaming over my cheeks, I ached to tell her that the flat Gary had spoken of had been a room in a house for one week. Then it had been a squat for months and then shop doorways. The jobs had been too lowly or too demeaning for us to take. And there were easier ways of making money. She had been right that Gary was a user and abuser and that he cared for no one but himself. She had been right about everything. Even the drugs.

At my lowest point, on my twenty-third birthday, I rang her. I wanted to tell her everything; that Gary was long gone, that I'd been living on the streets for years, that I hadn't closed my eyes at night without fear in my stomach for as long as I could remember. I wanted to go home. I wanted her to come and get me and take me back to the sleepy Worcestershire town with its single street of fairy lights. I wanted to confess every bad thing I'd done and beg for her forgiveness. She would accept me without judgement the way she always had.

But the second I heard her voice I couldn't do it. The words would not leave my mouth. I couldn't put those pictures in her head. I couldn't tell her what I'd become or what I'd done to survive.

Instead, I replaced the receiver and promised myself that I would find the courage to return under my own steam. That I would earn the money I'd need to get me home. Just one more hit and I'd leave this life behind.

And now she stands beside the place where I made that fateful decision.

Just one more hit.

I never spoke to her again.

She takes the photo from her pocket and shows it to anyone that stops to listen. Every approach is met with a shake of the head and in some cases a sympathetic touch.

Eventually she checks her watch. It is time to leave. She has timed the walk from Paddington Station and has left enough time to walk back to board her train home.

My heart grows heavier as she retraces her steps back towards Paddington. I consider another year of waiting for her to return. Twelve more months that she is paralysed by my absence. Another year that she fights to hold on to that shred of hope. I can't do that to her. It ends today. I have to make her understand that I can't leave. She cannot take me home.

This time I'm going to talk to her.

I call her. Every bit of energy I have goes into that one cry.

Mum.

She turns and looks right at me.

Mum, you have to let me go. Live your life. Move on.

She frowns, puzzled.

I can't leave because you keep coming back. You have to live your life.

Tears begin to form in her eyes. She hears me. I know she hears me and my heart is breaking for her loss.

'Jason.'

My name is a whisper on her lips. She feels me. She senses my presence.

Please, Mum, remember all the good times, the bond we shared. Keep that in your heart and know that I love you and that I'm sorry.

The tears are rolling over her cheeks. She cares nothing for the curious glances of onlookers.

She knows.

The tears slow as the acceptance grows in her eyes. She takes the photo from her pocket, looks at it and places it back in her bag.

She places her palm against her lips, kisses it and blows the kiss into the air.

Goodbye.

After a final look around she turns and heads into the station.

She can finally let me go.

She is no longer tied to this place. She can leave and be at peace.

And now I can too.

**

Angela Marsons is the Wall Street Journal and USA Today bestselling author of the DI Kim Stone series. She lives in Worcestershire with her partner and their two cheeky Golden Retrievers. After years of writing relationship-based stories Angela turned to crime, fictionally speaking, of course, and developed a character that refused to go away. Her books have been translated into more than 27 languages.

SANTA AND THE
HITMEN

BY DIANE SAXON

AT THE LOUD bustle of noise bursting through the green curtain, Dr Fiona Roberts' lifted her head from her study of the computer screen. She pushed half-moon glasses onto the top of her head to pin back long, silver-streaked hair.

'Right, who do we have here?'

'Santa Claus.'

She raised eyebrows speckled with grey and her lips parted in a weary 'oh!'

Her gaze took in the paramedic crew and their enormous, red-suited patient spilling over the sides of the gurney. Face up, his arms flopped either side, fingers almost grazing the floor.

She exchanged a look with Finlay, her head nurse. 'Funny, very funny.'

'Did I ever tell you I bloody love working Christmas?' Finlay snapped out a grin Fiona was well accustomed to. It wasn't a reflection of amusement, but annoyance.

He didn't want to be there tending to drunk Santas, elves and fairies. He wanted to be at home with his kids.

Fiona well remembered the years she'd worked when her

children were young. Babies, toddlers, infants, teenagers. Those days were gone. A faded memory. And she was more than happy to work over Christmas to give someone else with children time off.

All four of hers were grown with their own partners, their own homes. Not yet their own children but it wouldn't be long for Samantha and Lillian. How the years had flown. She'd stopped looking at the soft wrinkles radiating from her mouth, the lines that were no longer fine, feathering from once-bright sparkling green eyes.

For Fiona, this was her first year alone since Martin had left her back in February declaring he'd only stayed until the last of their children were settled. The cruelty still crippled her, bringing her to her knees every now and then. At a time of life when she was preparing for retirement, he'd gone. In her naivete, she'd never suspected for a moment that he didn't love her enough to stay.

Now she worked more than full time to get away from the complete loneliness of her empty house. She'd rather see happy faces around a gurney than the miserable ones of her children around the Christmas table. There through guilt and obligation.

In their thirty-nine years of marriage, Fiona had believed Martin had been truly faithful to her. There'd never been any indication otherwise. For the last seven years they'd visited the same resort in Portugal just to satisfy his love of golf.

She'd tolerated it. Knowing that when William, their youngest, left home, they would have more freedom. They would perhaps do more with their lives. Her husband would be ready to retire at the age of sixty-five. She was considerably younger than him, she'd throw in the towel too, happy they could go off around the world if they wanted to. Once their children were settled.

He'd cheated her of that.

Brought back to the present, Fiona stared at the man on the gurney. Thick sooty lashes reaching for his cheekbones.

'What happened?'

'Don't know really.' Trudi, short, rotund and eternally happy, grinned up at Fiona. 'His sleigh's parked in the ambulance bay, reindeer and all. Would you believe it? Santa here toppled off just as we pulled up behind, so we whipped him in here sharpish. Haven't had chance to check him over yet.'

From the healthy glow of the man's skin under his thick white curly beard, Fiona guessed he'd not had a heart attack. 'Too many sherries?'

Finlay tugged to remove the beard. Santa's skin stretched as the beard clung on and then pinged back. 'Uh, I think it's attached.'

'Bloody hell, he's the real deal.' Fiona's face stretched a wide and unfamiliar smile. She realised she hadn't done that in a long, long time.

Trudi snorted and then listened to her radio as it crackled to life. 'Gotta go. Are you okay if we leave this one to you? Apparently, Santa's little helper is stuck halfway up a chimney in an old manor house in Shrewsbury.'

Without taking her attention from her patient, Fiona smiled and waved them away. 'Off you go.'

As a shout sounded from the next cubicle, Finlay also disappeared, leaving Fiona alone with Santa behind the curtains.

She plugged her stethoscope, with a twirl of tinsel around it, into her ears and worked her fingers through each of the buttons on his heavy padded jacket. With a sweep of her hands, she pushed it wide.

Her mouth dropped open.

Instead of the portly barrel-chested grandfather figure Fiona expected, she'd exposed a deeply tanned ripped chest that rose and fell in steady rhythm to indicate a strong stable heartbeat. Which was more than could be said for hers.

She dipped her head to get a better look at the four, neat, circular red marks spattered in the region of his heart. She brushed her fingertips over them, tracing the shape of them.

She pressed the stethoscope to his chest and as the icy metal touched his skin, he took in a long deep breath, his chest filling like bellows.

Fiona dashed a look at him.

Eyes the colour of a summer sky popped open to clash with hers.

She bolted upright, her spine crackling in protest.

He reached out a white-gloved hand as she opened her mouth to cry out for help from security who were always close to hand, but Santa merely lifted a finger to his lips.

'Shhh.'

As he raised his arm, his jacket shrugged back into place spilling four grey metallic bullets from between the padded material onto his chest.

He smiled, his eyes twinkling. 'Kevlar.'

His scrutiny moved past her and before she could react, he whipped out a hand, encircling her wrist with his fingers. He yanked her over the top of him and off the other side of the gurney.

Winded, she raised her head from where he'd dropped her onto the floor and came face to face with a man in a smart tailored black suit who had just hit the ground on the other side of the gurney where she'd been stood a moment earlier.

Blood pooled over the tiled floor, pumping rhythmically from the wound inflicted by the scalpel sticking out from his jugular.

Vacant hazel eyes stared back at her as his hand loosened its grip on a large gun that was without a doubt real and, if she was right, that long bit on the end was a silencer.

An enormous pair of black boots slapped down next to her. The incongruity of the white fur lining the top hit her just as Santa jerked her to her feet.

'Out,' he growled in her ear.

With an unceremonious shove, he pushed her through the side curtain which led directly through to a long, deserted corridor. At this time of night on Christmas Eve, most of the patients on the wards would be settled. A peacefulness had stolen over the hospital.

Except, that is, for Fiona and Santa racing headlong towards the exit, the slap of their feet echoing off the walls.

At the sharp popping sound from behind, Fiona glanced over her shoulder but could see nothing other than Santa, his loose jacket flapping wildly as he propelled her along.

With a jerk, he slammed his hand against the double doors that opened into the stairwell.

'Down!'

Her knees melted and she dropped to the floor as the man charging up the stairs towards them raised a gun, similar to the one she'd already seen, and aimed point-blank at her.

'Pfft, pfft.' Gunshots gave half-hearted pings as though someone had muffled them with a pillow.

The man dropped to his knees and then slithered backwards down four steps to the halfway landing, blood oozing from two tiny dots in his forehead.

Fiona turned and stared at the blood-stained gun Santa held. The one she'd seen just moments before in the hand of the dead man in the cubicle.

Santa gave one shake of his head, the white fur ball on his hat dodging from side to side. 'Go.'

His deep commanding voice brooked no argument.

Fiona sped down the stairwell, ignoring the exits onto each landing, heading instead for the main exit leading out into the car park.

Icy air snatched the breath from her as they raced outside, the exit door banging hard behind them.

As Fiona paused for a peek back at the safety of the building, Santa took hold of her arm and drove her forward.

Ever grateful for her sensible black leather shoes in the deep snow, Fiona nevertheless wished she'd had a moment to grab a coat. Something more than just the overlarge, thin, green cotton scrubs that flapped around her limbs letting in more cold air than keeping it out.

Breathless, she huffed out, 'Stop. I can't...'

The exit door flung open, the sound of a gunshot echoed in the quiet of the night.

Santa's body gave a sharp convulsion before he wrapped a thick arm around her. He hugged her tight, her face pressed into the warm skin of his chest. His body juddered again.

'Pfft, pfft.'

The familiar sound of muted gunshot had her peering past Santa as another dark-suited man hit the ground, the spray of blood sparkling like rubies in the snow.

Fiona slapped her hand to her mouth to stop from crying out, but before she could draw more than a breath, Santa had whirled her around and was powering her along the path that led around the side of the hospital and back to the ambulance bay.

Bright lights beckoned them.

His breath came in stilted snatches with an underlying Scottish burr. 'I need to get to my sleigh.'

With a sharp appraisal, she took in his stiffened gait.

'Have you been shot?'

He gave her a slow blink as he placed a hand in the small of her back to encourage her forward. 'Let's go before more arrive.'

She came to a full stop and turned to face him as he tugged his jacket around his naked chest and buttoned it up one-handed while he held onto the gun with the other hand.

'You can let me go. I won't tell anyone what happened.'

In the face of his quiet contemplation, a small sob caught in her throat and she stared back towards the beckoning lights of the building. 'Please let me go.'

His beard moved like a living thing as he rolled his lips together. 'I don't think you want me to. You'll be safer with me.'

Shocked, Fiona took a quick step back before he grabbed her.

'Safer from who?'

He glanced sideways and nodded. 'Them, for starters.'

She turned her head to watch the three suited men lumbering towards them, their shiny shoes slipping in the snow. One stopped and raised an arm. A gun glinted in the moonlight. Fiona spun, darting off in the opposite direction with Santa's breath hot on the back of her neck.

She rounded the corner of the building and skidded to a halt.

Two more hitmen leaned against the sleigh, backs to them watching the entrance to A&E.

Santa charged past Fiona, grabbed one man in each meaty fist and smacked their heads together.

As they hit the floor, Santa turned and hauled Fiona up,

launching her bodily into the sleigh.

Her left cheek smooshed into the red leather seat, but she managed to turn her head. 'Please, God, tell me they don't fly.'

Santa snorted. 'I'm not God, and they don't fly. They're reindeer. They don't have wings. That would defy all the laws of nature.'

Fiona pushed herself upright, squished against the side of the seat as Santa settled his bulk beside her. 'I'm pretty convinced we've just defied the laws of nature by not getting shot.'

A sharp ping of a bullet slapped into the sleigh and Fiona ducked below the smooth flowing sides, her cheek once again pressed down.

'Yah.'

The slap of leather cracked in the quiet, pre-empting the surge of the reindeers as they dashed forward, knocking Fiona back in the seat.

She pressed a hand to her chest as the burn from their manic dash subsided.

She counted the reindeer.

Eight. There were only eight.

Dasher and Dancer, Prancer and Vixen, Comet and Cupid and Donner and Blitzen.

'Where's Rudolph?'

Santa leaned down and tugged a huge fur throw from the shelf in front of them. 'Rudolph's not real, you know. Just a fantasy.'

Santa turned and wrapped the throw around her one-handed as he held the reigns loose in the other hand.

Tension seeped from her body, her teeth stopped chattering as she buried her face in the soft warmth of the throw. Her murmured words slurred, 'I thought they were all a fantasy.'

Her breathing slowed.

Fiona let her eyes slip shut, the smooth slide of the sleigh through the deep snow a soothing rhythm. Comfortable, she leaned against the warm bulk of the man, tucking her feet underneath her.

Her eyes fluttered open.

Bright white gates glided wide and they rode through, the sound of the hooves and sleigh muffled by deep crisp snow.

They pulled up in front of a mansion with clean lines and panoramic windows.

In the silence, Santa dismounted, holding his arms out to help Fiona down.

Stunned by the sheer beauty, Fiona followed silently through a wide hallway. Their footsteps tapped against the gleaming ebony marble floor. The hall widened into a vast room with plush white leather sofas, glass side tables and elegant white marble statues. Ivory candles threw flickering light out to dance across the walls.

Entranced, Fiona left Santa behind as she approached the bank of floor-to-ceiling windows and stared out onto the vista below.

Ribbons of apricot and lavender streaked the clear dawn sky keeping the promise of a white Christmas.

Soft billows of pink-tinted clouds floated below her feet like pleats of cotton wool, parting occasionally to tease her with a peek of distant mountaintops.

She let out a breath she hadn't realised she'd been holding and turned.

With a hesitant smile, Fiona raised her hand and cupped the grey bearded cheek of the man before her.

Eyes the colour of a summer sky gazed down at her. A smile

curved his lips.

'Oh, Martin.' She wrapped her arms around her husband's waist and pressed her cheek to his chest knowing she'd come home. 'I missed you so much.'

'Time of death 06:53am, 25th December 2023.'

Dr Chris Simon blinked at the woman on the gurney. His colleague, his friend.

His voice held a husky whisper. 'She never stood a chance.' He still grasped the paddles, but the buzz of the defibrillator had been silenced. 'Her heart simply gave up.'

He gave a hard swallow. 'Who would have thought she'd go just like that? Right in the middle of her final shift.' He peered around at the rest of the medics, nurses, junior doctors. Friends of the woman they'd known and worked with for years.

He pressed his lips inwards to stop the sob escaping.

'She died doing what she loved the most.' Finlay swiped the tears from his cheeks as he stepped back to open the window and let Dr Fiona Roberts' soul fly free.

***

Diane Saxon lives in the Shropshire countryside with her tall, dark, handsome husband. She has two gorgeous daughters, a Dalmatian, two cats, numerous rare breed chickens, and a black Labrador called Beau—a name borrowed by her hero in For Heaven's Cakes. After working for years in a demanding job, Diane gave it up when her husband said, 'Follow that dream.' She subsequently had 12 Romances published for the U.S. market then turned to the dark side with her psychological thrillers.

Seventeen Minutes

by Emma Tallon

'KATE, Kate, quick! Get in the picture!'

Kate turned at the sound of her name and excused herself from the conversation she was having with another colleague, jumping into the frame just as the photographer took his shot. The flash went off and then he melted away with a smile, off to capture the merriment and fun throughout the rest of the grand hall they were holding the company Christmas party in.

'He's no fun, that one,' said the petite pretty woman who'd called her over.

'Who?' Kate asked, pushing her long thick auburn hair back over her shoulder and looking around the room.

'The photographer. He's single, I checked, yet not once has he actually glanced down at my perfectly bronzed bosom tonight, no matter how many times I put them in his direct line of sight,' she complained.

Kate laughed. 'Oh, Jen. You really are terrible.'

'How is that terrible?' Jen asked, her arched brows knitting together in a frown of confusion. 'There's something wrong with the guy,' she decided firmly.

'Maybe he does appreciate them, but instead of ogling, he decided to show you some measure of respect by looking at your face?' Kate offered. She was sure that most of the men in the room appreciated Jen's appearance this evening, single or not.

Jen considered this for a moment and then sighed. 'Well, that's all very well and good, but to be honest it wasn't respect I was looking for. What I *really* need is some downright fil– Richard!' Her tone changed abruptly as a tall man in his mid-fifties walked over to them. 'Such a lovely party. I was just telling Kate here how much I admire this venue. Such incredible artwork on the walls. It lends a real elegance.'

Kate kept her expression neutral with difficulty.

'I completely agree,' Richard replied with a good-natured smile. 'Though I cannot claim credit. It was Kate who suggested it.'

Kate smiled at her boss. 'How did everything go with Weisner? Has a date been set for trial?'

Richard was the CEO of the law firm they all worked for. Kate had joined years before, fresh out of university, and was now a senior criminal defence lawyer. Jen worked for her as a paralegal and outside of the office had become one of her closest friends in the nine months since she'd joined.

'Not yet. They won't look at it until January now,' Richard replied.

'What? Why?' Kate demanded, frowning.

'Because it's Christmas, Kate,' he replied with an amused grin. 'The office is closed. Everyone's breaking for the holidays.'

'Well, crime doesn't break for the holidays,' Kate replied with an irritated tut. 'Honestly, you'd think they'd keep at least one person in to deal with the things that need pushing through.'

'All right Ebenezer!' Jen replied with a laugh.

The music that had been playing pleasantly in the background came to a stop and the event coordinator took to the stage. 'Please could you all move towards the dining hall, where dinner will be served.'

'Oh, thank God,' Jen said with feeling. 'I'm *starving*.'

'You had a huge lunch; how can you possibly be starving?' Kate asked, following her through the grand hall towards the dining room.

'Kate, that was *hours* ago,' Jen said indignantly.

'Of course,' Kate replied with a wry smile. 'How silly of me.'

They found their places and soon a flurry of black-and-white-clad waiters filled the room, fine china plates carefully balanced on their arms. In one synchronised movement, which reminded Kate of a flock of birds turning in the wind, they all laid down their wares before disappearing to collect more.

'Oooh, what's that?' Jen asked, peering over towards her plate.

'Duck,' Kate answered. 'I don't eat turkey.'

'Really? You've got to have turkey at Christmas.' She grinned.

Kate sighed internally. She hated explaining this, but every year there was always someone she had to argue it with. 'I don't do Christmas,' she said with a curt smile. She picked up her wine glass and took a sip, casting her gaze around the room.

'What?' Jen asked in disbelief. 'What do you mean? Who doesn't do Christmas?'

'Me,' Kate answered.

'Why?' Jen asked.

'I just don't see the point,' she replied dismissively. 'I don't have any family and it's a family thing, so it's just a pointless holiday for me.' She shrugged. 'I'd rather be working on my cases and filling my time with something meaningful, not eating foods I wouldn't usually eat, or wasting money on tacky household garnishes that have to then be taken down two weeks later. There are criminals causing havoc every day out there, and *they* don't stop because it's Christmas, so why should I have to?'

She stole a glance at Jen and saw the look she'd already guessed was there. The one filled with sad horrified pity.

'Family aren't always the people you're related to, you know,' Jen said. 'People come together with warmth and cheer and fun...' she trailed off.

'It's just not my thing,' Kate said in a matter-of-fact tone.

The final plates were set down and she picked up her knife and fork, cutting into her duck breast and popping some into her mouth, savouring the flavour of the perfectly cooked meat.

'So what do you do on Christmas Day?' Jen asked.

Kate swallowed, disappointed that the conversation was not over yet. 'Nothing different to any other day. I get up, get dressed, work on my files... I get annoyed because all the offices I need to contact are closed...' She laughed and was relieved to see Jen smirk at this too. 'Then I read a book, have a glass of wine and go to bed.'

'Okay, well this Christmas you're not doing that,' Jen said assertively. 'This Christmas you're coming to–'

'No, Jen, I'm not,' Kate replied firmly. 'I don't want to be rude, but I'm just not up for it. It's not that I have nowhere to go. Richard has been trying to get me over for years. I just don't want to.' She pulled an apologetic grimace. 'Please don't be offended?'

Jen shook her head. 'I'm not offended, but I am sad. You're my best friend. And I can't bear the thought of you sitting there alone with no cheer at Christmas.'

'You're my best friend, too,' Kate replied, putting one arm around her and pulling her into a side squeeze. 'But really, I'm fine.' She plastered on a grin and picked up her wine. 'Let's cheers to a great month so far and continued success in the new year, yes?'

She raised her glass and Jen resignedly clinked hers against it. 'To continued success,' she agreed.

Stopping the taxi a few streets early, Kate decided to walk the rest of the way home. It had been a great night. The food had been fantastic, the venue a dream and the DJ had kept the atmosphere lively and fun. Everyone had danced and laughed and enjoyed themselves, Richard was happy and Jen had finally managed to get the photographer to go home with her. All was well.

So why was she feeling so restless? She knew why, really. This time of year was always hard. It brought back memories that usually stayed hidden, deep in the darkest depths of her soul. Memories that warmed and hurt her in equal measure.

She came to Muswell Hill high street and headed towards the warm light of the small local shop that always stayed open late. A selection of fruit and vegetables adorned the front and she slowed to have a look.

'Ah, my favourite customer,' came a deep voice from within. 'What will it be tonight?'

She twisted her mouth as she scanned the options. 'I think half a watermelon, six plums and some of your wife's baclava if there's any left,' she replied.

'There is,' he replied, pleased. 'I shall get it for you now.'

Kate waited patiently while he wrapped her purchases, her mind already back on the case she'd been working on before the party, then paid and carried on towards her flat.

She was defending a man who was on trial for his wife's murder, a high-profile case that was driving her crazy. He was innocent, she was sure of it, but she had yet to prove it. He claimed he was the other side of town when it happened and that he got back after the neighbour found her. But without evidence to support it, he was the main suspect. They'd argued that morning and she'd been having an affair. The murder weapon, a knife from their own kitchen, had been wiped clean and there was no sign of forced entry. But still, Kate believed him. And there had to be something in all the discovery boxes her team had put together to prove that. She just had to find it.

Picking up the pace she soon neared her building and, as she did, noticed a homeless man huddled in the mouth of the alley just before it. He'd been there that morning, she remembered, had wished her a good day. As she saw him shiver, she felt sympathy spear her heart.

Slowing, she reached into the blue plastic bag in her hand and pulled out the wrapped up baclava. Something sugary might help him get through the bitter night.

'Excuse me?' she asked tentatively. 'Here.' She handed it over as he looked up at her. 'This is for you.'

He took the package and smiled. 'Thank you for your kindness. It says so much about you.'

'It's nothing,' she said, embarrassed that he was thanking her for something so little when she had so much. 'Stay safe.'

She pulled her coat around her tighter against the cold and hurried into her building, resolving to bring him down a warmer blanket the next day.

Once she was inside and had changed into pyjamas, poured herself a glass of wine and turned on Sade in the background, she set about opening the discovery boxes for her case. Sitting down in the middle of her lounge, she pulled out the contents of the first and laid them in a circle around her on the floor.

The wife, Cassie, had been a piece of work, from what she could see. Pages of texts between her and her lover – his best friend from school, no less – showed her nasty streak in all its brightest colours. Cassie openly mocked Michael – her husband, and Kate's client – bragging about spending his money on their affair and complaining about everything and anything. Part of Kate wouldn't have blamed Michael if he *had* done it. But he'd been so genuinely devastated at her murder and shocked about the affair, that she was sure he was innocent. After years in this game, she'd become quite good at spotting the liars.

A low buzz came from her trouser pocket and she pulled out her phone.

'Hey.' She answered it and leaned back against the sofa, picking up her glass of wine. 'What's up?'

'Nothing much, just walking back from the photographer's place and thought I'd give you a call. I have questions,' Jen replied.

'Do you not even know his name?' Kate asked, amused.

'Now you're just being picky,' Jen replied dismissively. 'So, my first question is, what about New Year? Surely that can't be on your hit list too?'

'No, New Year I actually like,' Kate replied. 'I don't go out anymore, but I do celebrate.'

'How?' Jen asked, her tone suspicious.

'I buy all my favourite foods and I take a deckchair up to the roof of my building and I think about my year and make resolutions for the next one. And then I watch the fireworks.'

'I didn't know your place had a roof garden,' Jen remarked.

'It doesn't,' Kate replied. 'It's just got maintenance access, but I have a key.'

'Kate Gregory, you little rebel you,' Jen replied. 'Well, I'm glad you aren't a total holiday loss. Though I'm already guessing the answer to my second question will be a no.'

'Is your second question more of an invite?' Kate asked.

'It is.'

'Then you guessed correctly.'

She heard Jen sigh loudly down the line. 'Fine. I've just reached the tube. I'll catch you tomorrow.'

'Get home safe.'

She ended the call and took a deep drink from her glass. It didn't matter what Jen had in mind; she would never agree to go. She wouldn't ruin someone else's New Years Eve by being there. Christmas was always so hard and by the time New Year's came she was a depressed mess. It was why she chose to stay alone. That night was about one thing for her – getting back to a positive state of mind and leaving another dreaded Christmas behind her.

The memories she usually kept locked up and buried deep where they couldn't bother her crept forward and for once she let them. A picture of herself as a young child flashed through her mind, dressed all in pink. She was dancing. Her mother was singing and her father was clapping along. She let herself relive it for a moment, remembering that feeling of pure joy and innocence as she danced before the Christmas tree.

But as always, her adult mind eventually moved towards the rest of the room. Towards the things she hadn't noticed or understood as a child. Everywhere was a mess, the carpet filthy. Piles of dirty clothes sat on one end of a stained sofa, its cushions long gone. Plates crusted with days-old remnants of food were piled up on the fireplace next to mugs that housed fluffy green and white mould. And her father's shaking hand as he poured yet another glass of cheap vodka for both him and her mother.

When social services had taken her, she'd thought it would be temporary, that her parents would sort out the mistake and take her home. She'd cried and waited and tried to be strong, but eventually learned they'd signed her away. It had meant more to them to live the way they did, than to change to have her back. She'd been seven.

She wiped a tear that escaped and rolled down her face. The following years had been a jumble of foster homes. Each Christmas that came had been worse than the last. Not that they hadn't tried. Most of the homes had been okay. They'd fed her the turkey and given her a gift. But she had lacked the one thing she wanted most in the world. A family. A real family. People who loved her, who delighted in watching her smile. She'd sat quietly on the sidelines, an observer, whilst the real children of the family smiled in glee and the parents delighted, their eyes adoringly glued to their offspring. It was there she realised it was better not to have Christmas at all, than to be an outsider at someone else's.

When she'd aged out of the system, unclaimed and unloved, she'd vowed never again to put herself in that position. Christmas was not for everyone.

The following day Kate focused all her energy on the case, determined to find something that would prove Michael's innocence. Determined, also, not to spiral down through her memories again, the way she had the night before. That had been a slip of self-control, and she didn't intend to allow to happen again today. It was Christmas Eve, but as far as she was concerned it was just another day. One she was going to put to good use.

Matthew had left the restaurant, where he'd been having dinner with a friend, at 8.22pm and had gone straight home without stopping. The CCTV outside the restaurant showed that his car left the car park at 8.27. Route planners showed that his journey home would have taken approximately thirty-three minutes from the restaurant, which placed his arrival home at around nine.

At 8.41 his wife, Cassie, had ended a video call with her sister. A helpful timestamp. Then the neighbour took his bins out and noticed her body lying half out of the back gate at around ten past nine, when he called the police. Matthew pulled up at seventeen minutes past, which was logged on that call.

Matthew couldn't account for the extra seventeen minutes he'd taken over the journey, claiming he'd not stopped. And so the argument they were facing was that he could have come home through the back, killed her, then put up the pretence of arriving after she was found. There was no actual evidence, but neither was there an alibi. And seventeen missing minutes with no explanation was not working in his favour.

Kate sighed and rubbed her temples. She needed a walk to clear her head. Making her way down the hall she reached for her warm navy parka and cream woollen hat. It looked cold outside. This reminded her suddenly of the man in the alleyway and she nipped back to the airing cupboard, lifting the neatly folded pile of towels and bedding to reveal a large soft blanket at the bottom. It was old but thick and had been banished to the bottom of the cupboard for cold emergencies. This seemed like the perfect opportunity to put it to use.

She rode the lift down to the ground floor and walked out into the frosty air, making a beeline for the alley.

The old man was sat in the same spot he'd been in the night before, huddled under one thin blanket with his legs wrapped up in another. His hat looked as old as his wrinkled skin and the fingerless gloves on his hands had seen better days. Kate wondered what had happened to this man, to see him here, alone in an alleyway at this point in his life. Where were his family? Why was no one looking after him?

'Hello,' she said, announcing her approach. 'Can I join you?'

He looked up at her and she noted with surprise how clear and bright his blue eyes were, how they sparkled.

'Please do,' he said politely, gesturing towards an upturned crate opposite him. 'Though I'm not sure why you'd want to,' he added with a chuckle.

Kate smiled and took the seat, offering him the blanket. 'I thought you could use this,' she said.

'Thank you. Not that this old body needs much anymore. But the kindness does wonders for my soul.'

'Can I get you anything to eat? You must be hungry. I was just going to get something for myself,' she offered.

He shook his head. 'No. Like I said, this body doesn't need much.'

He searched her face and for a moment she felt oddly as though he was looking right into her head, reading her every thought. She fought the urge to look away.

'What brings a lovely young woman like you out here on your own on Christmas Eve?' he asked.

Another question she'd rather avoid and couldn't. 'I don't care much for Christmas Eve,' she replied.

'That's a shame,' he said. 'Do your family not do anything on Christmas Eve?'

She considered lying, for ease, then decided against it. 'I don't have any family.'

'Everyone has family,' he replied immediately.

'Not me,' she continued with a false brightness. 'I was in the system until I aged out and haven't met anyone worth settling down with. But that's not a bad thing. I'm married to my work, so there's really no space for anyone else.' She laughed to lighten her words.

'Family doesn't always mean those related to you,' he replied.

'What about you?' she asked, changing the subject. 'Do you not have anyone to spend Christmas Eve with?'

'I always used to spend Christmas Eve with my wife, preparing a huge feast for all our family,' he said warmly, his eyes crinkling at the sides as he smiled. 'It would take all day and many ovens,' he recalled. 'She would make her special cranberry meatballs in onion gravy. Oh, those meatballs...' He closed his eyes and shook his head, his smile growing wider. 'I can still taste them now. Gosh, I miss those. They were always a favourite with all the children in the family.'

Kate smiled at the picture he painted, despite herself. 'Did you always have a lot of people over at Christmas?'

'Oh, so many. And it was always wonderful. There's something so special about Christmas dinner. Filling stomachs and hearts simultaneously.'

Kate felt the wistful pull in her own stomach and looked away once more, wishing she hadn't asked. 'Do you have somewhere to go tomorrow?'

'I do,' he confirmed. 'And I'm greatly looking forward to it. My days of making Christmas dinner may be over, but I can still enjoy it.'

'Good.' She stood up. 'Are you sure I can't get you anything?'

He shook his head. 'I have everything I need right here,' he said in a confident tone.

Kate exhaled, wishing he would let her do more. 'Okay, well, have a lovely time tomorrow.'

'And you,' he replied.

With one last smile, Kate dug her hands deep into her coat pockets to warm them and set off in the direction of the high street. Luckily not everyone celebrated Christmas and she knew from experience a few of the shops and takeaways stayed open on Christmas Eve. She would treat herself to something naughty, something that was not diet-friendly, for once.

And *not* because it was Christmas.

She woke suddenly in the morning, jumping almost half out of bed as her phone pinged beside her. She put her hand to her head, as the pulsing reminder that she'd had a few more glasses of wine than she should have the night before kicked in with force. She'd only meant to have the one, but her conversation with the old man in the alley had prompted a few more unwelcome memories and she'd wanted to drink them away.

Reaching out she found her phone and pulled it back into the bed. Keeping one eye shut – which seemed to help the headache – she squinted at the screen with the other. It was Jen.

Merry Christmas Scrooge. You can ignore it all you want, but I still hope you have a merry day whether you eat turkey or not. Try not to work too hard, but if you do, go over box 7 carefully. Everything in there was done by the intern while I was off sick, and I haven't double-checked all of it. Love you. Jen Xx

Kate closed her eyes and pushed her phone away from her.

It was here. Christmas morning. This was the time, when she'd been a little girl, that she'd woken up and been convinced that there was magic in the air. That there was something special and wonderful about these few hours than transcended time and reality. She'd been such a fool, so naïve. And she hated herself for it. For falling for the stupid hype that society created. For feeling as though something special was lost. Because, in reality, nothing was lost. There had been no magic, there had been nothing extraordinary other than perhaps the fact her parents had cared enough about her to try and pretend there was, on the few occasions they'd still had custody of her for Christmas.

Feeling the weight of her past settle on her chest she suddenly threw back the covers and sat up, taking a moment to let her throbbing head adjust before standing up. Lying in bed thinking about it all wasn't going to help. She needed to get up and make herself some coffee – some strong coffee – before getting back to work and making a real difference in the world.

Padding through to the kitchen in her bare feet and rumpled pyjamas, Kate turned on the coffee machine and waited. After a few minutes it bubbled and sifted through, and she poured herself a large mug of the delicious smelling steaming dark liquid. Not bothering to get dressed, she took her mug into the lounge and resumed her position on the floor beside the semi-circle of discovery boxes.

Remembering Jen's earlier text, she decided to start with box seven. There were nine boxes of discovery in total, filled with all sorts of things the team had pulled together, anything and everything that could possibly be related to the case: the house, the victim, the suspect and their history. Jen was always incredibly thorough in her work, but she'd not double-checked everything in that box.

Kate pulled it towards her and laid the contents out on the floor, casting her eyes across them as she searched for the best place to start. Most of Matthew's personal items had been logged here, including his receipts and phone records. She'd been through those with a fine-tooth comb numerous times. But what else was there? The restaurant details, the transcript of the interview with the owner and blown-up images from the CCTV of Matthew driving out of the car park. She studied these for a moment then set them down and picked up the next file. This held a map printout with the route and timings on it. Her sharp eyes followed the line of the main A-road that made up most of the journey back, then the squiggly ones towards the end as the roads became smaller nearer his home.

Kate bit the inside of her cheek. There was nothing new there. She moved to place it down on top of the CCTV printouts, but then suddenly paused and pulled it back up, lifting the top image with the other hand. It was Matthew's car pulling out onto the road outside the restaurant; but he wasn't turning right, which would have taken him directly onto the A-road. He was turning left.

Ditching the printouts she grabbed her laptop and pulled up maps online, entering the start point and destination into the route planner. Immediately the route on the printout came up. She zoomed in and looked carefully at the roads to the left of the restaurant. There was a network of small country roads that, whilst they would be unlikely to be particularly fast, looked as though they might be a shorter route as far as mileage went. She played around with the route to find the shortest distance instead of the fastest, and as the details came up her eyes widened.

If she was correct, if Matthew had gone this way home that night, it would explain the extra time almost to the minute. Picking up her phone she scrolled through her contacts and pressed dial. It rang several times before finally being answered and she jumped in impatiently.

'Hi, yes, I need to speak to an inmate, a Mr Matthew Deeney, I'm his lawyer.' She paused. 'Yes, I'm aware it's Christmas Day. Please, it's extremely important to his case.' She closed her eyes and pinched the bridge of her nose. 'Yes. Thank you.'

The next few minutes were spent on hold and she began pacing the room, gnawing anxiously on her thumbnail. If she was right, the thirty-three-minute route had been no more than an assumption by the police team who'd put it together. A rookie error.

Eventually Matthew came to the phone. 'Hello?'

'Matthew, it's Kate. Listen, I need to ask you something.' She didn't pause for niceties. 'The night Cassie was murdered, when you left the restaurant, you turned left onto the main road. Why?' She waited with bated breath. She couldn't lead him there, he had to tell her.

'Oh, um...' He paused. 'I don't know. That's just where my satnav told me to go.'

'And the road you took, was it a main road or country roads?'

'Country roads, all the way. Why?'

Kate looked upwards, elation running through her veins. 'Matthew, that's brilliant!'

'Is it?' he asked, his tone confused.

'The police assumed you'd taken the A-road back, not the country roads. The A-road would have taken off a good fifteen minutes.'

'Except I didn't...' he said slowly.

'No, you didn't. Which means you have your alibi. I'll need to get hold of the ANPR data on those roads, prove you were there, but that won't be hard now that we know.'

'Oh my God,' he uttered, shock in his tone. 'So... I can go home?'

'It might be a few more days, being the holidays, but, yes.' She smiled. 'You'll be going home.'

'Thank you,' he cried, his voice wobbling with emotion. 'Thank you so much. Oh, God, I can't tell you how much of a relief that is.'

Kate nodded. 'I'm just glad we found a way to prove your innocence,' she said. 'We'll get you home soon and then the police can get back to finding who *did* kill Cassie. Justice will be served Michael,' she said sincerely. 'Just hang in there.'

'Thanks, Kate. Thank you so much, for everything. Merry Christmas,' he said.

Kate swallowed. 'Speak to you soon.'

She put the phone down and sat down on the sofa, letting the enormity of what had just happened sink in. She'd known he was innocent. She'd felt it in her bones. And now she'd proven it.

Warmth flooded through her and she allowed a happy laugh to escape her lips. She'd needed this win. She'd needed something to get her through the holidays, something to keep her mind from straying back to her broken past. Standing up she looked around and considered what she could do to celebrate. There weren't many options, everyone was busy and everywhere was shut. In the end she decided to get dressed and head out for a walk. Fresh air was good for the soul and she wanted to see the sky.

Ten minutes later she pushed through the front door of the building, wrapped up and ready to face and embrace the crisp cold air outside. She took a deep breath in and looked up into the clear blue sky, allowing her feeling of triumph to break out in a declaration of success.

'I did it!'

'Did what?' came a voice from nearby.

She jumped and her head shot around. It was the old man, still sat just inside the alley.

'Oh. I'm sorry, I thought I was alone,' she said, feeling embarrassed. She walked over. 'I, er...' She pushed her long auburn hair back over her shoulder and wondered how to explain it. 'I found seventeen minutes,' she said simply.

He nodded sagely. 'Every minute is valuable in this life. A

whole seventeen of them, well... There's a lot you can do with that.'

She smiled. 'I thought you had plans today?' She was sure he'd said he was going somewhere for dinner.

He looked down at his blanket-clad legs. 'I struggle to get anywhere on my own now. I can't make it without help.'

'Oh.' Kate immediately felt bad for him. Why had no one come to pick him up? 'I could help you get there,' she offered. 'I was just going for a walk; I have nowhere I need to be.'

'That's not true. You need to be with family today.' He smiled.

Kate looked away. Clearly he'd forgotten their conversation from the night before. Perhaps he had dementia. 'Where do you need to go?' she asked.

'This is it.' He pulled a small scrap of paper out of a pocket underneath his blanket and handed it to her.

She smoothed it out and read the messily scrawled address. 'Okay. I'll get you there. Give me a minute to find a taxi.'

'You'll come with me?' he asked. 'I need your help to get inside.'

She had planned to just put him in the taxi and pay for it, but his eyes begged and she felt as if she couldn't refuse. She nodded. 'Of course.'

A few minutes later they were in a taxi and he nodded off as they whizzed past streets and buildings. Bright lights danced and baubles twinkled and Kate focused hard on the architecture, ignoring the constant reminders of Christmas.

Soon they pulled up outside a large hall, its windows warm with light and the door propped partially open. She frowned and looked back at the paper in her hands and then up at the street address. It was the right place.

'Come on, it looks like they've already begun,' the old man next to her said, having woken.

'Okay then, let's go.'

'What's that?' the taxi driver asked, looking at her in the mirror.

'Nothing. Here, keep the change.' She handed him a twenty-pound note, then stepped out and closed the door.

'Come, this way. Less steps,' he said, eagerly shuffling away.

'Um, okay,' Kate replied awkwardly. She followed him around to the side of the building. 'I thought you were visiting family today?'

'Family is what you make it,' he replied. 'Family are those who care for you and want you around. Whose eyes light up when they've made you smile.' He turned to look at her, his piercing blue eyes seeming to cut straight through to her soul.

She blinked, surprised at his words. That was always how she'd defined family too. Real family. The ones whose eyes genuinely brightened when you smiled, rather than those who politely smiled back, congratulating themselves on doing their duty.

They reached the door and she moved to let him in first out of the cold. Inside, the hall was teeming with people. There were those who were bustling around serving the many dishes of Christmas dinner and offering small gifts to the children, and then there were those who were there to eat. The homeless and, she quickly realised from reading a small sign, those from the women's shelter next door.

The old man shuffled over to the side and found a seat at an empty table. 'I'll just warm myself here a while before I eat,' he told her.

She nodded. 'I'll get you a–'

'There you are!' came a voice from behind her and she turned with a start. 'Thank the Lord, we're really struggling to get everyone through the line quick enough. They're starting to queue out the door!'

'Oh, okay...' Kate looked at the line of hungry people. 'Um...'

'Here.' The woman reached around her and wrapped a pinny around her waist before Kate could say a word.

Her eyes flew open at the intrusion of personal space, and she glanced down at it with a look of disbelief. It resembled a pair of Santa's trousers. 'Listen, I–'

'It's fine, it's a spare, love,' the woman butted in again. 'Here you go.' She shoved a ladle in her hand and firmly propelled her towards the steaming trays of food. 'Whatever they want, just fill 'em up.'

Kate opened her mouth to explain that she wasn't there to volunteer, but the woman had already walked off. She blinked and made a sound of exasperation. What was she supposed to do now?

'Three potatoes please. Not two or four, *three*,' said a little girl the other side of the food, holding out her plate.

She looked down and felt something pull at her heart. The girl was skinny and pale, no more than six, clutching a threadbare stuffed monkey to her chest as she looked up at her with solemn eyes.

'Three?' Kate checked seriously. She was here now; she might as well help the young girl.

'Yes please. Two aren't enough but four are too much,' the girl replied seriously.

Kate nodded, placing three potatoes on the plate. 'I totally agree. It's a very well-thought-out plan.' She handed the plate back.

'Thanks,' came the reply. And then she was gone.

As Kate took the next person's plate she glanced over at the old man. He was watching her with a smile. She shot him one back. She might hate Christmas, and this was a complete misunderstanding, but at least she was helping people. For the next couple of hours she toiled ceaselessly, feeding people and chatting to those who talked to her. It felt rewarding and, if she was honest, was a great distraction from her least favourite day of the year.

She watched as tables came together, filled with people who'd never met, but who would share their food and their stories and their laughter as if they'd been doing it for years, and it stirred something inside her. Something painful, but also heart-warming, as she stood observing, an outsider again. But for once being the outsider didn't bother her. For once she didn't begrudge people finding such happiness in Christmas. They deserved it. And while it was hard to still her own personal demons, it didn't make her instinctively pull away the way it usually would.

Finally, once everyone was fed and the queue had whittled down to nothing, she paused and took a break. The woman who'd tied Santa's trousers around her waist called her over to the vat of hot chocolate.

'Here,' she said, handing her a cup. 'You deserve it.'

'Thanks,' Kate said gratefully. She glanced over towards the old man, but he wasn't there and the table was occupied by someone else. She frowned and looked around trying to spot him, but it was too busy to pick him out.

'How long has this place been running?' she asked, turning back to the woman.

'This is one of the oldest running mission halls in the city,' she said with a smile. 'It was set up by a couple in the early fifties. They provided meals to those in need every Sunday and every holiday. He was a banker doing well for himself and they couldn't have kids, so they plugged all their money and energy into this.'

'Oh wow,' Kate replied. 'That's amazing.'

'Yeah. He was a special man. I never met the wife, she died

years before I started volunteering, but he was something else. He'd be here every week without fail. Usually with a new stray or two that he'd picked up on the way.' She smiled. 'He used to hand them over and ask us to take care of them, saying they hadn't realised they were supposed to be here that day, even though they'd never even heard of it before. He'd trawl the streets for hours some days, would tell us he had to find those who didn't know they were lost yet.'

'How funny,' Kate remarked.

'Excuse me, miss?' She turned to see the little girl from earlier peering up at her.

'Yes? Do you want some more?' she asked.

'I'm okay,' the girl replied. 'I'm full. I had too many cranberry meatballs.'

'Cranberry meatballs?' Kate asked with a frown.

'Oh yeah, it's a mission special,' the woman replied with a grin. 'It was a recipe the founders used to make every year. Cranberry meatballs with onion gravy. It doesn't sound like it should work, but it does. It's delicious,' she said in a conspiratorial tone.

'But that's...' Kate trailed off. Could it be him? Was this the old man's mission hall? 'The man, you said he still comes in here every year?'

'Oh, he used to, but he died about five years ago,' she said sadly. ''Twas a real shame. He was a lovely man.'

Kate processed this. So it couldn't be him. Perhaps he was just confused about the dish. He had seemed confused about a couple of other things too. Maybe his memories of his wife and this place had begun to merge into one.

'Miss?' The little girl tugged at her sleeve. She looked down. 'These are for you.' She pressed something into her hand. 'To say thank you.'

'Oh, you really don't have to do that,' Kate said, trying to push it back. But the girl didn't take it.

'Please,' she said. 'We do it every year.'

'There's a group who make things for us in return for the food. It means a lot to them,' the woman said quietly.

'I chose these for you because of your hair,' the girl said.

Kate looked down. It was a pair of dark terracotta fingerless gloves. She smiled as warmth flooded her heart. It was such a sweet gesture. Probably the sweetest gift she'd received in years, if not ever. She looked down into the shining eyes of the child – who beamed with genuine happiness at Kate's acceptance of her gift – and her eyes suddenly clouded. The little girl had caught her totally off-guard, bypassing all the usual emotional defences she erected to keep people out.

'I love them,' she said, her tone much calmer than her churning emotions. She slipped them onto her hands. 'I shall treasure them.'

'Ladies and gents, thank you for joining us here today,' came a voice from across the room. A man was standing on a small stage, microphone in hand. 'It's been another wonderful year here at the Davis mission house, so many faces, some old, some new members of the family. As always, we take a moment to pause and remember our founders and give thanks for their generosity. Bill and Clara Davis were a lovely couple who created something truly special. A place that gave all of us here today a family to be part of, food and a warm place to go when we need it the most. Over the years they helped many people find their way, both practically and spiritually, and although they're no longer with us, their spirit lives on through all of us. Let's raise a toast,' he finished, his arm sweeping upwards to two pictures Kate hadn't noticed on the wall before now. 'To Bill and Clara.'

As she registered what she was looking at, the noise around

her faded away and her heart seemed to miss a beat. There he was, the old man, his blue smiling eyes piercing into hers. She blinked and shook her head with a frown, then swivelled around, her eyes searching the room.

'What's the matter, dear?' the woman asked.

'The old man I came with, have you seen him?' she asked, flustered. This didn't make sense.

'You didn't come with anyone. It was just you,' the woman replied, confused.

'No, I did, he was old and had a blanket around his shoulders. I brought him here. He gave me the address.' She searched her pocket for the piece of paper, but it wasn't there. 'I must have dropped it,' she muttered, looking around. 'He sat there.' She pointed to the table.

The woman looked and shook her head. 'No, dear. That's the Delaney family. They've been there from the beginning.'

Kate blinked and tried to make sense of it all. 'Okay,' she said eventually, aware that she sounded slightly crazy. 'Sorry, ignore me. Listen, I need to go. Are you guys okay?'

'We are. You go, sweetheart. And thanks again for today. You're part of the Davis mission family now.' She smiled. 'We hope to see you again.'

Kate nodded slowly. It all made no sense. Or it all made complete sense if she dismissed sensibility entirely. Which also made no sense. She said her goodbyes and left the mission hall with its warmth and laughter and people who cared just because they had care to give, and she thought about it all on the long walk home. There were no longer any taxis available, but she didn't mind. It gave her time to digest. When she reached home – still no nearer to understanding anything – she went straight to the fridge, having realised that whilst she'd fed everyone else all afternoon, she'd entirely forgotten herself.

As she opened the fridge door and searched the contents,

her heart skipped a beat. There, in the centre of the fridge was a box of baclava that looked suspiciously like the baclava she'd purchased and given the old man two nights before. But she hadn't replaced it. She closed the fridge and backed away with a frown, then after a few moments walked out to the airing cupboard.

Tentatively she opened this and – almost scared to do so – pulled up the bedding and towels to where the blanket she'd given him used to sit. A shock ran through her entire body as her eyes landed on it, folded neatly away as though it had never been moved. How was that possible?

She closed the door and sat down on the hallway floor, her stomach churning and her mind running in circles as she began questioning her very sanity.

'This isn't possible,' she muttered to herself, shaking her head.

And it wasn't. *Was* it? If she was to believe all the evidence in front of her, then she had met a ghost on the street, who had decided to save her the way he'd spent his life saving so many others, bringing her into the strangest family ever formed by using emotional blackmail. It was absurd. And entirely impossible.

But as she thought it over again and again, she realised that there truly was no other explanation. Either she was clinically insane, or ghosts were real. As, apparently, was the magic of Christmas – the very thing she'd spent her adult life actively railing against. And this man, who'd never even met her, had decided it was his duty even beyond the boundaries of *death*, to guide her into the heart of his family at Christmas. To care for *her* as family. To save her.

Tears ran freely down her cheeks as all the pain and the heartache of her childhood flowed out. And for once, she didn't force it back into the tightly contained box she housed it in. For the first time in years she allowed herself to feel. She allowed herself to grieve. And finally, after several hours had passed and her tears ran dry, she even allowed herself to hope.

Her muscles aching from the time spent on the hallway floor, and her eyes tired from the emotional release, she eventually stood up and went to find her phone. The family she'd been forced into tonight was a special one, and one she vowed to return to. But she had learned another lesson today, from a little girl carrying a pair of fingerless gloves. From the first person to break past her barriers. In order to see the light shine from someone's eyes, she had to give them the chance to be that close.

Bill was right. Family did come in all shapes and sizes. And if she was going to do some justice to his efforts from beyond the grave to teach her this, then it was time to make some changes.

She opened Jen's last message and, after a deep breath, began typing out a text.

Merry Christmas to you too Jen. I've been thinking. What was it you were going to suggest for New Year's Eve?

***

Emma Tallon is a British author of gripping, gritty, organised crime thrillers. With a number of bestsellers published by Bookouture since early 2017. Emma continues to write full time and has many ideas in the pipeline for future novels.

WHAT THE DICKENS!

BY EVA JORDAN

AN ICY BREEZE blew off the coast, pinching her cheeks. If she hadn't spotted the golden daffodils dotted along the roadside, or the blush-pink thrift sprouting from the cliff-tops, she would have sworn it was winter.

Still, maybe it was a good thing it was so cold because at least it put her in the right frame of mind for the task at hand. The magazine she worked for had commissioned her to write a piece about Charles Dickens. The editor suggested she visit all the places he'd either lived at, or frequented, incorporating each one into a final festive piece for the Christmas issue in December. It was only April, so she had plenty of time, but as there was no time like the present, Gemma had promptly booked a short trip to Broadstairs convincing fiancé Andy to tag along and keep her company.

Tomorrow, they were visiting Bleak House. Today they were heading to the Dickens House Museum on Victoria Parade; one-time home of Dickens' friend, Miss Mary Pearson Strong; the inspiration behind the donkey-chasing character Betsey Trotwood in *David Copperfield*.

When they arrived, the museum was locked, so Andy nipped off in search of takeaway coffee while Gemma waited for Adrian, the volunteer who had agreed to meet them and show them around. Gazing across the square, gravelled garden, Gemma stamped her feet and blew on her hands. It was getting colder, which was why, as she glanced up, she wasn't in the least bit surprised to see snowflakes tumbling from the sky.

Startled by the sound of the door opening behind her, she turned to see a bearded gentleman with wavy brown hair wearing a frockcoat, high collar, and necktie. She'd been warned that some of the volunteers liked to dress up.

'Good morning,' he boomed. 'You must be the reporter?'

'Erm... yes. That's right.'

'Do come in. And may I add, what a splendid yellow cape.'

Bemused, Gemma glanced down at her scruffy old poncho before following him into the parlour. It was decked out for Christmas, complete with a tree and a crackling fire, and where sat an elderly-looking lady introduced as, 'my dear friend, Miss Strong'.

Grinning, Gemma played along, sipping tea and eating almond cake, discussing the plight of the poor, donkeys, and the spirit of Christmas. At one point, another individual entered the room and took a photo of them using an old-fashioned bellows camera before Gemma suddenly remembered Andy and excused herself.

She found him up the road and apologised for her absence. Frowning, a look of confusion flitting across his eyes, Andy passed her a coffee then introduced her to Adrian, the volunteer, who had blonde hair and was wearing a Superdry jacket and jeans.

What? Gemma thought. *Who then... have I been talking to for the last hour?*

Leading them back to the house, Adrian unlocked the front

door. Inside, old photos lined the hallway. Most of the prints were black and white, while others were colourised – whereby colours had been painted directly on to the print – including one of Dickens seated beside two women; one of whom appeared elderly, wearing a shawl, while the other, much younger woman, wore a cape... a yellow cape.

Scratching his head, Andy studied the photo intently. 'If I didn't know any better,' he said, turning to face Gemma, 'I'd have sworn that woman in the photo was you.'

***

Eva Jordan was born in Kent but has lived most of her life in a small Cambridgeshire town. She is both a mum and step mum to four adult children and Nanny to two beautiful grandchildren, all of whom have, at times, inspired her writing and family-based novels: *183 Times A Year*, *All The Colours In Between*, and *Time Will Tell*. Her fourth novel, *A Gift Called Hope* is a heartfelt but at times heartbreaking family drama and is due for release in November this year. As well as writing novels Eva also writes short stories and is a columnist and book reviewer for a local magazine.

A CHRISTMAS CAROL

BY LOUISE BEECH

I WAS BORN on Christmas Day, so my mum called me Carol. Holly or Joy might have been better, but my mum liked to sing, with gusto, and the insistence that a rapt audience reward her song with applause. She loved Christmas; every window in our house was bedecked in something sparkly, glowing or snow-covered. Mum always began singing Jingle Bells at the end of November. By January, she had added a new verse.

Now, ten years after her passing, I ignore this too-jolly season. I split up with my boyfriend Josh last year because he wanted a life-sized Santa installed on the roof. 'You Feng-Shui the house with windchimes and crystals,' he said, 'but you won't entertain a cubic zirconia reindeer.' Josh was gone by December the third. Disrespecting my Feng Shui was the final straw.

I got home late from the office today – Christmas Eve – exhausted from the over-the-top excitement. Grown adults dressed as elves and screaming ecstasy at out-of-date chocolate snowmen in the Secret Santa. My first Christmas without Josh.

Tomorrow would be my birthday and I'd celebrate quietly. No tree. No turkey. I'd have steak and chips.

I drank a glass of wine and fell asleep by the fire. I woke to my mum singing Cliff Richard, wearing a shimmering white gown, and heavy chains that clinked as she swayed to her own song.

'Mum?' I whispered. '*How*? You're...'

'I know, love,' she said. 'It's clever, isn't it. You know who I am, don't you? I'm the Ghost of Christmas Past.'

I thought I was dreaming so I told her to bugger off. She didn't. She took my hand – hers was warmer than I'd imagined – and we were back in my childhood living room. As expected, every surface was covered in tinsel or fake snow. Gifts waited under the tree. The whiff of stuffing and cranberries filled the air.

'You loved Christmas when you were small,' Mum said.

'Because I was *small*,' I said.

'Childish joy is the greatest joy. Tell me this: why do you Feng Shui your house each year?'

'It's the Chinese art of placement.' I sighed. 'Certain items enhance your life depending on where you put them.'

'Like festive decorations. Do you know why I loved Christmas?'

I shrugged.

'Because that's the day I got you,' she said softly. 'We tried for years, and finally you were born Christmas morning. I was celebrating *you*. Before that, I ignored Christmas.'

I woke with a jolt. The fire had faded. Mum had gone. I was sad. I missed her. Maybe even Josh for a brief moment. I went to bed.

Just after midnight, I woke to my mum crooning Mariah Carey's mega festive hit. She still wore white and was wrapped in chains, declaring – between verses – that she was the Ghost of Christmas Present.

'Scrooge got a different person each time,' I complained.

Ignoring me, Mum took my hand gently in hers and we found ourselves in a house I didn't recognise. It was bare, cold, the kitchen cupboards empty. Charlene who worked in accounts was asleep on the sofa. In between belting out lines from Mariah's anthem, Mum explained that Charlene had divorced recently and was broke and depressed.

'She was dancing to Slade and wearing antlers in the office today,' I said.

'Just a façade, my darling. She cried in the toilets afterwards.'

'So did I. But that was when I saw the Christmas bonus.' I paused, looking at Charlene softly snoring. 'Poor woman. I had no idea. None of us did.'

'Who ever does?' whispered Mum.

I was about to ask why she was showing me Charlene when I woke in my own bed, the night still soft and slumbering around me. I went to the bathroom; when I returned, Mum was sitting on the windowsill, shrouded again in virgin white and bedecked in S&M-esque chains. She didn't sing now.

'Let me guess; you're the Ghost of Christmas Yet to Come. You couldn't wear a different costume?' I asked.

'Are you ready to see your future?'

'If you take me to my grave, I'll tell everyone you used pre-made pastry for your mince pies.'

She didn't; she took my hand once again and we were whisked to another room I'd never seen before. This time, a cheery one. It was dressed for Christmas, but tasteful, with matching gold baubles, stylish cream candles, a symmetrically decorated tree. Mum whispered that she had decided to show me the the bright future I could have if I opened my heart to

Christmas, not the dark one I was headed for. A small girl opened gifts with chubby hands, her smile shy, her hair a mass of curls.

'She looks like...' I couldn't finish.

'Yes,' said Mum. 'She's yours. Born Christmas Eve next year. But only if...'

'I'm not getting back with Josh.' I then sadly added the truth: 'He ... doesn't want children.'

'Do the thing you know you should,' said Mum.

'That Feng Shui class at the sports centre next year?'

I started to say I loved her even if she was emotionally manipulating me, but she'd gone. It was morning; I was in my bed. Fragile light slanted between the curtains, fingers touching the tiny ivory elephant on my dresser. I'd placed it in the Children and Creativity area of the room; a Feng Shui position supposed to grant the gift of a child.

I ignored the festive TV shows and opened birthday cards. I kept thinking about Charlene. Whatever I thought of this season, I didn't wish loneliness on anyone. It was a bleak one this year, especially with so many isolated, away from family.

I cooked my steak and chips, hearing Mum telling me to heat the pan first. But my appetite died when I pictured Charlene alone again. As the chips crisped, I messaged a friend to see if she had Charlene's address. When the meal was done, I covered it in foil and drove to a house just a mile from mine.

Charlene opened the door, bleary-eyed, wearing a Christmas Is Crap nightie.

'Carol?' she said, confused.

'It's not turkey,' I said, handing over the plate. 'But it's still warm.'

'Thank you.' She took it. 'Why?'

'Everyone should have steak and chips on Christmas Day,' I

said. She had tears in her eyes but tried to hide it. 'Merry Christmas.'

On my way down the path, I slipped on a devious patch of ice. Then he came out of nowhere. He was wearing a Santa outfit. He had eyes so blue they belonged to Mary in the Nativity. He helped me up.

'Careful there,' he said, voice cliche husky. 'You OK? Do you have far to walk?'

'Offering me a ride in your sleigh?' I smiled, motioning to his fur-trimmed jacket and fake round belly.

'Do you know what?' he said. I shook my head. He leaned closer and whispered, 'I bloody hate Christmas, but I'm wearing this for my niece. It'll make her happy. It's about the kids, isn't it?'

It is, I thought. Past, present ... and future.

Then he walked me to my car, and we exchanged numbers.

***

Louise Beech's debut novel, How To Be Brave, was a Guardian Readers' pick in 2015 and a top ten bestseller on Amazon. She has since gone on to have many more critically-acclaimed bestsellers, such as Call Me Star Girl which hit number one on Kobo, long-listed for the Not The Booker Prize and won the Best Magazine Big Book Award 2019. Her memoir, Daffodils, is out now in audiobook. She also writes under the name Louise Swanson, whose debut, End of Story, will be published in 2023.

A LITTLE CHRISTMAS WISH

BY STEPHEN EDGER

I WAS twelve years old when I stopped believing in Father Christmas. I inadvertently stumbled upon my dad's drunken return from the pub and caught him scoffing the mince pie and sherry we'd left out for the big guy. I might have believed he was just being selfish had I not seen him return the carrot to the vegetable drawer in the fridge, and that the sack from Santa was already under the tree. The fact that the present still bore the Woolworths price tag the following morning only cemented the truth.

So when my shift was near ending at 10pm one Christmas Eve, and Sarge asked me to do him a favour and chat with an arrestee, I didn't think twice before agreeing. After all, one good turn deserves another, right?

I could hardly contain my laughter when I entered the interview room and saw an old guy with a long, white beard, bursting out of a large, red Santa suit. Even by Sarge's usual standard of lame pranks, this took the biscuit.

The charge sheet read 'attempted burglary' and the arresting officer claimed neighbours had called 999 when they heard loud banging and saw an obvious flashlight through the curtains. The residents were away on holiday somewhere warm and expensive, and the suspect calling himself 'Nick' was apprehended attempting to flee the scene through the back door.

'I thought Santa only enters and leaves through chimneys,' I said, taking my seat across the table from him.

'Not when these modern homes have had them filled in, or they were never built to begin with,' he replied so matter-of-factly that I nearly choked on my gum. 'Much more of a challenge these days, but I do my best.'

Whenever interviewing a suspect, I always used an internal gauge to try and determine whether what they were claiming was the whole truth, a pack of lies, or something in between. It was clear that Nick wasn't intimidated by the cynical look in my eyes. What I would have given to spark a cigarette and blow smoke in his face, but that's why I had the gum.

'You couldn't use magic to get back up to the roof?' I gently probed.

'Why on earth would I want to go up to the roof when the sleigh was parked on the street?'

Again, not a trace of humour or fear in the deep, gruff, middle-class voice.

'Besides, magic is a finite resource not to be wasted. When there's a chance to use a door, I usually do.'

I pulled down my tie and chewed harder on the gum. 'Care to tell me what you were doing inside number five Galveston Square at 9pm this evening?'

A broad grin spread across his cheeks, reddening them in the process. 'Well, answering a special Christmas wish, of course.'

'No presents were located in the property or on your person.'

'That is because I was disturbed before I had the chance, dear boy.'

I bit my tongue at the condescending tone, reminding myself that I was supposed to be in control. 'There was also no report of a large sleigh and eight reindeer anywhere near the vicinity of Galveston Square.'

He stared at me blankly, and for a moment I wondered whether he was building up to some kind of diminished mental health defence.

'So, where's the sleigh and reindeer, Nick?'

'They're exactly where I left them, of course.'

I waited to see if he would explain further. 'Which is?'

'I already told you: parked on the street outside number five Galveston Square.' He paused at this moment and looked over my shoulder at the clock on the wall. 'I really do need to get back to them soon. Can you tell me when I can be on my way? This is all so embarrassing. Mary will be cross.'

'Mary?'

'My wife.'

I inwardly cringed because I hadn't seen the joke coming, but he'd delivered it deadpan. 'Your wife is Mary... Christmas?'

He nodded vigorously. 'Unfortunate, I know, but always breaks the ice at parties.'

I glared at my watch and then back at him. If it wasn't for this joker I'd already be clocked off and on my way to the shop.

'You chose not to consult with a solicitor, but you are still welcome to request one to advise you on the severity of the charges you're facing. There was no record of you on our system when we ran your fingerprints, so if you cooperate, the court is more likely to favour a more lenient outcome. Otherwise...'

I left the words hanging, hoping his imagination would fill in the blanks.

For the first time his affable mask slipped, the heat rising to his cheeks, his frustration building. 'Why on earth would I want to speak to someone on the naughty list?'

I slammed my hand down on the desk. 'You're facing jail time, Nick. Is that how you want to spend the festive season? Five years behind bars is a terrible way to start the New Year.'

He huffed. 'That simply will not do. With all due respect, detective, I have a job to do tonight.'

'A job? Another robbery?'

'Certainly not!'

I decided to change my approach and appeal to his better nature. 'Nick, help me out here, tell me why you were really in Galveston Square, and you might be able to get home to Mary tonight.'

He stared at me in silence for a long time. 'You don't believe in me, do you, Cory?'

My shoulders tensed. How did he know my name? I wasn't wearing any identification and hadn't had to announce it at the start as the interview wasn't being recorded.

I didn't respond, choosing to see how long he could keep the charade going.

'Most keep the faith until at least aged twelve,' he continued, 'but more and more forget sooner and sooner. It's all next-day delivery and interest-free credit these days. Children just aren't as patient as once they were.'

I needed to get home. I was wasting my time trying to help this guy. He might have wanted to mess about, but I had reason to sign off.

'We need to wrap this up, Nick, as I'm due home imminently. Are you going to tell me why you were in the house at Galveston Square?'

He fixed me with the sincerest stare I've ever seen. 'I will, but not yet.'

I looked at my watch again. Less than an hour until the shop would be closing.

'1991,' he suddenly said, with what could best be described as a whimsical look.

'Excuse me?'

'1991. That was the year when I last received a letter from you, Cory.' He stared off into the distance. 'If I recall you asked me for a new puppy to replace the dog you lost that year. Oh, what was his name...?'

I looked back to the door, half-expecting to see Sarge storm in, no longer able to contain his belly of laughter.

'I receive lots of requests for pets,' he continued, 'but they aren't something my elves can make in the workshop, so we endeavour to find something else that will bring as much joy... Now let me think... If I remember correctly, I brought you a... oh, I can't quite...'

I pictured the Game Boy game about running a pet store that bore the Woolworths' price tag. This guy was clearly a confidence artist reading me and waiting for me to give him some clue to grab on to. How he knew my name was beyond me, but maybe someone told him I would be the interviewer. It wasn't a huge stretch to guess my birth year, and as he'd already said most kids keep the faith until at least twelve, so 1991 could have been a lucky estimate.

I remained silent, allowing him to dig a deeper hole.

He snapped his fingers together a moment later. 'Pet Shop Professional.' A broad grin stretched across the old man's face.

My mouth dropped.

'I remember now because it was another item the elves couldn't make, and it had to be collected from a shop.'

I immediately fired a look of anger at the two-way mirror, picturing Sarge and his gathered audience laughing as my anger grew. My wife Samantha had to be in on the joke too, as nobody else could have told him about that lame game. I needed to keep my cool and show them their attempt to rile me would fail.

I stood to leave instead.

'Don't go, Cory,' he said, reaching a frail hand across the table. 'I know you stopped believing, and I'm sorry that you did, but now you have a little one on the way and she doesn't deserve to miss out just because you did.'

I could hear Samantha's words in his mouth and should have guessed sooner that she was behind this elaborate charade.

'That's why you're trying to give up smoking, isn't it? I know you want to buy her that stuffed elephant from the toy shop, but right now you need to get to the maternity hospital. Samantha is going to go into labour in the next hour, and she'll need you with her. Go now and be with your family.'

I shot back across the room, my feet almost failing me and crashed into the wall.

Nick remained seated at the table. 'Don't try to make sense of it, and don't ignore my advice, Cory. Have a little Christmas faith and all will work out.'

I stormed out of the room, heading straight for the observation suite, ready to catch them in the act, but as I barged into the room I found it empty.

No Sarge and no Samantha.

I charged back to the interview suite, and unable to control my fury, I grabbed Nick by the lapels of his fluffy red suit and hoisted him up. Slamming him into the wall, I demanded answers.

'How dare you bring my pregnant wife into your sick game?'

'She needs you, Cory.' He choked against the weight of my arm across his larynx.

'Stop it,' I snapped back. 'Just tell me why you were at Galveston Square, so I can get out of here.'

He coughed, and I eased the pressure of my arm a little.

'Because I made a promise to a little girl,' he gasped.

I eased the pressure of my arm a little further.

He took a moment to gather his breath. 'Please just go to the maternity ward. You don't have a lot of time.'

'Then you'd better talk fast.' I planted my feet and fixed him with a determined stare.

'Very well. I received a letter from a brave little girl who begged me for help. She said she didn't want toys or gifts this year, just one simple wish. She told me that she never got to meet her dad because when her mum went into labour, he was on his way to buy her a stuffed elephant from a toy shop and never made it. On his way, he witnessed an armed robbery and being the hero he was, he stopped to try and intercept those responsible, but he was shot and killed. She begged me for just one moment with her dad so she could tell him she loves him. That was six years from now, Cory. Tonight I made a special trip using a little Christmas magic so that I could convince you not to go to that toy shop.'

I lost my grip on his suit, not wanting to fall for his trick and yet unable to totally dismiss his words.

'She's waiting to meet you, Cory. Go to them now, and help me make that little girl's Christmas wish come true.'

I span on my heel and darted out of the door, and didn't stop running until I made it to my car. There was no answer from Samantha when I tried her phone and although I knew how ridiculous I was being in trusting the word of a man I didn't believe in, I drove straight to the maternity ward in time to see Samantha being rushed into theatre.

It was two days later when I was helping Samantha into the car with our new daughter in a car seat that I heard about the robbery at the jeweller's a stone's throw from the toy shop. I was about to tell Samantha about that strange meeting on Christmas Eve when I looked in the back of the car and saw the stuffed elephant staring back at me. Attached to its leg was a small note that simply read, *'Please tell Emily her wish came true.'*

And that is why I tell her this story every Christmas Eve. It's become our little tradition, and even though she's older now, and has a family of her own, she still visits to hear the story. Of course, she has no memory of sending that letter to him, but I wouldn't be here today unless she had.

I was twelve years old when I stopped believing in Father Christmas, but I was thirty-eight years old when I started believing again. A little Christmas magic should never be wasted, but it sure goes a long way to bringing loved ones together.

***

Stephen Edger is the Amazon bestselling author of psychological and crime thrillers, including Snatched, and the Kate Matthews series. Born in the north-east of England, he now lives in Southampton where many of his stories are set, allowing him to use his insider knowledge to deliver realistic and unsettling suspense on every page. Away from writing, Stephen loves to read anything that will keep him awake at night. He's also a passionate advocate for contemporary cinema and binge-watching the latest offerings from streaming services. He is married with a son and a daughter, and two dogs. Stephen also writes under the name M.A. Hunter.

A CHRISTMAS WISH

BY GINA KIRKHAM

'Twas the night before Christmas when all through the house
Not a creature was stirring, not even a mouse...'
— *The Night Before Christmas* by Clement Clarke Moore

WITH A TOUCH of her fingers the door to the bedroom opened just enough for her to see inside. The ghostly light from the bedside clock cast shadows onto the bed illuminating rumpled sheets that had been thrown back and a pillow that held a perfect shape where someone had been lying. She waited a while before turning to creep along the corridor, her bare feet making no sound.

She sat at the top of the stairs, her chin resting in her hand, her shoulders hunched to her ears in excited anticipation. She quizzically tilted her head, the *Night Before* story as fresh in her mind this year as it had been last year. She wondered what on earth a *t'was* could be. Maybe it was something that was bigger than a mouse. She giggled. It was true that no mouse was stirring, but she was. It was the night all children waited for, so surely nobody slept on Christmas Eve! She slid down each step silently on her bottom, a bit like being on an invisible sledge, until she reached the part that gave her a better view of the room. The Christmas tree was nestled in the corner, slightly wonky with twinkling lights and coloured baubles that reflected the dying flames of the log fire. Wrapped presents sat underneath in higgledy-piggledy piles next to a little plate decorated with green stars that held a mince pie and a carrot. She was so pleased they hadn't forgotten.

'It's beautiful...' she whispered as she tiptoed across the room to stand beside the man. He smiled and handed her a small box, the red bow almost dwarfing the gift. She held it briefly against her heart before placing it under the tree.

'And very special too, my child.' He turned to watch the young woman asleep on the sofa, a grey knitted blanket in folds around her, her face gently lit by the amber glow of the fire. The child, her eyes shining excitedly, nodded her agreement.

'So, little one, let's have some fun before you have to skip back up there...' He gave her a knowing look whilst pointing to the ceiling. He saw the child hesitate, a look of concern in her eyes, her small fingers twisting the cotton of her nightdress. He placed a kindly hand on her shoulder. 'Go to her...' he gently encouraged. 'It will soon be Christmas Day and there is still much to be done.'

Her tiny feet padded across the fluffy rug. She really wanted to stop, squish her toes and feel the softness but in a moment when time had begun to move again for her, she did not want to waste one second of it.

'Mummy...' she whispered. She waited for the woman to stir hoping she had heard her small voice. 'Mummy, it's Christmas. It's time to have fun.' She placed her tiny hand on the woman's arm and looked to the man for approval. He closed his eyes, bowed his head and nodded before turning back to the task at hand as more presents were placed under the tree.

The woman sighed, her lips moving as in silent prayer. A name so reverently called. A special name. Her eyes fluttered open and rested upon the child. 'I... Oh my goodness! Sweetheart, what are you doing here?' She raised herself up, throwing back the blanket. The warmth radiating from her child as she hugged her touched her soul. 'Has my Christmas started early?' She laughed.

The little girl placed a kiss on her mother's cheek and snuggled into her. 'Yes, Mummy, it's a wish... A big big big wish that I made.' She threw her arms wide into the air as if to evidence just how big her wish had been.

The woman placed her feet onto the rug, as bare as her child's own feet that were beside hers. She marvelled at their differing sizes and their ten toes apiece. She giggled as they scrunched them into the fluffy tufts. She sank into her child's laughter and her heart became full again.

In the precious time that followed they danced and sang together, played I-Spy and had a tea party and when exhausted from having so much fun, they flopped down onto the sofa where the woman's sing-song voice read her daughter her favourite story. The little girl, warm and loved, cherished every moment. She did not want the story to end but she knew that it would.

'*...Happy Christmas to all, and to all a goodnight.*'

She nestled herself against the woman who was now at peace, her sadness slowly melted away by the child's presence and unconditional love. Her finger traced a line across her cheek stopping at the lips that always kissed her goodnight. 'I love you, Mummy.'

The woman stirred, a small sigh escaping from the very lips the child had just touched. 'I love you too, sweetheart,' she whispered as she pulled the blanket over her shoulder to ward off the slight chill she had suddenly felt, the book slipping from her hand to the floor with a gentle thud. She nestled down into the cushion as the sleep still held her, for tomorrow all this would appear as if it had been a dream. The little girl, content to remain close, didn't need to shut her eyes like Mummy. She didn't need to sleep. She watched, taking in every small detail, every tiny line on her face, each wisp of hair and dark eyelash that curled upwards. These would be her special forever memories.

The man waited patiently, settling himself into the fireside chair to enjoy his mince pie. He silently watched the woman and child sharing a tender moment that would soon end, his part in the Christmas story complete. He had received many wishes in his time; he had created gifts, delivered happiness and made dreams come true but none had touched his heart like this one. He brushed the crumbs from his beard and eased himself up from the chair, his red suit giving a flash of colour. 'It's time, my angel,' he softly coaxed.

The girl looked at him. 'May I stay, just a little bit longer, please?'

He took her hand as a means of comfort, his gentle eyes crinkling at the corners. 'You know the rules, little one. It's time.'

As they walked together towards the staircase festooned with garlands and lights, he gave her time to pause by the window. She looked up at the indigo sky to search for the brightest star amongst a blanket of twinkling white. 'It's not there!' she exclaimed as she blinked to clear the patterns from her eyes. 'Has it gone out?'

The man looked down on the little girl, his heart full of her simplicity and innocence. 'Have you forgotten, my child?' his warm voice enveloped her. 'You, my dear, are the brightest star and always have been.'

She smiled, remembering, and now happy and content to dance and sparkle on her way, she let go.

Jasper the marmalade cat lifted his head and surveyed the room. The lights on the Christmas tree twinkled, the plate sat empty, the dying embers of the log fire sparked and his mistress still slept peacefully. A comforting silence now reigned over his domain.

As the little girl giggled and skipped across the snow to once again become the brightest star in the sky, her tiny feet left no trace on the pristine blanket of white, she left no door ajar or window open. It was as though she had never been at the cosy cottage on Cholomendy Lane...

... Apart from a little box with a red bow left under the tree that contained a single white feather – and a mother's special dream.

Did you know that Angels are allowed Christmas wishes too? And for one magical night only, little Sofia had just been granted hers.

***

Gina Kirkham was born in the late 1950s to a mum who frequently abandoned her in a pram outside Woolworths and a dad who after two pints of beer could play a mean Boogie Woogie on the piano in the front room of their 3-bed semi on the Wirral. After retiring from an enjoyable and fulfilling career with Merseyside Police, Gina's alter-ego, Mavis Upton, was born. Mavis was ready to star in humorous and sometimes poignant tales about the life, loves and career of an everyday girl who followed her dream and embarked upon a search for the missing piece of her childhood.

CHRISTMAS BONUS

THE FOLLOWING SHORT STORY WAS WRITTEN BY ASPIRING AUTHOR LILY DUNCAN (AGED TEN).

THE CHRISTMAS GHOST

BY LILY DUNCAN

'ARE WE NEARLY THERE?' asked Abbie Biltford, scanning the dusky horizon for some kind of sign.

'We'll be there in about twenty minutes,' answered her dad, John Biltford, looking at the car display and seeing 8pm.

Abbie groaned and rested her head on her fourteen-year-old big brother, who immediately shook her off and said angrily, 'Can you, like, get off me! I'm trying to like, play on my phone!'

Eight-year-old Abbie punched her brother's shoulder and cried, 'Shut up, Ollie!'

'Urgh, you just killed me!' yelled Oliver.

'Well, you don't look dead to me!' she fired back.

'On my phone, idiot,' he snapped.

'Hey!' cried Zara their mum. 'Stop yelling or you'll wake Benji up!'

Benji was their sixteen-month-old little brother, who was right now fast asleep.

'Here we are,' said Dad hastily, foreseeing another fight.

Skipper, their trusty black and white sheepdog, barked joyfully as he was let out of the boot by Abbie. He twisted

285

round and round her legs, barking as he went. Abbie clipped on his lead and yanked her suitcase down, narrowly missing the dog, and started to drag it across the stone drive.

Complaining about having to pause his game, Oliver threw his holdall over his shoulder and followed Abbie across the stones huffily.

A now stirring Benji was transported by Dad into his pushchair and bumpily taken across the stones whilst Mum dragged the two final cases towards the hotel reception.

In the quiet entryway, dimly lit for the evening with twinkling Christmas lights and glittering decorations winding their way up the staircase, Abbie gravitated towards a bookshelf and picked up an interesting looking paperback, scanning the back cover for an idea of what was inside.

Check-in was a short process and as the kind lady wished them a pleasant stay, she told Abbie to keep hold of the book if she liked, which Abbie did gratefully.

Walking up to their room, Abbie felt an inexplicable shiver run down her spine, like ice. She shook it off just as her mum opened the door to their room on the second floor. The Biltfords were having their house renovated for the New Year, but it wouldn't be ready in time for Christmas, so they were spending Christmas in the Sunset Hotel, North Yorkshire, instead. It was Christmas Eve.

On scanning the room Abbie saw two single beds, a huge double bed and a cot for Benji. There was a big TV on the wall, a wardrobe and the biggest mirror she had ever seen hanging above a lovely dressing table.

She let go of Skipper's lead, letting him sniff about his new surroundings and she pushed open a door to see what was behind it. To her delight there was a brightly-lit bathroom with two sinks, a huge shower and what looked like a tiny swimming pool.

Over her shoulder her mum popped her head round the door and gestured towards the 'pool' and said, 'It's a Jacuzzi, like a bubbly bath.'

Abbie's eyes lit up even more.

'Come on then; let's lay out a carrot for Santa and a cookie for Rudolph,' said Dad.

Oliver rolled his eyes; Abbie grinned; and Benji, now fully awake, babbled his delight. Dad did this every year. Picking up Benji and walking over to the small table by the window, Abbie helped her baby brother drop the carrot onto the waiting plate. After she'd placed a cookie beside it, she beckoned to Oliver. He scowled but came over anyway. As he poured milk into a glass, Abbie heard him say something a lot like, 'I'm getting too old for this.' Looking at her watch she realised it was nine o'clock already.

Her mum must have realised too because only a moment later she announced, 'Right kids, I only have one word for you. Bed!'

Oliver sulked about having to go to bed early; but Abbie was very good. She cleaned her teeth, went to the loo and helped changed Benji into his pyjamas before getting into her own, all without making a peep.

After they went to bed, Oliver was caught twice on his phone so his mum confiscated it. Abbie, though, was so worn out with Christmas excitement that she fell asleep within about 6.4 seconds of her head touching her pillow.

The next morning, Christmas morning, Dad was woken up by a long, piercing scream that startled a roosting flock of birds, causing them to take off in all directions. The scream was coming from Abbie.

'N-n-no p-presents?' she sobbed.

She was right, there were no presents to be seen.

'B-b-but, I've been so goooood!' she wailed, throwing her head into her hands dramatically.

'I don't understand,' cried her shocked mum. 'What's happened? Where are the presents?' she demanded, looking at her husband.

Dad was too stunned to speak. Benji started wailing like a siren. Oliver was still fast asleep. Mum shook the sleeping teenager by the shoulder, but Oliver just rolled over.

Abbie bounded over and screamed in his ear, 'GET UUUP!'

Oliver gave a yell and jumped up and scanned the room for a couple of seconds. 'Where are the presents?' he asked dumbfounded.

'W-w-what's that?' asked Abbie, pointing out of the veranda window of the hotel room. Tall fir trees stood either side of the balcony and one of them had a large scrap of what looked a lot like–

'Wrapping paper?' Abbie's dad said incredulously.

It wasn't completely daylight outside yet and a mist hung in the air as a backdrop to a light flurry of snow.

'But why?' asked Oliver.

'Look!' cried Abbie as she peered more intently out of the window. 'A ribbon!'

'That's the ribbon I tied your presents with, Oliver,' exclaimed Mum. The bright red ribbon was trailing on the ground, two floors down.

'How did it get all the way down there?' asked Abbie, hugging Skipper to her chest. Skipper was whining pitifully. 'Do you see that?' she asked quietly, almost a whisper.

Everyone followed her gaze out of the window to what looked like an old man in pyjamas, dressing gown and a woolly hat – with a big bag of presents. As if this wasn't a strange enough sight, he was an odd, eerie, blue colour and he seemed to be hovering in mid-air, or, a better description would be *flying*. Yes. Actually flying.

'GHOOOST,' gasped Abbie, who immediately fainted, taking a helpless Skipper down with her.

'HEY!' screeched Mum, surprising everyone. 'Give us our presents back.'

The ghostly figure turned, and looking quite guilty flew over to the waiting Biltfords, and said, 'I'm sorry. My family is too poor to buy presents, so I'm taking yours for my little granddaughter.'

And with that he turned and floated away. The Biltfords yelled from inside their hotel room and waved for him to stop, but he either ignored them or could no longer hear for the distance between them. He slowly disappeared from sight.

Abbie, having found her feet again, sniffed. 'This is the worst Christmas ever!' Her dad put his arm around her, but she shook him off and burst into tears.

'I'm going back to bed' she sobbed. She gathered Skipper back up into her arms and got into her not yet cold bed. 'Maybe I'll wake again to find this is just a bad dream.'

Suddenly, Dad made them all jump. 'Get dressed. We're not giving up that easily.' He strode across the room to his suitcase and started pulling his clothes out haphazardly.

Skipper, who had no idea what was going on, jumped after him and started barking in apparent agreement.

A short while later they all made their way down the stairs, tried hard to ignore the delicious smell of the hotel Christmas breakfast escaping the dining room, and broke out the main door and into the cold morning.

After piling into their old Ford Anglia, an excited Oliver shouted, 'He flew off in the direction of those woods.' He pointed out the windscreen over his dad's shoulder.

'Seatbelts,' warned Mum as the car shot forwards, down the drive and towards the woods.

On the right-hand side of the drive was a dirt track through the trees and Dad slowed ever so slightly to take the turning. They gathered speed along the uneven dirt track, a set of eyes searching in every direction.

Abbie began to feel that icy shiver up and down her spine again, a sign to her that they were getting close. She tried to concentrate on the scenery outside the window to shake off her nervous feeling. But it had the opposite effect. The woods looked cold and damp as the mist made the trees drip randomly. The huge fir trees dwarfed the small car and the track seemed to go on for ages. Where the water drops clung to the firs, they quickly fell all around them as the car caused vibrations to dislodge them.

Distracting her, in the distance, was a small stone building. Abbie realised after a second what she was looking at. 'There!' she shouted, bouncing her hand off the window as she tried to point in excitement, forgetting there was a pane of glass in the way. 'Ow,' she whimpered, shaking her injured hand to rid herself of the pain. 'A house, or cottage.' This time, she did not point.

'So it is,' said Dad, impressed but almost missing the sharp turn ahead of him.

He spun the wheel and the rear of the car slid round, allowing them to continue in the direction of the little house.

'Faster, Dad, faster.' Encouraged a now overexcited Oliver, hands on the back of the seat in front and bouncing about in the rear.

Mum had a slight fear he was going to make his way over the front seat and onto her lap in his eagerness for their task. 'Breathe, Oliver.' She chuckled, smiling for the first time that morning.

'THE GHOST MAN!' Oliver continued.

He was right: Abbie could just see a flash of red shiny wrapping paper waving around under the man's arm, as the eerie blue figure slipped inside the tiny building.

It wasn't long before Dad brought the car to a stop, a small distance from the cottage. He expected everyone to rush out, but there was an all-round pause. They each got out slowly, unsure of what they were about to uncover. After all, a ghost had just entered the cottage with their Christmas gifts. What if he wasn't alone? What if the house was actually empty when they got inside? What if it *wasn't* empty?

Mum scooped Benji out of his car seat and cuddled him closely so that he might be protected from the cold and damp of the woods. Perhaps it was her way of being at the back of the family as they slowly approached the cottage. They stopped at the step leading to the front door.

It was Abbie who went forward and knocked the door, louder than she actually meant to, surprising herself slightly, but standing her ground none the less. She tried the metal handle, which was freezing to the touch. A quick turn and a slight push, the door opened with, as you would expect, a creak.

There was no light or heat from inside the tiny entryway. If anything, it was darker and colder than outside. Abbie could see her breath and realised how loudly she was breathing into the silence. There were two doors in front of her to choose from, and just as she was about to ask her family which they should open, a voice was heard from behind the one on the right.

Glancing over her shoulder for reassurance, Abbie slowly opened the right-hand door and was surprised to see an old lady, the same eerie blue as the old man – another ghost. The only light in the room was what made its way through the small, cracked, dirty window at the back of the room. There was a rather large stone fireplace, but it was empty, only for a small pile of ash left behind from another day's fire. There was a threadbare rug on the floor, and a wooden table with three chairs that had seen better days.

Stood in the middle of the room were the ghostly figures of the old man and woman, who until just now had not noticed their uninvited guests. The man still had the big bag of presents over his shoulder and the woman did not look happy. She was wearing a tartan dressing gown, slippers and a hairnet keeping her rollers in place.

Dad positioned himself at the front of his family in the doorway and cleared his throat. 'We are here to—' he began, but the old lady grimaced and cut him off mid-sentence.

'You are here to retrieve the presents that my Charles took from you this morning,' she said glumly and with a sideways glance to the old man, Charles.

Dad's mouth was opening and closing like a goldfish.

'Yes please,' piped up Abbie.

Dad closed his mouth and just nodded in agreement.

The old woman smiled and looked over his shoulder at the remainder of the Biltford family. She beckoned them all into the small room. 'I am Agatha; this is Charles.'

The floorboards creaked as the Biltfords filed into the small room, filling it almost completely. The house smelled of damp wood and something else that Abbie couldn't place.

'I am John,' offered up Dad. 'This is my wife Zara and my children, Oliver, Abbie and Benji,' he said gesturing to his family and realising he had no idea where the dog had gone.

Then he wondered why he was introducing his family to a pair of ghosts, one of whom had just effectively ruined their Christmas. Right now they should be tucking into a hotel Christmas breakfast and chatting about their favourite gifts. Instead, they were deep in the woods, in an old cottage, conversing with a pair of ghosts.

There is only one explanation for it: he must be dreaming.

He jumped as Zara gently touched his elbow, bringing him back to the here and now.

'I said are you okay?' the old lady questioned, a concerned look on her wrinkled face.

Dad nodded.

Agatha and Charles moved apart from each other to reveal a man, woman and small child all cuddled together on the floor.

Abbie couldn't believe it: how had they not seen them when they entered the room? The child, Abbie thought a little girl but couldn't be sure, was holding a rather tattered book. Abbie could just see the title, *The Elephant's Adventure*. It was not one she had heard of.

More importantly, however, they were *all* ghosts. The eerie blue colour, the strange clothing, the apparent indifference to the low temperature or their surroundings.

'Who are you?' thundered the seated man, making the whole room jump. He gathered himself up from the floor and stood as tall as he could.

'We are the *family* you stole the presents from,' exclaimed Oliver, finding his voice for the first time since entering the cottage. 'And we would like them back. Please,' he added at the end.

'Well, I, erm...' Charles tailed off, unsure of what to say.

'Give them back,' Agatha said quietly. 'Just because we can't give presents doesn't mean we should take them from others who can.'

The little girl on the floor let out a sob and the woman – Abbie imagined she was the mother – hugged her closely and hushed her. Charles extended his arm towards the Biltford family, clutching the bag of presents.

Abbie stepped forwards and retrieved the bag from him. 'Thank you,' she whispered meekly, feeling a sudden pang of guilt in her chest. She turned and made for the door, catching her mother's eye as she went. Abbie stopped. 'We can help them,' she whispered.

'What was that?' asked her dad.

'We can help them,' Abbie said, louder this time.

All the eyes in the room were on her, none bigger than those of the child cradled in her mother's arms on the floor.

'You can have one of my presents,' said Abbie looking at the little girl.

'I'll give you one of mine, too,' said Oliver.

'And I will,' added Zara, looking at the lady sat on the floor.

'Muuum, you ruined my moment,' moaned Oliver, starting to sound like his usual self again.

'Sorry honey, you were great.' She smiled. Oliver beamed.

'Here you go,' said Dad, pulling one of his gifts out the bag and placing it on the floor in front of the family, not asking the question in his mind as to whether ghosts could use any of these gifts. The gesture was enough.

Ten minutes later everyone was sat on the floor of the small room chatting about their favourite Christmases. Dad had brought two blankets from the car and had found Skipper sniffing about outside. Oliver had gathered some wood from the forest and between them they had got a modest fire going in the oversized fireplace, providing heat and some light to the small room. Everyone had a smile on their face and everyone – apart from Benji – had a hard boiled sweet from the glove box in the car.

It wasn't much, but Abbie felt like she had turned Christmas around for this little family. It wasn't the Christmas day she had imagined – that any of them had imagined – but it had turned out just fine in the end. The feeling of giving even a single gift to a family who had nothing was so much better than opening her own presents, she decided.

When Abbie got into bed later that evening, she closed her eyes and said out loud, 'This was the nicest Christmas ever.'

***

My name is Lily Duncan I am ten years old. I currently live in the north of Scotland with my three younger siblings, my mum and my dad. I have always wanted to write a story and it feels amazing to think people will read this and know I was the one who wrote it. I love to write, it's fun to create the details and add twists and turns to the story. I hope you enjoyed it.

A NOTE FROM THE PUBLISHER

Thank you for reading this book. If you enjoyed it please do consider leaving a review on Amazon to help others find it too.

We hate typos. All of our books have been rigorously edited and proofread, but sometimes mistakes do slip through. If you have spotted a typo, please do let us know and we can get it amended within hours.

info@bloodhoundbooks.com

Printed in Great Britain
by Amazon

87765370R00178